MID THIRTIES SLIGHTLY HOT MESS FEMALE SEEKING BILLIONAIRE

J. S. COOPER

Copyright © 2024 by J. S. Cooper

All rights reserved.

No part of this book may be reproduced in any form or by any electronic or mechanical means, including information storage and retrieval systems, without written permission from the author, except for the use of brief quotations in a book review.

BLURB

To Whom it May Concern,

This is a long shot.

I'm seeking a billionaire; I will also settle for a millionaire. Sorry, I'm not interested in any salesmen looking to sell me a time-share or a part of their animal balloon company (been there, done that).

I am not a gold digger, though you may not believe that. I have references. Ask all my broke exes and my best friends.

To be fair, I am not a glamorous model, actress, or professional dancer. I do, however, take pole dancing lessons (for fun, of course, not dollar bills).

I am an educated (still have the student loans to prove it), open-minded (toy stores are fun, and not for games), fairly cute (when I try), only a little curvy (those last thirty pounds don't want to leave) single female. I want to be swept off my feet, wined, dined, and bedded in ways that make me forget my name.

I have a job (that I hate), with a boss that makes me

want to jump off a cliff. However, my friends make up for the day job. I'm ready for an adventure. And possibly a penthouse with a maid and a design budget.

If interested, please respond before Monday morning so I don't have to go in to work.

Love,

Sultry Sassy Sarah

~

Note to self. Don't write stupid ads while half drunk and hanging out with immature, obnoxious friends. Certainly, do not post them on the internal company message thread by mistake. Do not freak out when your boss says he wants to see you in the office first thing Monday morning. And please never make a joke, asking how many dollar bills he has to make it rain, ever again.

I'm dead meat.

1

Sarah

Dear Diary,

Ethan Rosser of Rosser International is a jerk. Yes, he is my boss and signs my paycheck, but he sucks. And yes, I would say that to his face.

Maybe.

Okay, not really.

Unless I won the lottery and a good couple of million.

Which is unlikely to happen anytime soon because I don't play the lottery.

Anyway, that's not important.

Today, I had the opportunity to go on an all-expenses paid trip to the Bahamas with fifty other members of the company staff for some new recruitment videos and brochures. HR came into our part of the building with the Kingpin himself. He looked around briefly and said, "Nope, no one from copywriting."

I was standing right at the front. And sure, I didn't look like a million dollars. But he could have at least made eye contact. But he didn't even notice me. It was like I was a piece of wallpaper on the wall. Invisible.

I can't stand that man.

That is all for now.

Plain Jane aka Sarah

Ethan Rosser is the sort of six-foot-two man with dark golden-blond hair and dazzling blue eyes that I love to hate. Add on the millions, if not billions, of dollars in his bank account and that know-it-all smirk, and you, too, will not be able to stand him. I'm willing to bet money on it. Unless, of course, handsome, sexy men with oodles of money turn you on.

Don't feel bad if they do. If he wasn't my arrogant boss, I may be a tiny bit interested myself.

"Look at you, feeling all handsome and proud of yourself." I stick my tongue out at the black-and-white image down below. An image I'm sure many other women are staring at in that moment, as well.

My fingers feel heavy as I hold the morning newspaper in my hands and continue to stare at his photo, gazing up at me. It's the only time the man has made eye contact with me. And it's not even real eye contact.

I shouldn't care.

I don't care.

Yes, he's my boss.

Technically.

I don't actually work directly under him, as he owns the entire company.

Nepo baby.

I try not to feel guilty about my diss as my eyes peruse the article. While it is true that Rosser

International is a family company started by Ethan's grandfather, Frederick Rosser, it was somewhat run into the ground by Frederick's son—Ethan's dad—Richard. It wasn't until golden boy Ethan took over that it soared to new heights. So, maybe, technically, he's not a nepo baby, but I don't care. It's still family money.

That I don't have. And likely never will.

Dad would laugh if I asked him to front me some of my inheritance money to take a sabbatical from work and spend time dedicated to my songwriting. Maybe I'd even summon up enough courage to play some gigs at local bars. There's a chance I could be discovered and signed to a label, or at the very least, hired for my songwriting skills.

However, there is no inheritance money, so that is a pipe dream. Honestly, I don't even mind that I come from a working-class family because my parents are the absolute best. They shower me with love, and while money would have been great, as well, there's not much to go around in our family. While we didn't have fancy clothes or toys, there was always food on the table and laughter in the room. Lots and lots of laughter.

I'm the youngest of seven. And the only girl. I've been the butt of many jokes, but I'm immune to them now. I give as good as I get. You learn to toughen up real quick when you're the youngest.

It also helps that I've been doted on my entire life. Not that that means anything, because being doted on also means I have six older brothers that love to constantly tease me and basically cockblock me at every turn. Wait, can women be cockblocked? If not, you know what I mean.

My eyes finally move from Ethan's photo to peruse the article again. This time, I read out loud, which is something I do to mask the silence in my home. I'm either talking out loud to my dog, playing music loudly, or I have the TV on in the background. Sound is important to me. It's weird that even though I live in New York City, one of the most populated cities in the world, I often still feel lonely. But I suspect that has more to do with living alone.

"Handsome playboy and billionaire CEO, Ethan Rosser, is once again named New York's Most Eligible Bachelor of the Year. The devastatingly charming head of Rosser International is known for his intellect, humor, and business savvy. While much is known about Ethan's business life, his personal life remains behind closed doors. Often seen with a beautiful woman on his arm, Ethan has no worries getting a first date, he just doesn't seem to want to go on a second one. Will the man on the top of our list ever settle down or is he destined to drive the women of Manhattan crazy forever?"

I alternate between wanting to laugh and roll my eyes as I pause. What a joke. No wonder the man thinks he's God's gift to womankind when editors write pieces like this.

"Idiot," I mutter as I fling the newspaper to the ground and get off of my cognac-tan leather couch that is one of the loves of my life. It is the most expensive piece of furniture I own and the most comfortable. I spent my entire first paycheck from Rosser International on this couch, and I don't regret it. I truly believe in treating yourself right. Plus, my last couch gave me a backache.

I half expect my dog, Johnson, to run over and grab the paper, but he's fast asleep in his bed. I head over to the small kitchen on the other side of the room and open the mint green retro fridge my family bought me when my fridge failed, and my landlord didn't want to replace it. I love my fridge; it makes me smile every time I see it. Not just because of how cool it looks but because it reminds me of how much I'm loved. When my brothers delivered the fridge, they threatened to beat up my slumlord, but a couple of beers convinced them otherwise.

I survey the contents of my fridge, debating between closing the door, walking away, or eating. I'm not super hungry, and I know I probably shouldn't eat, but food is a way to make myself happy. I know the technical name for what I am about to do is emotional eating, and I should likely go to a support group and find my Mike in the best *Mike and Molly* way, but I'm not going to.

I glare at the wilting green and brown celery and previously cut dry carrot sticks I'd made myself buy at the grocery store and then at the chunk of brie cheese. The crispy seven-dollar baguette on my countertop is begging me to grab the cheese, go to town, and eat all of my feelings. I even got a small jar of Nutella for when I finish the cheese, to feast on the last part of the crusty bread with. My mouth waters thinking of the chocolatey goodness. I have a weakness for anything and everything sweet.

"Go for the celery, Sarah." I try to amp myself up as my inner devil laughs in my face. "Yummy, yummy celery." I'm trying hard to convince myself as I grab the waning vegetable reluctantly. It's limp in my hand and reminds me of one of my ex-boyfriends, who shall not be named. He was always limp unless he watched porn. I stare at the celery and giggle, but then I let out a sigh as regret hangs over me. I haven't even eaten it yet, but I'm already disappointed in the choice. No one wants to eat a limp di—piece of celery.

"You will never be skinny if you don't make the right choices, Sarah." I continue lecturing myself, but it's half-hearted, and I already know I'll put it back in the fridge. I should dump it in the trash, but I know I'm going to lie to myself and pretend I'll eat it tomorrow. "Think of the bunny rabbits," I mumble as I place the celery back down in the fridge and push it to the back. I have no idea what I'm talking about, but I'm not going to question myself.

"You deserve this." My greedy fingers find a tub of Belgian chocolate pudding and grab a hold of it. "This is better than eating bread," I convince myself. The cheese and baguette can wait. Only chocolate can help to calm my nerves right now. "Stupid, Ethan Rosser, this is your fault," I say as I grab a spoon from my cutlery drawer, head toward the couch, and turn the TV on. I flick through the latest movies and TV shows on Netflix, Hulu, Peacock, Paramount Plus, Britbox, and Acorn, and let out a long sigh as nothing catches my attention.

Why am I paying for so many subscription services yet still have nothing to watch? I look away from the screen, and my body dances in joy as I take my first bite of the smooth, silky, and delicious pudding. For a few moments, I just enjoy the perfection that is this dessert and the immediate sugar high that hits me. My fingers flicker through my watching options again, and I settle on an old season of *Project Runway* that I've never seen before. I take a few more bites, settle back into my five throw pillows, and make myself comfortable.

Sometimes, it's not so bad being single and alone. I can eat what I want. Watch what I want. Wear what I want. And I can lie on the couch, scratching my stomach lazily without feeling self-conscious.

A life I'm sure women who date Ethan Rosser certainly do not have.

∽

I think I need a makeover. And when I say think, I mean, I know. The beautiful models and trendy designers on *Project Runway* have convinced me of that fact. I know I shouldn't compare myself to people on TV, but how can you not? Especially when you look down at your ugly black sweatpants and bright pink "I'm hot, and you're not" top. I don't wear the top out because I don't want someone to laugh and call me a liar.

I pause the TV and stroll over to the mirror in my

bedroom. I gaze back at my reflection, ignoring the smearing of chocolate on the top of my lip, emphasizing the mustache that is the bane of my existence. I get it waxed every week, but I swear it's becoming more and more obvious that it exists.

I grab my long, dark brown hair and try to style it. It sits flat and appears dull and lackluster. I know I need to get a cut, though I haven't bothered because it is almost permanently in a bun. I pull it up, tie a hairband around, and lean forward so I can examine my skin. I haven't had any acne in years, which is great, but I feel like I don't have any sort of glow. I hold back another sigh and stare into my eyes. My black horn-rimmed glasses make me look like Harry Potter's older, nerdy sister. Much older sister. Maybe even his spinster aunt. I suddenly remember the events of three days ago when I was in a store that shall not be named (cough, rhymes with castles) and the grumpy cashier who offered me a senior citizen discount.

"Excuse me, what?" I sputtered in bemused shock that later turned to anger. "I'm thirty-four."

The grumpy cashier glared at me like I was lying, while I glared back at her, waiting for her to apologize. Which she didn't do.

"I'm not seventy-four," I stated, waiting for her to cut me off and laugh and say she was joking.

Her deadpan face just stared back at me.

"Or however old you have to be to get the discount. I haven't checked yet, as I'm not even close to being that age," I continued to a disbelieving cashier. Okay, so that was a bit of a lie. I did know how old you needed to be to get the discount. Fifty-five in some places. Sixty-five in others.

But I digress. That wasn't important.

Instead of apologizing, the lady, who had no relation to an animal that goes moo, asked me if I was paying by cash or card. I covered the fifty-two dollars with my American Express card and prayed I wouldn't see decline before I left the store. Thankfully, it went through.

I try to dismiss the memory from my brain as I rub my forehead and straighten my shoulders. I could be beautiful if I tried a little harder. That's what all my idiot and too-honest brothers say. As they laugh and smirk. *Jackasses.* I know they love and support me, but I don't need their feedback on my looks. It's because of the fact that I have six older brothers that I'm a bit of a tomboy. And I never really learned how to apply makeup, wear sexy clothes or flirt well.

I walk over to my closet and open the door to see if I can find an amazing outfit to wear to work the next day. I'm not trying to garner the attention of anyone specific, but I would like to look good enough to be included in a company brochure. I would like to not be as dull as wallpaper. However, as I look at my drab and tired pieces of clothing, I understand why I haven't drawn the eyes of Ethan or any other hotties.

My clothes have seen better days, as well. But it's not like I have money to go out and buy a brand-new wardrobe. My savings account is an unhealthy three thousand five hundred dollars. Granted, my 401k looks a bit better than that, but I can hardly see HR or the government cutting me a break if I say I'd like to loan myself five grand to buy some new clothes. It would more than likely make me get audited, and the last thing I need is for the IRS to know that the twenty-five dollars I listed as an office lunch expense on my last tax return was really a me-bitching-about-my-boss event with my two besties, Isabel and Ella, at a local bar.

No, I would just have to make do with the clothes I already own. No matter how dated they make me feel. It's not like I have anyone to impress, anyway.

2

Ethan

"How many times do I have to tell you to tell these people to stop putting me in their newspaper?" I fling the paper down on the table in disgust and glare at my assistant Edith. She doesn't bat an eyelid as she glances up at me over the top of her purple glasses. Her blue eyes take me in keenly and then glance back down at her desk. She doesn't even acknowledge the paper as she swipes something on her phone. She's looking at photographs of her grandkids and is not bothered with me and my bad mood whatsoever. "Did you hear me?" I ask her, irritation clear in my voice. I fold my arms, square my shoulders, and stare her down.

"I heard you, Ethan." There's not a note of concern in her voice as she nods and holds up a photo of a blond baby in a bath. "Isn't Jeremiah such a cutie?" she gushes as she waves the photo back and forth in front of my face.

I hold my breath and count to ten. For the twentieth time this week, I want to fire her. She deserves to be fired. She's the worst assistant to exist in corporate America, yet I know I can't get rid of her. Edith Pisa has been at the company since my grandfather started it and even worked for free for my dad when he almost ran it into the ground. Edith knows the Rosser family loves her and that she has a job for life, even if she doesn't actually do much. And by much, I mean nothing. She's entitled to a full pension. She is set for life but says coming to the office gives her purpose.

"He's okay." I press my lips together as she flickers through more photos of her grandchildren, like I care. "Are there any messages for me?"

"Not that I know of." She shakes her head as if I'm asking her a dumb question. "Oh, there is something. Janet, you know Janet, she works in the cafeteria. She makes the coffee. Not the bad coffee, that's Sylvia. Who I daresay should have been fired long ago, but I guess after she got over cancer, it would have been heartless to fire her."

"Edith, please. What is the point of this?" I hold in a huge sigh as I grab a stack of letters from her desk.

"Well, Janet told me that she was speaking to people in the IT department this morning. They love her cappuccinos, you see. She gives them free biscotti, with each cup. Homemade it is, very nice. I think her husband's mother was from Sicily."

"Edith."

"Well, they said that there's an internal website

going live this week. An internet for everyone who works here at Rosser International. Just for us."

"Intranet."

"That's what I said, internet."

"No, it's an intranet. It's a private network for all employees to communicate with each other. Post memos, etcetera." I nod. "And yes, it's going live later this week. I am the one that approved it."

"Well, well, well, look how far we've come." Edith sits back and opens her handbag. I can see some knitting needles and several skeins of wool. She's probably knitting me another scarf for my birthday or a blanket for another one of her grandkids. I wasn't going to bother asking which one, though I hope it's not for me. The bright red wool I can see is not appealing to me whatsoever.

"I'm going into my office. Hold all calls for the morning. I need to concentrate on some contracts Nicholas has drawn up for our new line of pendant lights." I may as well be talking to myself. Edith is no longer listening. I walk into my office, close the door, and pull out my cell phone. It rings twice, and then I hear a long groan.

"What is it?" Pamela, my real assistant, answers, and I know she's not happy to hear from me. I don't care.

"When are you back? Edith is not handling shit." I grunt as I head toward my desk. My office is vast, with a majestic view of the New York skyline. I can see Central Park in the distance. I think of the people walking about leisurely at that very moment. None of whom are as rich as me. No one who is walking around in the middle of a workday has close to the amount of money I have.

"Next week."

"Next week?" I glare into the phone. "That means I have to handle the entire week by myself."

"I'm sorry, Ethan, but you've known that I was going to be away this week for over a year." I can hear seagulls in the background as she talks and whispers something to someone and giggles.

"It's just not a good time to be away..." My voice trails off as I pause and wait for her to offer to get back to the office to help me out. There's silence on the other end of the line, aside from the sound of waves crashing against rocks and little kids screaming in the background.

"Ethan, I am on my honeymoon. You're lucky I even answered the phone." She sounds annoyed now, and I can picture her pinched white lips. Pamela often gets annoyed with me and isn't shy to express her sentiments, which is why we get on so well. Pamela, like Edith, is not in love with me, has no desire to impress me, and doesn't want to date or marry me. And she isn't trying to get her hands on my fortune. That is part of the reason why she's worked alongside me and Edith for the past five years without issue. In fact, Pamela used to be a workaholic until Carl came along, swept her off her feet, and then proposed to her. Carl Poveroski is the worst thing that has ever happened to me and my work life.

"Aren't honeymoon's overrated?" I ask, grunting as I take a seat behind the mahogany wooden desk that my grandfather had once sat behind. His father made the desk, and it makes me proud to use it to work from every day. A real piece of family history.

"Mr. Rosser." She changes to my formal name and I know she's lost all patience with me. "Was there something important you wanted to ask me before I hang up in five seconds?"

"Make sure I'm not on that list of eligible bachelors again next year," I snap as I lean back and check my email. I groan as I see dozens of new emails from eager women who have gone to our company website and found my email address. I close my eyes and press my lips together. "I don't need every desperate woman in the United States and beyond trying to make me fall for them."

"If you got married yourself, then you wouldn't have to worry about being on the list," she says smartly and then laughs because she knows her words are not what I want to hear. "Carl wants to go swimming now. Have a great week. I'll see you soon." Before I can respond, she hangs up the phone, and I put my cell down on the desk.

"Never going to happen," I mutter to no one as I think about her words. The thought of getting married does not excite me. I don't see myself married. Or having kids. Or settling down with one woman. My grandparents think it's because I've never met the one, but I already know there isn't a one. I've dated hundreds, if not thousands, of women, and I have not once wanted to have a serious relationship. I know many women think I had my heart broken when I was younger, and that's why I'm not looking for anything serious, but no such thing ever happened. I've never been in love and never wanted it, either. The last thing I need is a bunch of women trying to garner my attention to try to be the one to make me settle down.

Bang. A loud rapping on my door makes me stand up and walk toward it. I know it's not Edith because she doesn't bother to knock.

"Who is it?" I call out as I open the door abruptly. I try not to roll my eyes as I see my CFO, Jackson Pruitt, standing there with a bouquet of roses in his hand and a dopey grin on his face. I already know he's about to get on my nerves with some foolishness. Jackson is my best friend, colleague, and probably the only person in the world who can tease me and get away with it.

"Mr. Rosser, please take me on a date this evening," he says in an overly high, squeaky feminine voice as he walks into my office. "I promise I can make all your dreams come true." He pretends to bow and flutters his fingers. "I've looked all my life for a mighty fine man like you," he continues, barely able to keep a straight face as he jokes around.

"Really, Jackson?" Fireworks spark from my eyes as I glare at his grinning face. He thinks he's funny, and I know he will be teasing me for the next couple of days, as he does every year when the article comes out. I wish the sparks were real so that they'd burn him and make him shut up.

"But, sir, I'm sure I can make you fall in love with me," he says with a wink as he saunters to the desk and sits in one of the leather chairs. "How many emails have you gotten already saying the very same thing?"

"No idea." I walk back to my chair and sit down and face him. There's a stupid expression on his familiar face that makes me want to laugh and smack him at the same time. Our relationship is one of the most important in my life. He is like a brother to me. "Just so you know, I don't read any of the emails I receive. I delete them. I wish I could delete my email address from the website, as well."

"But we both know that Rosser International is a company that stands for transparency. From the CEO to the clerks in the mailroom," he reminds me of my mantra, and the policies I instated years ago, and chuckles. "Isn't that why stocks are up thirty-one percent this year? Or is it that all the women in the world want to invest in your company because they think they will have a chance with you if you know they're a shareholder?"

"Or maybe they are hoping to have a chance with you?" I suggest as I take in his short, dark hair and vivid green eyes. Jackson Pruitt was the second most handsome man behind me when we were at Harvard getting our MBAs. At least, that's what I always teased him and said. I know that many women prefer his looks to mine. They definitely prefer his lighthearted, flirtatious personality to my overly serious one. I don't have time for small talk or banter. I didn't have time for it in college, nor do I now. Back then, I focused on saving the family company. Now that I've saved it and have plenty of money, I should be more lighthearted. But the responsibility of thousands of families rests on my shoulders, and I take that very seriously. I have money to continue to make and families to support, including my own.

"They can have a chance." Jackson winks and places his palms on the table. "And if they can blow my mind on the first date then they get a second date, where I'll actually spend some money on them."

"You're a dog."

"I'm not the only one that dates a lot," he shoots back at me.

"But I don't sleep with them all."

"You sleep with some of them though." He grins at me. "Don't pretend to be a monk with me, Ethan. You forget we date in the same circles. There are many women who talk about your prowess in the bedroom."

"What can I say?" I shrug, a certain smugness in my tone. "I like to fuck. What red-blooded male doesn't? I can't help it if I'm so amazing in bed that women always want more. Sorry the women you date don't feel the same."

"Most men don't have a five-date rule though." Jackson leans forward on the desk. "And most don't tell women on the first date that there will not be a sixth date or sex after the fifth time."

"I like to be clear about what is available when going out with me." I grab some folders and hand them over to him. If he's going to waste my time and annoy me, then he might as well be given more work. "Enough about my love life. Nicholas sent over some contracts between us and several department stores for our new line of pendant lights. We need to have these read by tomorrow as we're meeting with Home Design Depot in the morning to finalize the details for the first shipment. We have ten thousand items being sent out and a massive campaign starting next month."

"Didn't Nicholas say the terms were good?" Jackson's eyes are keen as he gazes at me, his brain back into work mode. "You still want us to go over them to find stuff he may have missed or just to be more knowledgeable?"

"We need to ensure we know exactly what they say." I remind him of my mantra, "Let there be nothing going on at the company that we don't know about." I trust Nicholas; he is one of the best corporate attorneys in America, but I need to ensure I know everything I am agreeing to in every contract I sign off on. Since I was a young boy, I'd been taught by my grandfather Frederick that one should always have knowledge of everything going on in your own business. This was stressed to me as he watched his son and my father running his business into the ground. My father was not astute, lacked knowledge of basically everything, and had a gambling and woman addiction that led to a predilection for buying my mother anything and everything she wanted, no matter if he could afford it or not.

"I know." He nods. He knows all about my family history and my need to be diligent. "I actually came up to talk to you about the marketing campaign for the brass and gold dome lights designed by Lord Chambers. He wants to have a jingle created." Jackson smirks as I run my fingers through my hair in exasperation. It had been my idea to have a Royal Lighting Line, but dealing with the various members of different royal families was proving to be extremely tiring. Especially seeing as the lighting section of my corporation was only one percent of what we did. Yet the named royals designing some of the lights had expectations out of this world.

"A jingle?" I raise an eyebrow. "What does he think he's creating? A new cereal for kids?"

"Hardly." Jackson laughs, and a light comes on in his green eyes, and I can tell he's just had what he thinks is an ingenious idea. He stands up and heads over to me. "Though General Mills has had a—"

"Stop right there." I cut him off. "We're not going into the cereal market."

"But..."

"But nothing." I lean back in my seat and think for a second. Lord Chambers, though not particularly talented, has a large social media following due to his handsome, good looks and daredevil lifestyle. He can sell several hundred thousand lights for us if we hit the market just right. If it's a jingle he wants, it's a jingle he shall get. I stand up and head back toward the door. "The cereal line is not going to happen, especially if we're focusing on branching out into entertainment and, specifically, new musical artists. Shall we go down to copywriting and see if anyone can come up with a jingle?"

"You want to venture down to the copywriting department?" He grins in surprise as he jumps up and puts the folders under his arm. "Going to hang out with the peasants."

"They're not peasants. I am accessible to everyone in the company."

"Sure you are." He laughs, and I know he wants to add something else but thinks better of it. Jackson and I have been best friends since high school. We both went to undergrad together and got our MBAs at Harvard. When I took over Rosser International, he was the first hire I made, even though he'd been recruited by Fortune 500 companies for far more money. He helped me grow the company into the huge success it is today and is my right-hand man. I love him like a brother, and even though we have different personalities, we get on like a house on fire.

"You coming?" I ask him as we exit the office. Edith is now on the phone and eating a sandwich, and all I do is smile as she gives me a happy wave. She might be an awful assistant, but she is like family, at this point. "Edith, Jackson and I are headed down to copywriting. I'll be back in a bit."

"Sure thing, Ethan." She smiles at me as she lowers her phone from her ear. "Watch out for all the ladies who might want to marry you."

"There's a no-fraternization policy at Rosser International," I remind her. "Everyone knows that."

"Yes, Ethan." She nods and then looks over to Jackson. "And what about you, Mr. Pruitt? Are you in the market for a wife?"

"I think that neither of us is in the market for a wife," he says as he hands her the bouquet of roses.

"These are for you. Turns out, Ethan doesn't want them."

"Ooh, thank you very much." She beams as she pushes her chair back. She places her phone down on the table loudly and grabs the flowers. "Let me go and find a vase. I don't want these to dry out. Oh, what will my Frank say when he sees I've been given roses? He'll be so jealous." There's excitement in her tone, and I don't question why she wants to make her husband of decades jealous.

"Sounds good." I nod and wrinkle my nose as I see my face beaming up at me from her table. The newspaper article is mocking me as it lies across her desk, and I turn back to Jackson with an annoyed frown. My furtive expression causes him to smirk, but I don't acknowledge his holier-than-thou look. "Come on, let's go. Hopefully, no one else in the office thinks they can talk to me about my love life."

3

Sarah

Dear Diary,

Isabel thinks I should have a stripper name. She thinks that's the way to reel men in on my now-defunct dating profile. I reminded her that I'm thirty-four and not twenty-one. I'm not going to start calling myself Flexible Barbie or Sexy Kitten. For one, I don't look like Barbie and secondly, I'm not that flexible. Plus, no one would believe I'm a stripper.

Trust me, I once attempted to audition at a private club. I was laughed off the stage, but that's a story for another time.

Sarah

"So, there she was, on this yacht being fed grapes by this man, and she sits up, and she says, 'Do you or don't you have a billion dollars?'" My coworker Ginger is eagerly recapping some reality TV show she watched the evening before, and even though I've never watched it before, I feel like I know all the stars of the show like family.

"Wasn't she just sucking his toes the night before?" I ask, trying to remember what she'd said happened in the last episode. "Shouldn't she have asked him about his bank account before that?"

"Well, the problem was she thought he was related to some A-list actor, at first, but then he told her that he was actually—" Ginger pauses and jumps up abruptly, giving me whiplash at her sudden change of attitude. "So, Sarah. I will need the copy for the Monsoon account by the end of the day." Her tone is high and nervous, and I blink in confusion. Monsoon, who? What on earth is she talking about?

"Huh?" I blink at her. "What about Bridget or Janelle or whatever her name was and the billion-dollar question?"

"Now is not the time."

"That's what she should have said to him before she decided she was going to suck on his cheesy—" I pause as I realize I can smell a distinct male cologne and look up. I freeze as I see Ethan Rosser and Jackson Pruitt standing at the front of our department, looking around. My heart races as I watch the two handsome men who run the company. Both are super rich, super handsome, and out of my league. I look down at my desk, pull my keyboard toward me, and start typing. I now understand why Ginger is acting so weirdly. I only hope our voices didn't carry across the small room. I hear footsteps approaching my desk, and I take a deep breath and look up. If Ethan Rosser heard Ginger and I talking about toe-sucking, I would die.

"Good afternoon, Mr. Rosser." Dave, another coworker, jumps up. He is normally engaged in the shows that Ginger recaps every morning, as well, but he'd wanted to check his stats in some game he was playing online. "Good afternoon, Mr. Pruitt. How can we help you today?" Dave is grinning like he's an exemplary employee, not someone who sings show tunes all day while eating Cheetos and doughnuts.

"Is Mr. Wayne around?" Jackson speaks up, and I peer at him from behind my glasses. He's so hot that he could be a Hollywood movie star. He looks around the room, and I feel his eyes on me briefly. He nods slightly but continues looking around. I can't take my eyes off of him though. He's wearing a navy suit with a white shirt and an emerald-green tie that matches the color of his eyes. You can tell that he did it on purpose. He knows he's gorgeous.

"He just popped out to grab a sandwich," Dave answers, and heads over to the two men. "Can I help you?"

"We need to talk to him about creating a jingle for Lord Chambers' new gold dome pendant light designs," Ethan Rosser says sharply. I can tell that he's not happy that Todd Wayne is not in the office. Little does he know, but Todd is barely in the office. He started dating a nurse that works at night and likes to spend his days with her; even though she sleeps most of the time. He says it's worth it because she loves to make love every time she wakes up. I'm sure Mr. Rosser doesn't want that information though.

"A jingle?" Dave asks, a questioning expression on his overeager face. Dave is very much like a puppy dog, and anytime anyone brings up anything vaguely related to music, he gets excited. He initially moved to New York with the idea that he would make it big on Broadway or be discovered at a karaoke night and made into a pop star. Neither of which happened because the simple fact of the matter is that he can't sing to save his life. Not that I or Ginger would ever tell him that. Sometimes, it's nice for people to live in their own worlds. Plus, as someone who would love to be a songwriter, I don't want to burst his bubble. It feels like karma would fire right back at me and tell me I won't make it, either.

"Yes." Ethan nods but doesn't elaborate on what he means. Most probably because we're mere peons, and he doesn't even know who we are. Though, maybe I am being unfair to him. Maybe he does know us. Maybe he's heard great things about what we've done on the Jerry Catnip campaign. Maybe I'm too self-analytical and down on myself. I need to have more confidence. That's what Ella and Isabel always say. I push my chair back and stand up. I am going to be a part of this conversation. I am going to be assertive. Especially as I am the creator of most of the work in the department. Even if Todd pretends it is him.

Ethan turns to Jackson and lowers his voice. "What do you think? Do we wait a few moments to see if—"

"We can help," I say, though my voice is little more

than a pip from a squeaky toy. I need to take an assertiveness class or something because this is ridiculous. My brothers wouldn't believe how shy and quiet I am at this moment, since they considered me loud and annoying for all of our childhood. Though, that's because they're my brothers, not two very handsome billionaires that every woman in the world wanted to date.

I mean, aside from me. I couldn't care less about dating either one of them.

Neither man looks at me as I approach, but that doesn't surprise me. They most probably didn't even hear me talking. I make my way over to them, hoping they will both turn to me with huge smiles of awe, but they're too engaged in their conversation. I play my this or that game, something I've been doing since childhood. Basically, I have to choose in my mind which option I would take. Often, the game is about items or possibilities that would never actually exist to me, but I don't care. I once spent a good hour debating with myself whether I would go with a black sports Range Rover or a white Tesla Model 3. After going through all the options, I went with the Range Rover; it just looked like a cooler car. I didn't care that I could barely pay my bills that month and that the Range Rover dealership would laugh me out of town if I went in to purchase one.

Now I'm debating which one between Ethan and Jackson I would choose if I had to give them a rose on *Bachelor in Paradise*. Both men are more attractive than is fair. Both are rich. Both have bodies that look muscular. Jackson seems friendlier and more open to flirting, but Ethan has that dark, brooding look in his eyes that drives women like me crazy. And when I say women like me, I mean women who fall for emotionally unavailable men. I am the bane of my existence. Constantly lusting over and dating the wrong men.

"We can..." I am louder this time, though I pause as Ethan looks at me, his blue eyes keen as he glances at me. I can feel myself flush as I am finally acknowledged by the big boss. I swallow hard and plaster on my best, most winning smile. For some reason, I push my shoulders back and my breasts forward and start to play with my hair. "I was just saying that we can—"

"Jackson, I have to take this." Ethan pulls his phone out of his pocket, glances at the screen, and heads out of the office without a single word to me, Dave, or Ginger. I'm mortified, embarrassed, and annoyed. Suddenly, I remember why I do not like him. He is a jerk. I stand there and look at Dave for a few moments before looking over at Jackson.

"I was just going to say that we can help you. We do most of the work in the office, anyway," I say to Jackson, who smiles at me in a way that tells me he's being nice but not trying to get into my pants. I know it's the glasses, the bun, and the fact that I have no makeup on, but still, it burns a bit. I've heard he's a huge flirt, normally.

"Oh, don't mind Ethan." Jackson chuckles. "His mind is all over the place. He's in a bad mood because an article has come out about him and now, he'll be the focal point of every woman's eyes for the next two months."

"Oh, the most eligible bachelor in New York article?" I ask, silently chiding myself for admitting I know of its existence.

"Yes." Jackson's eyes are alight with glee. "He hates when newspapers and magazines feature him in this way, but I sure notice that he hasn't given them my name and address so they can feature me instead." He cocks his head to the side and smirks slightly. "I don't think I'd mind so much being bachelor of the year."

"I'm surprised they haven't asked you," I say honestly. Jackson Pruitt is just as eligible of a bachelor as Ethan is, as he's the heir to the Pruitt fortune. He's old money, and sometimes there's talk in the tabloids that he's going to leave Rosser International and take over his family business, The Pruitt Company; however, the rumor at the office says that that's unlikely to happen as there's a reason that he doesn't work there in the first place. Though, no one knows what that reason is.

"Do you think I'm eligible?" He winks at me and then tilts his head down and spins around. "Before you answer that and offend me, I must go..." He looks back at me. "What's your name?"

"Sarah," I say breathlessly.

"Nice to meet you, Sarah, in copywriting." He heads out of the office, and Dave, Ginger, and I stare at each other for a few moments before Dave starts singing "Moon River" in a very off-key voice.

"What was that all about then?" Ginger asks,

ignoring him and looking at me with narrow eyes. "You trying to reel yourself in a big fish?"

"No." I roll my eyes at her and then take my glasses off to clean them on the hem of my shirt, which I know is a bad idea, but I always forget to bring my lens-cleaning cloth with me to work. "Why would you say that?"

"You were all over Ethan." Dave stops singing, and there's a slight sulk to his tone as he realizes that neither of us is paying attention to him. "I've never seen you smiling like a vulture before."

"What?" I glare at him, annoyed. "I was not smiling at him like a vulture, plus, vultures don't smile."

"Sure they do. And when Ethan wasn't interested, you went for Jackson, who obviously wants to bed you," he says, and heads back to his desk before I can argue with him. I shake my head and try not to fume because the fact of the matter is, I had been smiling with all my might, but the great and mighty Ethan had not cared in the least.

I look down at the half-eaten ice cream tub on my lap and feel guilty for all of ten seconds. The chocolate fudge brownie ice cream certainly isn't going to help me look like a cover model for *Sports Illustrated*, but at least it's saving me therapy money. I lean back on my comfortable leather couch, pull my cream cashmere throw over my body, and reach for the remote control. Johnson, my mini golden doodle, jumps up and settles on my lap, his little nose twitching as he inches closer to the ice cream tub.

"Nope." I tap him on the nose, moving the ice cream out of his reach. "You can't eat this, Johnson." Johnson was named after Lyndon B. Johnson because he came into my life after reading his biography. I'm a bit of a history nerd. But I don't tell many people that. Not when I already look like Harry Potter's older sister. Being a nerd is only cute when you could also be a supermodel. No one cares if you're just a regular nerd.

Johnson gives me a dissatisfied look, jumps off the couch, and heads toward his bed to do who knows what. I pick up my phone and call Isabel, who doesn't prefer to go by Izzy, even though I'm trying to make it happen after being a latecomer to *Grey's Anatomy*. She answers after one ring.

"What are you up to, Sarah?" she asks as if there is a possibility that I could be up to something amazing. Sadly, we both know that's highly unlikely.

"Oh, you know, just getting ready to head into a sex club with my dominatrix, Arnold." Johnson stares at me with judgmental eyes, and I avert my gaze. I will not let my dog make me feel like an idiot or a hoe. He, better than anyone, knows I'm not. I haven't had a man back in the apartment in years.

"Oh, you've gone back to the Austrian?" she asks with a giggle, then pauses. "What happened to Ricky?"

"Ricky, who?" I wonder if there's a Ricky I've forgotten about flirting with? It's unlikely, but not impossible.

"The hot Puerto Rican guy that was a world-famous singer—"

"If you're talking about Ricky Martin, it turns out he doesn't want me. He's gay."

"But she bangs..." she interrupts her own sentence by bursting into laughter. I listen and shake my head. Isabel is much younger than me, but we get on like a house on fire. I think that's because I am still young at heart. And when I say much younger, I mean more than five years, though it's not anything either of us thinks about.

"Have you heard from Ella?" I ask, bringing up our other best friend. "Is she still in Paris?"

"Nope, the lucky bitch is in London now," she says, and we both sigh in happy jealousy for her good luck. Ella is now dating her brother's best friend, Colton, who is also her boss, and he has decided to take her to Paris for their first date. A place I have never been to but want to go to so badly. I can picture myself eating croissants while flirting with a hot French man or two.

"Wow, when is she back?" I ask, not because I envy her dating a billionaire but because I miss her and our weekly girls' nights.

"I think she said she's back next week unless Colton surprises her with another destination." Isabel half laughs, and I know she's on the same page as I am. We're happy for our friend, but we want love, as well. Frankly, I would settle for good sex. But I'm not going to advertise that fact. I know if I create a dating profile saying I'm looking for good sex, I'd have ten thousand applicants. And not because they were good in bed, no, but because men have super huge egos, and they all think they've made you have the best orgasm of your life, even if you barely even felt them inside of you.

"Awesome. She's living her best life," I say and then let out a deep sigh. I am not living my best life whatsoever. "You wanna go for a drink tonight?"

"Don't you have work tomorrow?"

"Yeah, and what is your point?" I retort without even an iota of guilt. My job sucks. My work as a junior copywriter in the marketing department of Rosser International means nothing. I am a peon in a conglomerate, and I hate my job. I don't get to write cool copy for ads or anything. No, I write copy to send in press releases to market and sell the thousands of crappy products we sell. Not that I would say that out loud to anyone out of my small friend group.

No one else at the company feels the same way though. Everyone else drinks the Kool-Aid that Ethan Rosser, the CEO, is distributing. Not that he's ever distributed any to me. I'm not important enough at the company for him to know I exist. Even though I have been in the same room as him twice, he hasn't acknowledged me properly once. Today didn't really count.

I cringe and die inside a little bit when I think back to earlier in the day when I tried to give him my best flirtatious smile. I do not want to remember that moment though. Even if Dave and Ginger won't let me forget it.

It's slightly embarrassing how hard I was staring the man down without even one flirtatious smile or admiring glance in response. And when I say slightly embarrassing, I mean a momentous amount of embarrassment. He most probably thought I was after him because of the article. The joke's on him, though, because I also think the article is trash.

"You want to get drunk on a work night? I mean, I'm down, but I'm just checking. I know you work in corporate."

"Not like I'm high up and it will matter if I'm slightly hungover tomorrow morning. No one around me cares." I laugh as I think about my little cubicle at work. I interact with my two workmates, Ginger, an early-sixties woman who loves to gossip, and Dave, a mid-forties man from Kentucky who originally moved to the city to be on Broadway. But it was obvious today that we're just lowly peons to those at the top. "I'm a nobody at Rosser International. It's not like you see me on the list of the most eligible New York City singles."

"Maybe not officially, but you are definitely one of the most eligible women in the city," Isabel says, and all I can do is laugh because I'm not sure that's quite true. There's nothing to make me an eligible woman other than being single. And certainly, nobody at work would look at me twice, seeing as I look like a dowdy librarian every day. But the reason why is a story for another day. "Don't laugh," she continues. "You are wanted by so many men."

"In what dreamworld? Must be yours because it's certainly not mine." It would be nice to be highly sought after though. I could get on board with hundreds of hot men chasing me down to date me. Actually, that's not true. Hundreds of men sound fairly tiring. In reality, I could most probably handle three men wooing me at the same time. A couple of dinner dates a week and maybe one date dancing. I'm already exhausted just thinking about it.

"Well, maybe tonight I can show you just how wrong you are."

"So, you're up for going out?" I ask hopefully, though I have no doubt what she will say.

"Was that ever in question?" Isabel says, and reminds me why she is one of my best friends. "So, where are we going?"

"I have no idea." I think for a moment and put her on speakerphone. "Hold on, let me pull up my Insta account. I think Dave posted about some cool new bar he hit up last weekend. He was raving about it at work."

"Do we trust Dave's taste?" she asks skeptically, and I know she's thinking about the time Dave took me dress shopping for a night out, and I ended up looking like a nurse from the 1940s. And not a cute one, either. Dowdy is the word that comes to mind.

"He might not know women's clothing styles well, but he does know bars," I respond, and scroll through my feed until I remember I can just go to his page and scroll through his posts. "He told me there were lots of hot guys there that night."

"Straight or gay?" she hits back quickly. "I don't care, but I want to know if there's a possibility I am going to get my flirt on tonight or not?"

"I don't know that Sam is going to be there," I quip, and she groans.

"Like I told you before, I do not have a crush on

Sam Wynter." She is way too emphatic in her denial, but I decide to let it go. If she's not ready to acknowledge that she's in love with Ella's brother, then who am I to force her?

"The Owl and The Pussycat is the name of the bar," I exclaim, changing the subject. "It looks pretty cool, very trendy. I see a lot of Wall Street types in the background."

"We don't do Wall Street types though."

"Right now, we're not doing anyone, so I'm not too picky. Are you?"

"Guess not." She giggles. "Meet you there in an hour?"

"Perfect," I say, jumping off the couch and watching my forgotten ice cream tub fall to the ground, spilling melted ice cream everywhere. "That is why I should have just eaten the entire thing," I mumble as I hang up the phone and get some paper towels. I'm looking forward to going out and perhaps meeting and flirting with some guys.

I even imagine going home with one. I'm not normally the girl to go for a one-night stand, but Ella had attempted to have one and ended up with the love of her life. Perhaps something similar would happen to me. Though, I know that's doubtful. I'm more likely to have a one-night stand with a homeless man, and then he'd never want to leave, and I'd have to feed another mouth until he finally stole all my money and left me and Johnson, heartbroken and hungry.

4

Ethan

"The best way to get out of your funk is to go out and grab a drink." Jackson strums his fingers against my desk, and I look up at him irritably. There's nothing I dislike more than when people tell me how to get out of a funk I'm not in.

"Not your best idea." I look back down at the files on my desk. It will take me a good three to four hours to finish going through them. Then, I have to head to the gym and work out before heading home for bed. "I don't want a drink, and I don't want to be accosted by dozens of women as soon as I enter the bar."

"Since when?"

"Since when what?" I snap, giving him the evil eye. If I had a magic power that allowed me to shoot laser beams from my retinas, I would activate it now. "Don't you have something else to do, Jackson, other than get on my nerves?"

"Ooh, I'm getting on your nerves now?" Jackson

acts like he can't believe what I've said. As if I haven't said it a million times before now. "I think that is a definite sign that you need to leave the paperwork for the night and come out and grab a drink."

"Why do you want me to get a drink with you so much?" I question him, my patience wearing thin. I do not want to be around giggling, flirtatious women, the entire evening telling me how amazing I am.

"Maybe because you're Mr. Popular?" He shrugs. "And if you are popular, then I'm popular."

"You don't need me to be popular," I say, looking at him in his expensive, crisp navy-blue suit. The top button of his shirt is undone, and I know that women will hurry over to him as soon as they see him. Jackson needs me as much as he needs a skunk to be popular.

"Oh, come on, Ethan. I know you're in a bad mood, but this is not going to make you feel better. Like I said we—"

"We nothing," I growl.

"Look here, old chap, let's grab a drink. There's this new bar that opened called the Owl and the Pussycat. We can check it out, then we can come back. Maybe we can even come up with a jingle ourselves. Todd Wayne never got back to you, right?"

"No, he didn't." I frown, wondering why the man never emailed me back.

"So, then, I guess we come up with something."

"You and I come up with a jingle?" I say stoically as I glance at him. "Copywriting isn't really our wheelhouse."

"Well, I actually had an idea already."

"You did?" I raise a single eyebrow and lean back in my leather chair. I tap my fingers against the solid wood desk and stare at him for a couple of seconds. "Go on, then."

"Go on what?"

"Let me hear the jingle you created. Now."

He walks toward me and takes a seat in the chair opposite the desk. Our eyes are locked and honed in on one another, almost as if we're battling. I know I'm going to win. I always win. Be it a staring contest, an arm-wrestling match, or a mental showdown. I never lose.

"Fine," he says, tapping his foot against the ground. I hold back a smile as I wait for him to sing the jingle he's created.

He clears his throat and counts, "A one, a one, a one, two, three, four."

He starts snapping his fingers, and I'm holding back laughter now. If there's something about Jackson, it is that he always commits to what he's going to do.

"Get yourself some light," he sings. "Some beautiful lights. Do you want to feel like royalty, like the king and queen of France, or the king and queen of England, or the king and queen of your pants? Get yourself some lights. Get yourself some lights from Lord Chambers. He is not a stranger."

I can't stop myself; the laughter erupts from me. Jackson has a nice voice, but he's not talented with his wordsmithery.

"What? You don't like it?" He pouts like he's wounded. I know he's not.

"I wouldn't say I don't like it, but I would say it's kind of crap."

"Fine. Now, can we go grab a drink? You made me embarrass myself to get you to come out to the bar."

"Well, you chose to embarrass yourself," I say and then nod. "But fine, one drink, then I have to come back and work." I watch as he stands up, and we head toward the door. As we exit, I notice that Edith is long gone. However, the newspaper is still sitting there. I grab it from the desk and study my photo.

"Where did they get this picture from anyway? I look like a douchebag."

"Women love douchebags though." Jackson watches as I throw the newspaper into the trash. "Isn't that crazy?" Jackson says as we make our way to the elevator.

"What do you mean? Isn't what crazy?"

"That you hate the fact that lots of hot women want you? You're totally in another world, aren't you?" he asks as we step inside the elevator, and he presses the button for the lobby. He leans back against the wall and checks something on his phone.

"No, I'm not in another world. I'm just frustrated. I've called the newspaper several times. I've spoken to several different editors, including the editor in chief, and all of them have told me that I was put in the paper by popular demand. But really, who are these people who want me so badly? Who is voting for me to be the most eligible bachelor in New York City? The editor in chief said I come highly recommended each year."

Jackson looks away from me, then, and my eyes

narrow as he runs his fingers through his hair and taps his foot against the ground—telltale signs of some sort of guilt.

"Is there something you're not telling me?"

"What?" he says in an innocent tone, and I can feel something clicking in my brain, but I'm not sure what.

"*You* didn't nominate me, did you?"

"Me? Nominate you? Would I do such a thing?"

"Yes. Yes, you would. I remember when we were getting our MBAs and you nominated me to be president of the tennis club."

"What, you liked to play tennis."

"I've played tennis ten times in my life. I could take it or leave it."

"But you were really good."

"No, I wasn't."

"You were very sporty."

"I'm sporty, yes, and hey, I can hit the ball across the net. Didn't mean I wanted to be the president of the tennis association."

"Well, you should have told me you didn't want that job."

"I would've told you if I wanted it." I let out a deep sigh and press the stop button.

"Oh, boy," Jackson says, folding his arms and focusing on me. "What is it?"

"Tell me this. Did you, or did you not nominate me?"

"I didn't nominate you, but I may have told someone late one night that my best friend was really eligible and really rich and really good-looking. Not knowing that she would nominate you." He bows his head, but I can still see the knowing smirk. "In my defense, she was giving me the hand job of my dreams."

"Really, Jackson?"

"Sorry," he says, his eyes light as if he's remembering that night fondly. "But the good news is she hates me now, so it's very unlikely that she'll nominate you or put you in next year."

"I've been listed for the last five years. How long ago did you date this lady? What's her name? How do I get in contact with her?"

"To be honest, we were on and off for a couple of years. She liked to play, if you know what I mean. Ironically, her name was Primrose, but she went by Prim. I can see if I can find her number, if you want." He shrugs and presses the button for the elevator to continue. "Now, are we going to talk about this all night, Ethan, or are we just going to go out and have some fun?"

"Whatever," I say. "I can't believe Todd never got back to me. You haven't heard from him?"

"No." He shakes his head. "By the way, one of the girls down there was trying to say something to you before you left."

"Oh?" I stare at him. "Which girl?"

"I don't remember her name."

"I don't remember seeing anyone. I just remember that guy, Dave, or whatever his name is. I've spoken to him before and I did not want to be there when he burst into song again." I shudder as I think about him.

"That makes sense."

We exit the elevator as it arrives at the first floor and walk through the white marble floor of the lobby. I notice several of my employees having hushed conversations as they notice me. I nod at several members of staff and continue to the door. I know that my employees both revere me and are scared of me, which is the way that it should be. They should love me and want to work well, but they should also be in fear that if they don't do a good job, they will lose it. At least, that's what I think is my leadership style. I've been going to a therapist who says that might not be the best way to treat my employees. I'm still thinking about whether or not I agree with her.

I step outside of the building and look over to the right. My chauffeur, Randy, is standing there and hurries over. "Good evening, Mr. Rosser. Good evening, Mr. Pruitt," he says as he turns to Jackson. "Am I driving you somewhere tonight or will you be walking?"

I look over at Jackson. "How far away is this bar you were talking about?"

"It's on the other side of the city," he says. "Randy, do you mind driving us? It's a new bar called the Owl and the Pussycat."

"Not at all." Randy hurries toward the limo and opens the back door. "I'm here at your service, as always."

"Thank you, Randy," I say as I get into the back of the car. Jackson gets in beside me.

"You want a whisky?" he asks, opening the small fridge at the side. I nod, and he takes out a decanter with some of the finest Scottish whisky sold, pours me a glass, and makes one for himself.

"It's been a long day," he says, handing me the glass. "But I do have some good news."

"Okay, and that is?"

"The manufacturing plants in Ohio are scheduled to be completed next month, so that's a month ahead of schedule."

"We have enough people power to work them?" I ask him, raising an eyebrow. "I thought HR said they were having a hard time finding qualified applicants."

"We haven't gone into full-force yet, Ethan. We didn't want to do that until we knew when we were going to officially open, but now we have a date. I will speak to someone in HR about contacting some more recruitment agencies to get the word out. Everyone needs jobs."

"But do people want to work the jobs?"

"We pay three times minimum wage," he says. "We have excellent benefits. I don't know why they wouldn't."

"Yeah, I guess. Because that's going to be of the utmost importance if we're going to meet quotas." I pause as I see my phone ringing. It's my granddad. "Hey, hold on. It's Granddad."

I answer the phone. "Hey, what's up?"

"Hi, Ethan. I was just speaking to your nana, and we were wondering if you'd like to come over to dinner tonight."

"It's seven p.m., Grandpa."

"Oh, yes... Well, maybe not tonight. Maybe this weekend. Lunch."

"Yeah. Is everything okay? You sound weird."

"I'm not weird. I'm just..." He pauses. "Hold on, your nana wants to speak to you."

"Okay," I say, sitting back, staring out the window at the lights as Randy drives us through the hustling and bustling streets of Manhattan.

"Ethan, darling," my nana says in her sweet older voice. I wonder if she wants something.

"Hi, Nana, how are you?"

"Oh, darling, I saw the newspaper today." Of course.

"And I assume you're talking about the article?" I say sarcastically. "Who knew I was so eligible?"

"Yes, and I've had so many phone calls from so many of my friends with granddaughters who are also single. And I was thinking that..."

"No, Nana." I cut her off because I know exactly what she's going to say. She's going to say that she wants to have a luncheon, and invite over a bunch of eligible women to see if I like any of them. As if I were Prince Charming and the luncheon was instead of a ball for me to find my Cinderella. Nana knows better than this. I'm not looking for a Cinderella. I'm not looking for a princess. I'm not looking for anyone.

"But, Ethan."

"Nana."

"Oh, Ethan. You know how much I worry about you. I just..."

"There's no need to worry about me. I'm living my best life."

"But, darling, all you ever do is work, just like your grandfather. That's why I made him quit and hand over the company to your dad."

"And we both know Dad ran it into the ground, Nana. That's why I'm working so hard, remember? Because if I wasn't, then you and Grandpa might be out in the streets and Mom and Dad might be out in the streets, and the thousands of people that work for Rosser International might be out in the streets, as well."

"You know we appreciate everything you've done to turn the company around and it is doing so well because of you and that Jackson, of course."

"I'll let Jackson know," I say, glancing at my friend. He's looking at something on his phone, but I can see the smile on his lips. I know he knows exactly what this call is about because, every year, Nana tries to do the same thing, and every year, I tell her no, I'm not interested.

"Oh, but Ethan, I..."

"Nana, Jackson and I actually just headed out somewhere. Can I give you a call back later?"

"Well, you know what I would prefer?"

"What's that, Nana?"

"If you would just come to Sunday lunch."

"I'll come to Sunday lunch if you promise there won't be any eligible women there."

She lets out a deep sigh. "Fine, fine," she says again. "And you invite that friend Jackson of yours."

"I will. I'm sure he'd love to come, Nana. Love you."

"I love you, too, darling," she says.

We hang up, and I look back over at Jackson. "Nana wants you to come to lunch on Sunday."

"Ooh, I'm down," he says. "I love your nana's cooking."

"I know."

"If your nana was younger and single, I totally would have married her."

I roll my eyes. This is the hundredth time Jackson has said this to me and my nana. Nana loves it because he's so handsome, which makes her blush, but I know it's not true. Jackson, for all his talk, has no interest in getting married, either. He comes from a very wealthy family that is even more messed up than mine, and even though we don't talk about his reasons why, I know that he also doesn't believe in true love, and he also doesn't believe in a happily ever after.

"So, I was thinking," he says. "What about we change the company photo shoot from..." He pauses. "Wait, where were we going again?"

"I don't think we actually decided on a place, but I was thinking Hawaii."

"Did you finalize which of the employees would be coming?"

"Not yet," I said, shaking my head. "I did go around to the different offices with HR, but I guess, apparently, there's been some complaints because I went into a couple of offices and immediately said no. And they think it was based on me looking for people I thought were good-looking so the photos would be filled with the 'beautiful' people who work for me. But I don't see looks in the office. You know that."

"I know, because if you had, you would have totally noticed that smoking hot girl in copywriting that was trying to talk to you."

"What smoking hot girl? What are you talking about?" I rack my brain to think about the different people I'd seen in copywriting. "There was that guy Dave, and then that old lady, and then that librarian-looking lady."

"Oh my gosh, Ethan. You totally didn't check her out, did you?"

"Um, no, and you're telling me you did?"

"She was smoking. Sure, she had her hair in a bun and those big glasses, but I looked into her eyes and she was really pretty. She had a pretty face. I mean, she needs a makeover or something, but..."

"But nothing. You know you're not allowed to sleep with or date anyone at the office."

"Well, I'm not interested in dating her," he says. "But one hot night?" He smirks and puts his hands up as I glare at him. "Don't worry, I'm not going to sleep with the hot girl in copywriting."

"You better not," I say, shaking my head. "Plus, I think maybe you need to get laid, because I don't remember seeing any hot girl in copywriting." I shrug. "Are we nearly there yet, because I really do need to do some more work tonight."

"Don't worry," he says. "We'll be there in, like, ten minutes. We'll have a drink or two and then you can go home and bust your ass."

"Uh-huh," I say, shaking my head. "You're lucky that you're my best friend or you would not be able to get away with half the stuff you say to me."

"But I am your best friend and I can," he says, winking at me. "And that's why you just love having me as your CFO."

"Oh yeah," I say. "That's why. You're as welcome as a bullet in my head."

Jackson throws his head back and starts laughing because we know we would be lost without each other, and I couldn't run Rosser International without his help. Yes, sometimes I can be grumpy, but I know I wouldn't want to do it alone.

5

Sarah

Dear Diary,

Tequila is the devil. Or the drink of the devil. Or something like that. I swear that if I hadn't had tequila, I wouldn't have acted like the fool that only my friends know me to be.

Also, note to self: Boasting about your prowess as a stripper in a bar is not a good idea. Especially when you've never really been a stripper and are not interested in being one. Same goes for lap dancers. Saying that you once got a thousand dollars for a lap dance is not the flex you think it is when you're drunk.

Especially not when the CEO of your company is sitting in a booth in the corner of the bar, watching and listening to the entire conversation.

Kill me now.

Shameful and hungover,

Sarah

"This place is popping." Isabel grins as she bops her

head back and forth in time with the music blasting through the open doorway of the bar. "We are going to have so much fun tonight." Her entire body is practically buzzing in excitement as we walk into the crowded bar. She looks me up and down and beams as she takes in my sexy, slightly uncomfortable outfit. It's an outfit from when I was twenty pounds slimmer and ten years younger, but I wanted to sexy it up for the night. Something about being ignored by a hot guy makes you want to look your best. "You look so pretty, but I'm going to take your glasses off."

"What?" I exclaim, shaking my head. I know my glasses make me look nerdy, but they are a part of me. "I won't be able to see if you take my glasses off, and I kind of need to be able to see."

"You only need to be able to see if you're going to make a mistake tonight, but I'm not going to let you make any mistakes."

"Isabel, no," I say as she grabs my glasses and takes them from me. I feel naked without them on my face. I reach up self-consciously to touch the side of my face. I miss having my glasses there. They are like a part of me.

"Don't worry. I won't let you make out with anyone fugly and I won't leave your side to make out with anyone myself." She cocks her head to the side. "Unless Bradley Cooper shows up and says he must have me right away." She licks her lips. "Or Brad Pitt. Or both of them. I've never been interested in a threesome before, but if they both want me, I don't know that I'd be able to say no."

"Isabel," I whisper-shout, blinking my eyes, trying

to adjust to the dim light of the bar. "I can see you and that's about it. Everything else is blurry." I tap her shoulder. "Glasses, please?"

"You're able to see, right? Just not everything?"

"Yes, but..."

"Just enjoy the night. Plus, you look absolutely gorgeous." Her eyes run up and down my face and body. "You're the belle of the ball."

"This is not a ball."

"You're Cinderella and your Prince Charming is going to see you and want to sweep you up into his arms because he can't resist your stunning aura."

"You mean I look absolutely gorgeous without my glasses?" I fake a frown. "So, with my glasses, I'm the ugly stepsister?"

"No, silly. But why don't you wear contacts?"

"I told you why. They irritate my eyes, and I always feel like I'm going to lose an eye when I put them in and take them out."

"You just have to practice." She sighs deeply and motions putting contacts in and out of her eye. "When I first got contacts, I hated it, as well. But after the first month, I got used to it. You will get used to it, too. I can put them in and take them out in my sleep now."

"I'll think about it." I shrug and look around the bar. It's packed in here with wall-to-wall people from every sector. I can't see many faces clearly, but I can make out suits and skirts, and there is a lot of laughter in the room. The music is too loud, but what bar really gets the music level right.

"Oh, I love this song," I say as I hear Noah Kahan's

song, "Stick Season" playing. He's no relation of mine, even though we have the last name. Though, it would be cool if we were related. Maybe then I could play a song with him at one of his shows.

"Oh, it sounds cool." Isabel nods her head. "Totally your type of music." She sways back and forth to the folk-rock song. She's right. I am definitely into bluesy folk music. I'm a one singer with a guitar sort of person. "Written anything recently?" she asks, and I nod. "When can I hear it?"

"Soon." I'm too self-critical. I know that. I want everything to be perfect. My therapist blames it on my family. She says that even though I love my family, my brothers' constant teasing caused me to lack self-confidence. I don't know if that's true. It makes me feel guilty to assign blame to them for any of my negative traits.

"Hey, hold on," Isabel says as she reaches over and pulls out my hairband and lets my hair down. "You do not need your hair in a ponytail tonight."

"I didn't get to flatiron it and I need to get a trim." I run my fingers through my tresses and try to fluff it up.

"Or you don't have to do anything. It looks really cool and sexy, wavy like that." She grins. "You look hot."

"You mean I look hot without the glasses and with my hair down."

"Yes. I look better without my glasses, as well. It's not like you got plastic surgery, and I'm saying you only look hot after that." She links arms with me and hugs me to her. Even though Isabel is younger than me, she reminds me of a big sister. She's blunt and honest at all times, but she's the most loving, caring person I know. Also, the queen of bad decisions. However, that's not saying much because I am a close second in that realm. "Come on, let's go and get some drinks. Tequila shots on me."

"I don't know about tequila." Worried thoughts fill me as I follow her toward the crowded bar of other people waiting to drink away their woes and have a good night. "Tequila goes straight to my head." And that was an understatement. Tequila is a liquor that makes me need to throw my phone in the ocean so I can't drunk dial or text any men I've loved and lost or loved and never had.

"It goes straight to my head, as well. We need to have a good night, and if we are in our heads, we're not going to have as much fun as we could." Isabel dances and holds my hand up. "Tonight, we get out of our heads. Tonight, we are living our best lives."

"I don't need tequila. I can have fun with you being sober," I say honestly. Isabel is one of those friends that makes everything more fun. I watch as she twirls around, her skirt flying up as she spins. She's got a wide smile on her face, and I love how carefree she is in life. I want her to find love just as badly as I want to find love. Though, she says she's not looking for anyone. I know it's because she's in love with Sam and has been since she was young. I don't even know if she realizes how badly she has it for him. I don't even know if Ella realizes how deeply Isabel feels for her brother. But I know. I'm really intuitive when it comes to feelings. Though, I don't know how Sam feels. He's a typical man: clueless and caught up in the rat race at his law firm. He seems to spend every hour working and trying to make partner.

"Yeah, we always have fun just hanging out, but tonight we're going to flirt, and we're going to just do whatever we want to do." Isabel raises her hands in the air. "Tonight, we are free."

"Why do I kind of feel like that's what you said to Ella when she hooked up with Colton that night at Sam's holiday party?"

"Is that so bad though? Look how that worked out for her." She giggles. "Don't you want it to work out for you, too?"

"But there is no Colton in my life. There is no one that I want in any way." Which is sad and maybe not totally true, but that's what I'm telling myself. "So, if I go home with a guy tonight, it truly will be a one-night stand. And I don't do one-night stands. Especially not without my glasses on. I don't want to go home with a grandpa."

"Doubt any grandpas are here right now."

"Well, I can't really see, and I don't know that we have the same standards, so I'm not sure I want to rely on your discretion."

"Oh, my gosh. Get out of your head. Please, Sarah. It's going to be fine." She grabs my hands and jumps up and down. "I won't let alcohol take you down the mistaken hookup path tonight, I promise."

"Fine, but I am holding you to that." I smile; her energy is contagious, and I do like having fun. I look around and see a couple of guys at the bar to the right staring at us. I bet they think we're easy pickings because we're already acting like we're drunk. Little do they know, we're just high-energy. As we get closer to the men, I can see that they look kind of cute, but I can't really tell how cute because the lighting isn't great. I feel Isabel nudge me in the side, and I look over to her.

"Hottie alert. Two o'clock," Isabel says under her breath. She's noticed the guys, as well. She's running her fingers through her hair, so I assume that the men are very cute.

I smile automatically because that's the first thing I do when I hear there's a hot guy in my presence. "Are you sure?" I whisper, then speak louder because she can't hear me, at first.

"Yes." We stop next to the guys by the bar and she turns to me. "Now, we'll get some tequila shots and then maybe they will buy our next drinks. What do you want after the shots?"

"What about a...?"

"If you say sex on the beach or a white Russian, I will throw up and then pinch you. We are not in college anymore."

"I wasn't going to say either of those drinks. I don't drink sex on the beach anymore." At least, I hadn't in a few months. "I was actually going to say I would like a strawberry margarita."

"With salt or sugar?" She's leaning back against the bar now, and I can see that we have the full attention of the men next to us.

"Sugar, baby. You know I'm sweet all the way." I giggle coquettishly, look over to the side, and then turn back to Isabel. The hottie next to us is looking pretty good.

"Fine." She nods. "But you know all that sugar is just going to go to your bloodstream."

"I almost had an entire tub full of ice cream today. I'm not worried about my sugar content at the moment, but thank you for your concern." I shimmy back and forth to the Hozier song that's now playing.

"Hey, you two," the hottie to our immediate right says, interrupting our conversation, and we both turn to look at him. I smile at him and nod. I can see him a little bit closer now. He is handsome with his light brown eyes and ginger hair. He's slightly taller than me but really skinny. I have a thing about dating guys who are skinnier than me because it always makes me feel fat, and even if they don't mind, I have an issue when my arms, thighs, and stomach are bigger than his. "What's your name, sexy?" I can't tell if he's speaking to me or to Isabel, and I don't think he really cares which one of us answers because his eyes are darting back and forth. I have a feeling whichever one of us gives him the time of day will be the one of us that he wants. I decide to keep quiet. He's not my type. I nod toward Isabel to let her know she can have him. Then, I look past the guy who's talking to see if his friends are cute, as well.

There are two other guys, but they're with gorgeous girls that look like models. I try not to feel bad about myself as I watch them flirting and doing the pickup dance. I don't know why I feel jealous when I see cute guys and cute girls in a bar flirting with each other. Maybe it's because it reminds me of my own pitiful, lonely self and how much I suck at flirting.

I realize that I do want to be in a relationship. I want to meet the love of my life. I want to be loved and told I'm beautiful every single day, but that just hasn't happened for me yet. I've met some guys that have really been into me, but they haven't been great. And when I say they haven't been great, I mean, they've been absolutely awful. I'm just hoping that one day, my knight in shining armor will come and ride me off into the sunset because I don't know how many more Shreks I can deal with. And just because Fiona was okay with Shrek doesn't mean that I am.

Looks like Isabel isn't particularly interested in the man, either, because she's ordering our shots, and he's now talking to his friends again. Which is fine by me. We came out to just let loose, not to hook up.

"Here are your tequila shots," Isabel says, handing me two shot glasses. The shimmering gold liquid glistens in the glasses, and I know that if I take them both, I am opening myself up to a crazy, yet carefree night.

"These are not both for me, right?" I ask and let out a groan as I stare at her offered hand. She has another two shot glasses in her other hand. "Really, Isabel, two shots of tequila to start the night?"

"We've got to get this party started quickly, honey. We only have so many hours."

"We're not late and we don't have to get totally wasted in the next half hour. It's only…"

She holds her hand up. "Sarah, drink the tequila shots already."

"Fine, you sound like my brothers, by the way." I wrinkle my nose at her as I down my first tequila shot quickly. The warm liquid goes down my throat smoothly and I cough as I feel the warmth hit my belly. "This is potent." I know this tequila is going to fuck me up, and I know I really shouldn't drink the other one, but I down it just as quickly as I did the first. Within what feels like seconds, I can feel the alcohol going to my head. I don't know if it's the placebo effect or if the alcohol has really hit me that quickly, but I'm feeling giggly and like I'm on top of the world already. I shake my hair around and start dancing like I'm auditioning for *So You Think You Can Dance.*

"So, how did you know that..." I pause as my brain freezes, and I forget what I was going to say.

"How did I what?" Isabel pays for the drinks and then looks back at me with a confused expression on her face.

"I don't even know what I was going to say." I giggle. I look back over to the guy at the right, and he's staring at only me now. I can see his eyes on my cleavage, and I congratulate myself on wearing a very tight, very plunging neckline. If there's one thing that a lot of men like, it's boobs, and granted, every man is not a boob man, but at least fifty percent are. And I've got some pretty nice ones, if I do say so myself.

"So, you girls looking to have fun tonight or what?" he asks and elbows his friend, who is no longer talking to one of the models. I look at his friend, a blond guy with dark brown eyes. He's grinning and looking at me and Isabel, and I can tell he also doesn't care which one of us he gets, which isn't exactly a compliment. I want a guy that wants me. Not a guy who wants any woman who's interested in taking him to bed.

"Sorry, guys. Tonight's a girls' night," Isabel says as she hooks her arm through mine again. "If you know what I mean."

"Holy shit." The ginger guy gawks at us, and I can see a million fantasies running through his head. "You girls aren't lesbians, are you?"

"You would like that, wouldn't you?" Isabel says, winking. I try not to roll my eyes. I don't know why Isabel bothers with men like this, but she loves to be a tease. Maybe I need to learn to be a better one.

"I mean, are you guys open to experimenting with two hot, packing men?" The ginger guy nods toward his crotch. "The real thing is better than a strap-on, trust me."

"How do you know?" Isabel asks at the same time that I answer him.

"No, we're not." I shake my head quickly. "Come on, Isabel." I turn to Isabel, and she winks at me as she picks up two more glasses. She hands me a tall margarita glass with bright red liquid and I take a sip. It's delicious. I know I'm going to regret drinking so much alcohol tonight, but right now, I don't care. Not after the day I had. "Come on, let's go to the corner," I say. "Let's dance."

"You should have been on *Dancing with the Stars*." She takes a sip of her colorful cocktail and we head away from the bar. "You love to dance, you and Ella both. I'm just, like, what is going on with you two dancing queens? You know I don't have rhythm." She moves her hips back and forth as we make our way through the crowds of people, and I can't help but giggle at Isabel's self-critical comment. It's true, she doesn't have the best rhythm, but if I'm honest, I'm not the most rhythmically inclined, either, but that doesn't stop either of us from letting loose on a dance floor.

"You kind of have to be a star to be on *Dancing with the Stars*," I remind her as we make our way to the corner of the room. There's a makeshift dance floor where three other girls are dancing, and we stop and start dancing next to them.

"Hey, *chicas*," a girl with long, dark hair says with a wide, friendly smile. She's wearing a crop top that shows off incredible abs and underboob, and I'm impressed by the fact that she's dancing and not exposing any private parts. Her black skirt ends right under her ass, and I know even if I could carry off such a look, I wouldn't be able to wear such attire. I don't have the confidence, and I'd be scared that my ass cheeks and tits would be hanging out. Though, I can see half the men surrounding the dance floor are hoping for the same thing to happen. Their eyes are watching her every move. And she seems to love it.

"This is fun," Isabel says as she sips her drink and nods at the girl. I'm surprised she's drinking a cocktail, not wine, because she loves white wine. Especially Pinot Grigio. If she could marry a winemaker whose sole focus was Pinot Grigio, she would be a very happy woman. "I just love going out on a weeknight," she says, holding up her glass. "Cheers." I clink my glass against hers and then take another sip of the drink. I'm feeling warm and happy, and I dance to the beat of the music as best as I can. I'm not sure who's singing, but the song must be really popular because many people have joined us on the dance floor, jumping up and down, screaming and dancing. I would love it if I could write a song that would affect people that way.

"You're right, this really is so much fun." I take another sip and look around to see who else is dancing. It's mainly other women, but I can see a couple of guys standing on the edge of the makeshift dance floor like vultures, waiting for their opportunity to swoop in and grab someone they fancy. There are also some other men sitting in different booths watching us. It's voyeuristic and weird, but it doesn't stop me from enjoying myself and moving to the beat of the music. "I kind of feel like I'm a dancer on display. I wish there were tables that we could get on so we could dance and spin around," I shout over at Isabel.

"Oh, what? Like *Coyote Ugly* or something?" Isabel responds, and I nod in affirmation. "Dance up and down tables and poles?"

"It's not like I'm a great dancer, and it's not like I've ever been a lap dancer or stripper or want to be, but I have taken pole dancing lessons, and while I'm not good, I really enjoy it," I admit. There's a thrill to pole dancing lessons, and even though I'm the worst student in the class and can't get up the pole, I do think I am getting better.

"We can always get on a table and dance around and wait for the bouncers to tell us to get down." Isabel looks around. "Maybe they will even lift us down with their big, strong arms."

"You would not get on a table with me, would you?" I ask, surprised.

"Yeah, of course I would. Do you not know me?"

"True. Yeah, you would be all about it."

"Come on, Sarah. Should we do it?" She points over at a booth table. "That can hold our weight."

"Oh, you're serious." I take a huge gulp of my drink. "What if I fall 'cause I can't see well?"

Isabel looks slightly nervous, at first, and then laughs. "You won't fall, Sarah. What happened to my best friend that wants to be more adventurous?"

"What? Me? More adventurous? The nerdy librarian with the glasses?"

"Your glasses have gone. Your hair is down. Let's find a table." She grabs my hand and guides me to the booth she pointed at earlier. There are two guys sitting there, and she takes a seat next to one of them as I stand there. I cannot believe that she's doing this. "Hi, guys. Do you mind if my friend and I get on the table and do a quick dance?"

"Hell no," one of the guys says. He's muscular and handsome, and I try not to lick my lips like he's a meal waiting for me to taste him. He's the sort of guy that I would go for in a heartbeat. He stares at me, and I can see him looking me up and down. He has dark hair and dark eyes. He's built like a football player and is wearing a tight black shirt. "Hey, what's your name?" he asks as he scoots closer to me. "Come here, beautiful." He motions me closer to him.

"It's Sarah," I say, stumbling, feeling like a fool. "What's yours?"

"My name is Mr. Right," he says, winking, and I giggle at his answer. Not because I think it's funny, but because I don't know how else to react.

"Well, nice to meet you, Mr. Right."

"Yeah. It's nice to meet you, too, Sarah. I don't know if I'm Mr. Right Now or Mr. Right Forever, but hey, hop up on that table and then we'll see."

"Oh, it will definitely be Mr. Right Forever if you see her dancing on the table. Sarah is known as the best dancer in the city." Isabel leans forward and tells Mr. Muscles, "She's been called the Pole Whisperer by some men and the Slutty Stripper of Manhattan by others." My eyes dart to Isabel and I try not to glare at her. What is she doing? Is she out of her mind?

"The Slutty Stripper of Manhattan?" Mr. Right jumps up eagerly. His dark, glassy eyes are staring directly into mine now. I can see that he has a hint of green in his irises and some stubble. He also smells like whiskey and cigars. Now, he's so close to me I can see that he's even more handsome than I thought. And even more built. This is a man who spends several hours a day lifting weights.

"Well, you know," I say, blushing furiously. "I don't like to advertise it, but I am known around town as a girl with some moves," I lie, and I can't help but wonder what it would be like dancing for a man like this. I have a feeling his hands would be all over me as soon as the dance started.

"Ooh, baby. So you are a dancer or a sexy-ass, blue

ball-giving stripper?" His words make my head spin, and I nod slowly as he runs a finger down my belly. Oh, boy, this is going way too fast for me.

"Yeah, that's why they call me the Slutty Stripper of Manhattan, the best dancer on the Lower East and Upper West Side." I grin, feeling like an idiot, but I'm enjoying the attention. "I once got a thousand dollars for a lap dance, and I didn't even have to remove my panties." I don't know where the words come from, but I know I'm out of control. Isabel starts laughing, and I briefly turn my attention to her as she wiggles her eyebrows. Oh my gosh, what the hell am I saying? Why would I be lying about being a stripper?

"Let me see your moves. Get on the table, Slutty Stripper," he says as if he can't believe his good luck. I can't believe his good luck, either. I step onto the bench and then onto the table and start dancing, imagining that I am a sexy vixen here to turn men on. After the day's events, I quite like being admired and paid attention to. Even if it's not for the best reasons.

I'm swaying my hips back and forth and enjoying being the center of attention. I run my hands down the front of my chest and gyrate my hips. I'm about to start twerking when I hear a deep voice that makes me still.

"Sarah." The voice is loud and surprised. Why does it sound so familiar? "Sarah, from copywriting." I squint to try to make out who's talking. It's Jackson. Jackson Pruitt, the CFO of Rosser International. I'm going to die. I can't believe he witnessed me dancing on a table.

"Oh, hi," I say, raising my hand in the air. I can't see

his face properly, and I know there's someone standing behind him, but I'm not sure who it is.

"You like dancing on tables on weeknights or something," he says, and I want to close my eyes and stop time. However, I'd also be okay with a huge sinkhole opening up and swallowing me whole.

"She's not only a stripper on the weekends. She's..." The muscular guy starts talking, and I yelp.

"Can someone help me down?" I say quickly, and I watch as the muscular guy heads toward me, reaches up, and lifts me down.

"Thanks," I say gratefully. I can see Isabel grinning like a Cheshire cat.

"If you guys want a dance from..."

"No, Isabel," I say quickly, shaking my head. "This is Mr. Pruitt, my boss."

"Oh, the sexy CEO who was in the most eligible bachelor article?" she asks too loudly and checks him out.

"No, that's Mr. Rosser."

"Yes, that's me," Mr. Rosser says from behind Mr. Pruitt. And it's now official.

I'm dead.

I've died and gone to heaven.

Or maybe hell because that's where I deserve to go for being so stupid as to dance on random tables when my boss could be around.

"Oh, hi, Mr. Rosser. I didn't see you there." I blink and try to pretend to be happy to see him.

"Apparently," he says in a slow drawl. "So, you work for me?" he asks as if he can't quite believe it. My heart sinks in slight sadness. It is now one hundred percent confirmed that he has no idea who I am, even though he was in my office that very afternoon, and for some reason, that makes me feel even worse about my situation. I want to slap him across the face for not noticing me, but I know that's an overreaction. Violence is never the answer.

"I guess?" I say nonchalantly, pretending I don't care or even know who he is. I want to tell him that he's not all that and he should pay attention to the people who work for him, instead of just saying that he does to look good in the press. But instead, I just stand there for a few moments, saying nothing. I know I'm in over my head, but I can't stop myself. "Are you the CEO or just someone pretending to be him to get women?" I sneer like I think he's an impersonator, and I know that this is the worst comeback of my life.

I am never drinking tequila again.

6

Ethan

"What is going on here?" I look at the blushing woman who just asked me if I'm impersonating myself. She's standing in front of me and next to an amused-looking Jackson. She is blinking rapidly, and I wonder if she's high. She looks slightly familiar, but I'm not sure why. "Jackson? Did you say this lady works for me?"

"I'm standing here." She sounds annoyed. "You can ask me again if I work for you. You've only met me like —"

"Don't tell me I've met you a billion times." I cut her off and smirk as I give her a once-over. "I'm not even sure I've met my parents a billion times."

"You were in my office this afternoon." She's squinting now, and I wonder if I need to implement drug tests at work. I take a step closer to her and breathe in a dainty rose scent. Her face is glistening with a glow of perspiration, probably from dancing on the table, and her cleavage looks like it's ready to pop out of her top. Her dark hair is tousled and frames her face in a wild way, and I know this is a woman I would not have forgotten meeting.

"I was?" I cock my head to the side. I have never seen this lady before in my life. I would put a hundred dollars on it. "And don't you mean my office? I do own the building."

"I know you own the building. I know you're the CEO. You're the big bad wolf of Rosser International. Who doesn't know you?" She's definitely pissed, and I'm not sure why. What have I done to this woman? She's acting like I slept with her and left her without saying goodbye or something. Had I slept with her in a past life and not remembered? I stare at her face carefully to see if I recognize her. She's very pretty with big, well, sometimes big, violet-blue eyes. Her hair is a long dark brown and cascades in waves down her shoulders. She's wearing a bright red top with a very low V. She's generously proportioned, and my eyes take in her heaving bosoms. I know I shouldn't stare, but she's obviously cold or not wearing a bra because her nipples look hard under the tight material. I ignore the sudden hardening in my pants. Surely, I would have noticed this lady if she worked for me?

"Are you going to offer me an autograph or something? I bet you want to because your head is so big." My lips twitch as she continues to berate me. She sounds angry. Like I've done something to her. This is a woman who is not impressed by a newspaper article calling me eligible. She certainly is not trying to get on my good side.

"Are you mad at me for something, Ms...." I wait for her to supply her full name.

"Sarah." She presses her lips together and then squeals as the muscular guy that lifted her off the table slaps her ass. I wonder if that's her boyfriend. I frown as she moves away from him and glares. Maybe he's not her boyfriend.

"Don't be so modest, Sarah." The bulky guy slides his arm around her waist. "Gentlemen, this is Slutty Stripper Sarah, the hottest stripper in Manhattan." He stares down at her cleavage rather obviously and licks his lips. "How much for a motorboat, Slutty?"

"Don't call me that," she gasps, and I understand why. What woman would want to be called slutty?

"Five hundred?" he offers, and I watch as he pulls his wallet out of his back pocket. The man is not seriously going to offer her money to motorboat in front of her boss. Granted, I had no idea who she was, but it seemed inappropriate, and I could tell she was offended. This was definitely not her man.

"Sarah, you okay?" I step toward the man and block his view from Sarah. I position myself in a guarding position and stare down at her. "What's your last name?"

"Kahan." She seems reluctant to tell me.

"That's it!" Jackson exclaims. "I knew you were from copywriting. I've memorized every employee's name in every department."

"I am." She looks surprised as she stares at him. "You remember that well?"

"I also never forget a pretty face." He's flirting now.

"Jackson!" I chastise him. He knows the fraternization policy at the company.

"What?" He grins. "Everything okay here, Sarah?"

"She's good. I'm here," a blonde girl interrupts and steps forward. "I'm Sarah's best friend, Isabel. Well, I'm Ella's best friend, as well, but we're all really close." She hiccups. "Oops, silly tequila."

I frown as she continues hiccupping. I really hope she doesn't say she works for me, as well. I'd have to speak to HR about their hiring policies. I don't want the company full of drunk women, no matter how pretty they are. I can't stop looking back at Sarah. She's staring at Isabel and blushing again. The bright red hue is cute on her face. She's playing with her hair now, and I wonder if it's because she's nervous. I don't think it's a bit to try to turn me on. For some reason, I'm captivated by her. What's her deal? And why was she dancing on the table?

"Dude, you're interrupting a business deal," Bulky guy starts up again and tries to brush past me.

"Let it go." I stare him down. "Step back and have a seat. Your time with Sarah is done."

"Fine." He shrugs. "Not like I can't go to the titty bar later anyway. Dime a dozen." He moves away, and I turn back to Sarah.

"So, what's the deal here?" I ask her, frowning.

"We're leaving now." Sarah grabs her friend Isabel's hand. "Nice seeing you both. I'm sure you have other women you want to talk to. Women you will remember in the morning."

"You don't think I would remember you?" I ask her, not wanting her to leave just yet.

"I don't really care if you do or don't." She shrugs and moves to the right but trips over something and rubs her eyes. "It would be the first time that you did," she blurts out, and I frown.

"Have we dated?" I ask her bluntly. She's acting like we've fucked and I never called her again. "Have I been inside of you and didn't know it?"

"No." She blushes and shakes her head vehemently. "Of course not."

She's so taken aback by my question that I can't help but laugh at her reaction. She's acting like that would never happen. Like she would never be interested in me. Which is frankly hard to believe because I've never met a woman who wasn't interested in me.

"No offense or anything," she says as if that makes it better, then laughs. I can't help but smile at the sound. Her laugh makes me warm. It's silky and loud, and it pleases my ears.

"No offense taken. Just checking so that I don't have to fire you."

"Fire me?" She freezes, and the laughter is gone. Which I regret because I like the sound a lot. *Weird*. I'm not even sure why I'm drawn to her laugh. What I really need to be doing is going back to the office to finish going through the paperwork and figuring out what Lord Chambers wants from his jingle.

"You couldn't work at Rosser International if we'd

fucked. It would make it too awkward," I explain, then pause. "You work in copywriting?" I ask her, and she nods slowly. I try to think back to being in that department earlier in the day, but I don't remember seeing her. I'd remember those eyes, and that smile, and those breasts. Though, I know I'm not supposed to be noticing any breasts.

"So, Slutty, what's..." The bulky jackass is back, and I turn around to face him.

"Sit your ass down," I say in a low and very distinct tone. He stares at me for a few moments, and I know he's wondering if he can take me, which is not likely. He is most definitely drunk, and I'm sober as all get out. He's also a bit top heavy, and I'm evenly muscular. He doesn't want to take me on. It wouldn't be a fair fight whatsoever.

"Whatever." He shrugs. "She'll be dancing on my table after she's done with you." He looks back at Sarah. "You're cute, but you got eye issues, or what?"

"I don't have my glasses on." She glares at him and blinks rapidly. "Isabel, give me my glasses now," she demands, and I watch her friend wordlessly handing back a pair of thick black glasses. Sarah puts them on, and they take over half her face. She's still cute, but they aren't the most attractive accessory I've ever seen. She presses her lips together as she continues playing with her hair.

"So, you work for me and as a stripper?" I ask her because I don't know what to say at this point. Was that why she'd been dancing on the table?

"Um, kinda, not really, I mean..." She looks away

and shrugs. She seems to think something over, and I watch as she squares her shoulders and stares me directly in the eyes again. "A girl's got to do what a girl's got to do, right?" She gives me the sweetest smile a woman has ever given me, and for a few minutes, we take each other in. I feel like I feel when I'm at the beach and staring at the waves of the ocean. I'm awed. And my heart stills for a second. My breath catches as I stare at her lips. Lips I want to kiss.

"I guess so." I nod slowly and take a step back. "So, it's jingles in the day and dances in the night?"

"You know it. Something like that." She takes a step toward me. "I am the top dancer in the region." She spins around. It's not the daintiest spin I've ever seen, but I can't seem to take my eyes off her. "Tap, ballet, hip-hop, you name it, I can do it."

"I'm sure the men only care about one sort of dance though?" I can imagine her giving me a lap dance, pressing her breasts against my lips. Telling me I can't touch.

"Yah, my pole work is excellent." She puts her hands up in the air and pretends to start climbing. "All I need is a pole and a thong." She presses a finger to my lips and heat consumes me. "Then they don't forget me." She's got my heart racing now, but I don't respond. "Have a great evening, Mr. Rosser." She grabs her friend's hand and they leave in a flourish. I stare after her for a few seconds and then shake my head. How am I hard right now?

"What was that?" I ask a dumbfounded Jackson. "She actually works for us?"

"She does and shit, she's hot." He licks his lips. "Think we can change that fraternization policy?"

"Not at all," I snap and look at my watch. "We've had a drink. Now we need to go back to work."

"What?" He's aghast and sighs. "We're not going to discuss what just happened with little miss hottie and her thong comment?"

"Nope." I shake my head. "What my employees do outside of work hours is up to them. Now, if she were to do such a thing in the office, I'd have her fired so quickly for being unprofessional." I ignore my burning lips and the images in my mind. I can picture Ms. Kahan sliding up and down a pole, a thong in her ass cheeks as she dances around, breasts bouncing in glee. I need to get the thought out of my mind. I am not going to break my no-fraternization policy for a copywriting stripper, no matter how intriguing I find her. Though, I suppose I do have a duty to find out where she works at night to ensure that it's not dangerous or shady. I can't have my employees mixed up in anything too salacious or seedy. Rosser International doesn't need any bad press. Not right now, when we're about to expand even more. That would completely ruin our new lighting launch. And the announcement of our new home chain stores.

Business is the most important thing right now—the absolute most important thing in the world. I'll make sure Sarah Kahan's night activities aren't going to mess up anything, and then I'll promptly forget who she is and what she's doing in her life.

7

Sarah

Dear Diary,

I touched his lips. And told him I liked to dance on a pole in a thong. Why, oh, why did I say that? A thong? I haven't owned a thong in years. They are so uncomfortable. How can I go in to work tomorrow? Maybe he won't remember? Maybe he was drunk, as well. I have no idea if that's true or not because I could barely see him for more than half of our conversation, and then for the other half, I was just embarrassed.

The "he" I'm talking about is my boss, Ethan Rosser. Why, oh, why is his name popping up in my diary so much now?

I mean, you would have been embarrassed, as well. I don't know what possessed me to pretend I was a stripper on the side. I literally have never stripped in my life. Not even with a boyfriend. I'm not going in to work tomorrow. Well, maybe I am, but only because I need the paycheck.

Why couldn't I have been born to rich parents? My family has really let me down.
Stupid Sassy Sarah

The previous evening feels like a really bad dream. A part of me wishes that it was one. Yes, nightmares suck, but then you get to wake up and join the real world again and banish all the bad memories—no such luck when your nightmare is real life.

Yes, I've been waiting for Ethan Rosser to notice me, but that is not how I wanted it to happen. Frankly, I was slightly miffed that he'd been so shocked that I worked for him. He really hadn't recognized me. I know I look different with my hair down and my glasses off, but I don't think I look that different. Though, I can't worry about that too much now. My stomach tenses as I get closer to work.

I make my way to the office timidly, much different than how I'd been acting the night before, fueled by liquid courage. I hope I don't see him. I don't want to see him. I also don't want to hide behind my glasses anymore. I'm ready to get rid of them, though I'm not quite ready to take the leap to LASIK surgery. I'll take it one step at a time and start with contact lenses.

I decide to find an optometrist who can see me this week so that I can get my eyes tested and fitted for contact lenses. It's not that I'm vain. I actually like my glasses. But it would be nice to go out without them on and be able to see. My phone rings when I'm a few blocks from the office, and I see Isabel's name on the screen. I answer it immediately, and all I can hear is laughter on the other side of the phone. I know why she's laughing. But I'm not going to let her off that easily. She could've got me fired. She could've gotten me put out on the streets. I know that's a little bit of hyperbole, but I didn't care.

"Hello, Isabel," I say dryly. "You can stop laughing now."

"Sure thing, slutty stripper."

"Ugh, do not remind me of that stupid name. Whose bright idea was it to call me slutty stripper? As if anyone would actually go by that name." I almost forgot the moniker bequeathed to me the night before. I know lots of women like to make up fake names for themselves when they go out at night, but normally, it is a complimentary name or something sultry. Slutty stripper is trashy and not something I ever wanted to be known as. In fact, I don't even remember how it came up that I was a stripper, as I am the furthest thing from one that a woman could be. Not that I am a nun or a saint or anything. But if I had to come up with a fake profession, why couldn't I have gone with something glamorous, like museum curator or dolphin whisperer.

"Not sure." There's a guilty expression in her tone, and I immediately wonder if she coined the term. Memories come crashing back to me, and I recall that she was the one who had called me that. "But guess what! Ella is back tonight. Colton has some big project, so they will be back this evening. Exciting, right?" she exclaims quickly, and I know she knows I'm about to go off on her.

I decide to let my anger go. There's no point in being upset about something that has already happened; plus, I am excited to see Ella. I want to hear all about her trip, and I know that she'll have brought back gifts for Isabel and me. Ella is one of the most thoughtful and kind people I know. But I'm a little bit embarrassed to tell her about my interaction with Ethan last night. I still feel like a bit of a fool. Though, I know I need to stop calling myself that. I once read a book that said you should only refer to yourself with positive attributes, but somehow, I feel like this morning, I will be unable to do that. Though, I suppose I could congratulate myself on having the courage to dance on a table in the first place. It was certainly an adrenaline rush.

"She's going to think I'm crazy when we tell her what happened last night," I say, my mind still trying to process the events of the previous evening. I'm feeling hot and shameful again. Partly because Ethan Rosser is frustratingly annoying and sexy at the same time. I'm ready to sink into the earth in shame at the way I acted before I left the bar. "But of course, I'm happy to see her and ask her about her trip. Not like when we meet up it will be all about me."

"She suggested we all go to brunch this weekend with Colton and Sam." Isabel tries not to sound excited, but I know the thought of seeing Sam most probably has her panties in a twist. She *lurves* him, and no one can convince me otherwise, at this point. Maybe someone seeing the way I interacted with Ethan and Jackson would make them think I was in love with one of them, as well. Which is an absolutely ridiculous thought. "She said if she's not jetlagged, maybe we can all go out tomorrow night for a catch-up."

"Sounds good." I stop outside of the grand Rosser International building and take a deep breath. "Okay, I've just arrived at work. I'm going to head inside now and try not to throw up."

"Tequila got you feeling bad about your life?" Isabel asks like she doesn't know exactly why I'm feeling nervous.

"No, my big mouth last night does." I want to keep on walking down the street. I don't want to enter the building. I don't want to face Ethan or Jackson. Though, maybe I won't even see them. Maybe they've already forgotten the previous night.

Maybe that's even worse.

Maybe being forgotten by the two hottest men I've ever interacted with in real life is more scarring than dancing on a tabletop. Going back to being wallpaper is not the promising alternative I'm looking for.

I don't know if that would make me feel any happier.

A wash of sadness hits me as I stand there. It's weird to be someone that doesn't exist to someone else. I'm so used to men's eyes going past me, like I'm nothing. Last night was different, even if it wasn't for the best reason. Last night, all eyes were on me. Maybe I wouldn't be as crazy next time. But I don't want to go back into my shell.

I don't want to go back to being invisible.

"You okay, Sarah?" Isabel's voice is soft. "You want me to bring you eggs and soup and tea and stuff?

Maybe some headache tablets and..." She pauses. "Anything you think you'll need to feel better?"

"I'll be okay." I debate telling her what's on my mind. That I'm feeling waves of sadness. That I've fallen into a hole of self-doubt and pity and overcompensated the night before. "It just hit me that I might be so nervous about going into work, and it could be for naught. Maybe they won't even remember last night. It's not like they care what a peon at their company gets up to. Ethan didn't even realize I worked for him." The hurt hits me in the stomach like a gut punch once again. I don't want to think about why it hurts so badly.

Every time I've been overlooked in the past sits upon my shoulders—the feeling of not being pretty enough, memorable enough. I don't know why it's hitting me now. I should be happy to be a nothing at this moment. But in my heart of hearts, I don't want to be a nothing. I don't want to be the funny friend or the shoulder to cry on. I don't want to be the overgrown weeds in the garden next to the beautiful fragrant roses.

"There is no way they will forget you or last night. Trust me." There's silence on the phone for a few moments, and she continues. "I know what it's like to be ignored, Sarah. To feel like you're unnoticed and not good enough. You, me, and Ella. We were always the girls that no one noticed. That's how we all met. And maybe that's manifested itself in us being dramatic and outlandish at times. But it's also why we're so fun, and cool, and unique. Ella got her Mr. Right and you will, as well."

"I don't expect my boss to be my Mr. Right," I say quickly, though my heart races at the thought. "Or even Mr. Right Now." I giggle as I think of the muscular guy.

"I think your boss wanted to be a Mr. Right Now, for sure." She's lighthearted again. "If you saw the way he was looking—"

"Wait, which boss? Jackson or Ethan?" I ask, my heart racing. I see a limo pulling up next to me, and I wonder if a star is going to pop out. My jaw drops as I see Ethan sliding out of the back seat. "I gotta go," I whisper into the phone and hang up. I'm standing there, watching Ethan as he heads toward me. I know I need to head inside, but I can't seem to move. Maybe it's because I want to see if he will remember me. I'm playing with fire, and I don't think I care if I get burned. I'm the one who lit the candle in the first place.

"Good morning, Ms. Kahan." Ethan's voice is dry and sarcastic as he stares at me. "Were you debating if you're going to come in to work today or just going to go to the club to make it rain."

"Good morning, Mr. Rosser." I tilt my head to the side and smile sweetly. "The dance club doesn't open until the evening and there's no prediction for rain today in the weather forecast." I feign ignorance.

"We both know I'm not talking about the dance club." He takes in my appearance, and I think he's frowning. "Is that part of your schtick?" He looks at me from my head to my toes and back to my eyes.

"Sorry, what are you talking about?"

"Dowdy librarian to begin the day to dance and sexy temptress when you end?"

I don't know whether to be offended or complimented by his comment. It's nice to know he thought I was sexy, at some point, but hearing I look dowdy now is not nice. Even though I've come to a similar conclusion only recently, it's still never nice to hear someone confirming your own negative thoughts. Especially when the word dowdy is used.

"Really?"

"You're in your beginning dance attire. Though, I assume the club expects you to dress up a bit more than this." He waves his hand at my outfit like a game show model. "But I guess it makes the transformation even more powerful."

"I have to get inside and do some work," I say stiffly. I hold my handbag to my side and nod my head at him. I can feel a warm hue on my face. "Have a good day, Mr. Rosser."

"I'll be down in the copywriting department later." He nods, a thin smile on his face. "Perhaps I shall see you then."

"Perhaps you shall," I say formally. Too formally for someone who was giggling about wearing thongs not twenty-four hours prior to that.

I move toward the entrance and realize that he's walking beside me. I sneak a peek at his side profile as he holds the door open for me.

"Thanks," I say curtly and walk through. I fully expect him to give me a snide *you're welcome*, but he doesn't respond. He holds the door open for a few more people and I continue to the elevator by myself. My heart is racing from the interaction, and I feel like I need to splash my face with cold water. My body feels like it's on fire, and I don't want to analyze the feeling too closely. I walk into the elevator, and I'm about to bury my face in my hands and scream when it dings and the doors open again.

"Fancy seeing you again." Ethan walks into the elevator and presses the button for the top floor. "What level are you on?" he asks as his long, tan fingers hover over the numbers.

"Seventeen," I say. "Thanks."

"No worries. I should have remembered that." He presses the number and steps back. "Copywriting is seventeen."

"Yes, I'm in the copywriting department," I say as if we both don't already know this. I should be happy that he has not forgotten me. I am a little wired by the previous interaction, though he still has a knack for irritating me in the most tantalizing way. I want to push him up against the wall and both smack and kiss him.

"And you enjoy it?"

"The seventeenth floor?"

"The copyrighting department."

"Oh." I grin. "It's okay."

"Not as much fun as a stage, huh?"

"Well, it's not like I'm part-time on Broadway." I shake my head and try not to roll my eyes. "I'm not the new lead in *Wicked*."

"You've got the dance moves for it though."

"You don't actually know if I do have the dance

moves, if you're quite honest. You've never seen me really dance."

"Is that an offer?" He raises an eyebrow, and I wonder what he's thinking inside that handsome head of his. Is he flirting with me? He couldn't be flirting with me. Not Ethan Rosser. He's not a flirt. He dates a lot, but everyone knows he doesn't seem to be big on romance or flirting. Is he trying to test me? I don't even know how to respond. This entire encounter is blowing my mind. A part of me wants to press the emergency button and start doing a dance right then and there. He's hot and I'd love to have my wicked way with him. "So, is it?" He takes a step toward me, his eyes crinkling as he smooths down the front of his shirt. I have no idea what I'm going to say in response.

8

Ethan

Sarah's eyes are wide as she stares at me, and I internally ask myself why I asked her such a question. It's not like I really want to see her dancing. As she stands dumbfounded by me, I think about the previous evening. I reflect on the fact that she looks so different with her glasses on and her hair up. No wonder I hadn't noticed her before. However, I must admit I can still see her beauty. That's undeniable.

"What did you just say?" she asks, her lower lip jutting out slightly. I want to suck on it. I dismiss the thought quickly. "Um, excuse me?" she snaps, and I can tell she's intrigued and annoyed. I half expect her to tell me off.

"I was just joking, wanting to see if you were going to take that bait," I say quickly. She tilts her head to the side and considers me. I know she's wondering if she should call me out for the obvious lie or not. I hope she does. I quite like bantering with her. It's stimulating and something I haven't indulged in since I took over the company.

"Okay," she says slowly, and I'm waiting for her to tell me off. Or move closer to me. "Well, just so you know, I..." The elevator beeps, and she pauses as it stops. The doors open and a petite blonde with a wide smile walks in.

"Good morning, Mr. Rosser." There's a sassy tone to her voice as she comes to stand next to me. I can see Sarah rolling her eyes, and I smile. I want to roll my eyes, as well, but I know I can't.

"Good morning," I say with a deft nod. Unfortunately for me, the conversation with Sarah is over. She knows it, and I know it. In fact, if I were a smart man, I never would've begun the conversation in the first place. "So, Sarah, will you come up to my office in about an hour?" The words are out of my mouth before I can stop myself.

"What?" she says, blinking at me, showcasing the same surprise I feel. I have no idea why I've just invited her to my office. Maybe it's because I don't want the conversation to end. Maybe it's because I worked too late last night, and now I've lost my mind.

"Be in my office in an hour," I say, staring at my watch to check the time. I have two meetings I will now have to postpone due to this sudden appointment. I don't care, and I'm not going to second-guess myself. "We have things to discuss."

"Um, okay," she says, nodding as if she knows what I'm talking about. I see the blonde looking at me furtively and then looking at Sarah and wondering what's going on. I press my lips together and tap my foot. I don't even know what's going on. The elevator beeps again, and Sarah moves toward the door. We're on the seventeenth floor. "Have a good day, Mr. Rosser," she says as she exits.

I don't respond. I know that's rude, but I don't really know what to say. I can hardly say, "I'm going to see you in my office in an hour and then it will be much better." That sounds like too much of a proposition. Plus, why would seeing Sarah Kahan again today improve my mood?

"Mr. Rosser, I was wondering if..." The blonde touches me on the arm, and I stare at her bright red fingernails.

"Yes?" I'm irritated.

"It's so good to see you, sir," she starts again, and I look down at her big blue eyes gazing up at me. Pretty, but not the same violet-blue as Sarah's. Sarah's eyes are perhaps the most mesmerizing I've ever seen.

"What's your name?" I need to see if I can have her transferred to another office.

"Chantelle," she says, "But you can call me C-Money."

"Sorry, what?"

"C-Money." She giggles. "I used to be a little bit of a rapper when I was younger and the name stuck."

"You were a rapper." I look over the petite blonde girl and frown. "Really?"

"Well, I was in a dance group, and we had one rap song, and my name became C-Money. You know how it is, right?"

"No, I really don't." I shake my head. I don't want to continue this conversation any longer. The elevator dings yet again, and I decide to get out.

"But this isn't the executive level," she points out the obvious with a pout.

"I know, I needed to speak to someone on this level," I lie as I exit the elevator. I don't want to deal with her this morning. I don't want to deal with any more women trying to hit on me, especially those that work for me. "Just so you know, Chantelle," I say because I refuse to call her C-Money. "There is a no-fraternization policy here at Rosser International."

"A no what?" she asks. "Don't worry, I wasn't in a fraternity. I was in a sorority."

"What department are you in?" I ask. If she tells me accounting, I will call HR to my office right away.

"Oh, I'm in sales. I'm working on the new lingerie line for the Macy's and Dillard's collection."

"Oh, okay." That makes more sense. I can see people buying from her, people who aren't me, of course. I would not buy anything from her, but I'm smart and CEO for a reason. I know when to spend my money and when not to, and I'm not won over by a pair of big blue eyes with an empty brain. "You have a good day, Chantelle."

"Thank you. You too, Ethan." She says my first name like we are old friends, and I walk away. I'm not going to tell her off, but I'm not going to acknowledge it, either. She doesn't get to call me Ethan. No way. I'm her boss, and I don't want her to think she has a shot with me. I don't want it going around the cafeteria at lunchtime that she and Ethan, the CEO, are now a thing. I sigh as I head to the emergency exit and make my way up the steps. I've got twenty floors to go. It's not like it will kill me. I'm in great shape, and sometimes, I even take the steps just for fun because I like to see how quickly I can get up several flights. Though, initially, today had not been one of those days.

Today, I just want to go to my office, sit in my chair, and think. Think about the previous evening and think about Sarah. I need to process what I'm going to do with an employee I'm attracted to who used to be a first-class stripper.

Right now, all I can seem to think about is ripping her clothes off. I can imagine her arriving at my office and asking why I'd called the meeting and me saying, "Oh, I want to see you dance for me, baby." I groan at my thought. It's not that I would ever use those words. I don't say *baby*. I'm not a *baby* sort of man. No woman has ever heard me use the term baby, honey, sugar, sugar plum, or... I pause my thoughts. This is not the time for me to be thinking about random pet names I will not be calling Sarah. I have actual work to focus on.

I set the timer on my watch and start running up the stairs. I am going to try to make it up within five minutes. I know Edith will wonder why I am sweaty when I reach the office, but she'll just have to wonder. It's not like I answer to her. She's not a great secretary. She doesn't actually do anything. So, it's not like she can call me out, even though she does, indeed, call me out on stuff all the time, because she seems to think she's my second grandma. To be fair, in some ways, she is my work grandma. Not that I would tell her that, even though she knows how much the Rosser family loves her.

An hour later, I'm sitting in my office when I hear a knock at the door. I already know that it has to be Sarah, but I'm going to pretend I forgot because I'm already regretting my impulsive decision to tell her to meet me in my office. "Who is it?" I call out in a husky tone. "I'm quite busy."

"Mr. Rosser, you have a visitor," Edith says as she opens the door slightly. "There's a girl from copywriting here to see you. I told her that you're full for the morning, but she says that you have an appointment, though I don't see it on the calendar, so—"

"Send her in, Edith." I shrug and sit back. Of course, this is the one time Edith pays attention to my calendar and who comes in and out of my office.

"Yes, sir." She shrugs nonchalantly, as if to say, *if she tries to hit on you and marry you, it's not my fault. I did my due diligence.* The door opens wider, and Sarah walks in, looking slightly bemused and confused.

"Hello, Mr. Rosser. I'm here for the appointment," she says, standing there uncomfortably.

"Yes, close the door behind you and have a seat," I say, standing up. "Would you like some tea, coffee, water?"

"How's about a gin and tonic?" She grins widely as she closes the door. I raise a single eyebrow, and she turns to me with a nervous giggle. "That was a joke. I don't really drink in the morning, and I don't drink gin and tonic anyway. It was just..."

"It's fine. Have a seat," I say, keeping my face even-tempered. She really is an odd one. She heads toward me and takes a seat in the chair on the left. I can see she's playing with her fingers. I don't know if it's because she's nervous or something she does. I remind myself that I don't know anything about her, really. I didn't even know she existed before yesterday, but for some reason, I want to know more about her. I want to take her glasses off. I want to reach up and take her hair ties out of her bun and let her hair down. I want to bring her closer so I can give her a morning kiss. I want to stare into her big blue eyes and tell her she's beautiful, but of course, I'm not going to do any of those things because it's temporary insanity that I'm even thinking them.

"So..." she says, tapping her foot against the carpet. "This is a cool office." She looks out of the large window into downtown Manhattan and appreciates the view that I love staring at every single day. "Wow, what I wouldn't do for a view like this."

"Oh?" I ask her, leaning forward. "What wouldn't you do for a view like this?"

"Lots of things." She giggles nervously. "I mean, I wouldn't give you a..." She pauses, her face going red. "I mean, I wouldn't do anything naughty, you know?" She wrinkles her nose. "So, why was I summoned here?" she asks, and I want to start laughing again because she really doesn't have a way with words. I kind of like her awkward demeanor though. I kind of like that she's not polished. I like that she says what's on her mind. It makes me trust her, which is something I don't often do with women, especially when these articles come out and I find clusters of them around me.

"So, last night we were talking and—"

"Oh, my gosh, you're not talking about my nickname, Sarah the Slutty Stripper, are you?" She makes a face, and I sit back.

"Sorry, what?"

"Look, I know we told you my nickname was Slutty Stripper because I'm really great at... never mind that. I know I said I love to wear a thong and dance around, but I'm past those days. Well, I mean, those days were never really true... I mean, I'm not a liar. I know it sounds really stupid that it would be a lie, but it's kind of a lie... I was never really a stripper. I was never really called Slutty Sarah. I do wear a thong, but do not have a thong on right now. I'm not going to take off my clothes and dance around for you. I do take pole dancing lessons." She rushes out her words, and I have no idea what she's talking about.

"You take pole dancing lessons?" I ask her because she has me confused by her conversation, but I did catch that part.

"I mean, for fun. Not because I want to be a stripper." She takes a deep breath. "I have never made lots of money on the stripper pole or... Oh, I am just making this worse, aren't I?" She throws her hands up in the air and leans back in the chair.

"Yes," I say honestly.

"Long story short, I'm not really a stripper. Never

was, never will be, never want to be. So, if you invited me here for a dance, the answer is no."

"Hmm, I don't really know what to say because I don't really know what's going on here, Sarah. I didn't ask you to come to my office so you can strip."

"Oh, so you didn't call me into your office to give you a lap dance?" She blushes.

"I mean, are you offering to give me a lap dance?"

"Well, that's what you asked me earlier, and that's why I thought you wanted me in here to..." She pauses. "I should just stop. Maybe you can tell me why I am here and how it pertains to last night."

"You're in the copywriting department, right?"

"Yeah," she says. "Oh, please don't fire me. I can't afford to lose my job right now."

"No, I'm not about to fire you, Sarah. I want your help writing a jingle."

"Oh." She looks confused. "But yesterday when you came to the office, you didn't want to speak to any of us. You wanted to speak to my boss."

"Well, now I do want to deal with you and only you. I want to see how good you are at copywriting." I'm not sure where the idea came from, but it's a good one. I do need someone to write me a jingle, and she's as good a person as any; maybe this will be a chance for her to shine and win a promotion. Not that I'm going to tell her that because I'd hate to tell her that her jingle sucked and the promised promotion was off the table.

"So, that's why you called me to the office?" she asks, reaching up and pulling her hairband out unconsciously. Her hair cascades down her back, and I want to reach over and touch her silky tresses. Of course, I don't though. That would be highly inappropriate.

"I do. Do you think you're up for the challenge?" She nods slowly.

"I mean, I know I'm up for the challenge. I'm always up for the challenge." She grins wickedly, and my stomach flips. "I am known as—"

"Please don't tell me you're known as Slutty Stripper Sarah, the dancer that can also perform the best jingles in the world," I say, cracking a smile, and she laughs.

"Huh? You're kind of funny when you want to be, aren't you, Mr. Rosser?"

"Call me Ethan," I say, going against everything I've ever thought or believed when it comes to dealing with employees.

"Okay, Ethan. So, when do we get started?" She leans forward eagerly and clasps her hands together. "I think you're going to be really impressed at my way with words."

9

Sarah

Dear Diary,

I think I have to admit that I am one of those women who loves positive feedback from other people. Especially men. I've always aimed to be someone who's self-sufficient and doesn't need compliments to make me feel good about myself. But I suppose that hasn't quite worked.

Two days ago, I got assigned a project by Mr. Rosser. Yes, the CEO. The guy I was just trash-talking a few days ago. I know what you're thinking, "Wow, it didn't take much to turn her mind," but I'm here to tell you that I still think he's a womanizer.

I still think he's full of himself, but I will give him a couple of points for having a better sense of humor than I thought. I know, I can't believe it, either.

He almost makes me want to write a song, but I'm not going to write one. I mean, not for him anyway. I'll write a song for me. It might be about him, but not in a Taylor Swift sort of way.

Though, I guess that is obvious because Taylor Swift writes about men she's dated, and I have never dated Ethan Rosser, and I never want to. I swear, I really don't.

Love always,
Sassy Sarah.

"So, you're telling me that your boss wants you to run a new ad campaign?" Ella asks as we eat mozzarella sticks. She, Isabel, and I are at our favorite bar catching up, and I am so happy to see her. She's glowing from being in love, but aside from that, she looks just the same. I don't know why I expected an epic trip to change her in some way.

"Not quite run it." I shake my head and enjoy the salty goodness of the fried cheese. "And you just got back to town. We really don't have to talk about me right now. I want to hear more about you and Colton and—"

Ella holds her hands up to stop me. "Colton and I are boring. There's not much to say. We went to museums. He bought me jewelry. We made mad, passionate love everywhere." She pauses as Isabel groans. "What? I'm just being honest."

"Way to make us feel better about ourselves. Am I right, Sarah?" Isabel grabs the last mozzarella stick, and I look around for a server so we can order more. I need a lot more food to keep up with all the alcohol we're consuming.

Isabel looks at me, and I nod slowly in agreement. "Yeah. we're not trying to be haters, Ella, but we don't really want to hear about your mad, passionate lovemaking with your gorgeous billionaire boyfriend, who's most probably soon going to be your husband." I snort with laughter. "We have empty beds back home."

"I hope you know I'm not trying to rub it in your faces," she says, looking sad.

"I know," I say quickly, not wanting her to think that I'm being serious. "I'm really happy for you. And trust me, I want to hear all about it."

"Me too," Isabel adds. "We're just joking with you. We don't mind that we're going to be spinsters."

"Speak for yourself, Isabel. I hope not to end up a spinster. I'm not that old."

"True, true. I'm just joking with you, as well."

"You two." Ella reaches her hands out to us, grabs both of ours, and squeezes them. "I've missed you both so much."

"You weren't gone that long, Ella." Isabel sips on her sangria. It's the third pitcher we've ordered so far, and we're all past tipsy.

"I know, but I was wishing that you guys were there with me. I was wishing that we could go shopping along the Champs-Élysées, and..."

"I would love to go shopping along the Champs-Élysées," I say, picturing myself in France.

"I would love to have the money to go shopping along the Champs-Élysées." Isabel makes a face, and I laugh.

"True. I don't think my credit card has much left on it to spend."

"You mean your limit? What's your limit?" Ella

asks.

"I mean, my balance is a lot. I don't think my credit limit is saying much. The bank does not want to loan me any more money than they already have. For some reason, they feel like I can't pay back thirty grand," I say in a haughty voice. "Do they not know who I am?"

"I guess not." Ella snorts and then beams at the waiter. "Can we get another pitcher of sangria, another serving of mozzarella sticks, and some chicken wings, please."

"Yes, ma'am," the waiter says before sauntering away like a ghost in the night.

"So, anyway, tell us about your boss. Exactly what does he want you to do with this ad campaign?" Ella inquires as she leans back in the booth. "This sounds like a great opportunity for you."

"I already told you guys. He called me into the office and said he wants me to write a jingle for a new ad campaign for our new Royal lighting line. I guess he came down to the office earlier this week to ask someone to work on it and decided he wants to give me a chance. David was a little upset, but I know I'm up for the challenge. I'm going to meet him again tomorrow for more information."

"That's amazing. He's most probably hoping you'll bust out some moves, as well." Isabel winks, and I glare at her.

Ella frowns in confusion, and my stomach sinks as she leans forward. "What are you guys talking about? Bust out what moves?"

"Do not bring up the nickname you gave me." I glare at Isabel.

"I won't," she says innocently. "Plus, I didn't know that anyone would take it seriously."

"Take what seriously?" Ella asks. "Tell me. Tell me."

"Long story short, Isabel pretended I was this world-famous stripper, and I was slightly drunk, so I embellished the story and may or may not have told my boss that I like to prance around on a stage in a thong."

"What?" Ella says, her jaw dropping. "You're kidding, right?"

"I wish. But I told him it was a joke. Well, at least I think I told him it was a joke. I told him something stupid. I was rambling and I think he was a little bit confused, but he didn't bring it up again." I shrug. "It doesn't matter now. Everything between us is professional."

"Oh, Lordy, Lordy, Lordy." Ella shakes her head. "You guys have been up to a lot of mischief since I've been away."

"Well, you're the queen of mischief, so who knows what else we'll get up to now that you're back." Isabel has a twinkle in her eyes.

"So, anyway, he wants to see me tomorrow and go over the exact details of the jingle," I continue, the excitement clear in my tone. This could be the chance to show what I'm really made of. I want to impress Ethan Rosser more than I've wanted to impress anyone before in my life.

"Did you tell him that you're a songwriter?" Isabel asks, her fingers gripping her glass.

"No, because I'm not."

"Yes, you are." Ella gives me a pointed look. "You're an amazing singer and songwriter."

"Just because I've written some songs for myself doesn't make me a songwriter. No one famous has ever sung the songs. No one outside of you guys and my brothers has ever heard me singing."

"So, maybe you should change that. You've got a beautiful voice and I think—"

"No." I cut Isabel off. "I'm not going to tell my boss that I actually want to be a singer-songwriter and not a stripper."

"Why? Maybe he will..."

"Maybe what?" I interrupt Isabel again. "My dreams of being a songwriter are not going to get me a promotion with the company in the copywriting department," I say. "'Oh, hey, why don't you head up copywriting because you want to be a singer-songwriter.'" I roll my eyes. "And a dowdy singer-songwriter at that."

"You are not dowdy," Isabel protests, with Ella nodding enthusiastically in agreement.

"Well, that's not what my boss thinks."

"He's a jerk," Ella says, and then pauses. "I mean, sometimes you do go into work looking a little bit older than you are."

"Girl, with her glasses and her bun, she looks like a grandma," Isabel interjects.

"Thanks a lot, Isabel."

"Okay. Maybe not a grandma, but close to a grandma."

"Thanks, guys."

"What? It's true. I mean, I've never called you dowdy though. I wouldn't do that because I'm one of your best friends and—"

"I know. You guys love me, and I know my look could use some updating." I sigh. "I did make an appointment with the optometrist and I'm going to see about getting contacts."

"Yay!" They both start clapping enthusiastically.

"That's the best news I've heard all year," Ella adds, and I roll my eyes.

"Really? Even better than the man you fell in love with telling you he's also in love with you and wants to be with you for the rest of your life?"

"Okay, so maybe not quite as good as that, but still pretty good."

"Uh-huh. Anyway, I need to have a makeover. I really want one, but I don't want to have a makeover now and have *him* thinking I'm doing it for him."

"Well, then don't do it for him. Do it for you and all the other gorgeous men you're going to meet." I can see the excitement in Isabel's eyes. She's been waiting for me to get a makeover for years.

"What other gorgeous men?"

"I don't know. Some other gorgeous men. He's not the only gorgeous man in Manhattan, you know."

"Exactly," Ella adds, and I can see she's also invested in my makeover and love life. "There are plenty of handsome billionaires that would love to take you out."

"I don't think so. More like zero."

"Don't be such a pessimist, Sarah." Isabel frowns. "I

think that you should write an ad, and I bet you a billion different billionaires will want to apply."

"Write an ad about what?" I think she's crazy.

"I don't know, like a personal ad. You know, like in the newspaper. 'Sexy Sarah is seeking billionaire'."

"I'm not calling myself Sexy Sarah," I say, finding humor in this whole idea. "And I'm not putting up a personal ad."

"It would be fun though." Ella nods and thanks the waiter as he brings another pitcher of sangria and refills our glasses. "Wouldn't it be cool to see if you got any responses?"

"I don't think it sounds like a good idea at all." I take another long gulp of sangria and giggle uncontrollably. "Though it would be hilarious if I did get a response. I'd feel like a princess dating a billionaire."

"Okay, what about 'Sultry Sarah seeking billionaire'?" Isabel speaks dramatically.

"No."

"What about 'Slutty Stripper seeking billionaire'?" Isabel giggles.

"Stop with the slutty stripper names. It's so not cool. Imagine if I really was a stripper. Would you call me a slut then?"

"If you were fucking all of your customers, I'd call you a slut," Isabel says honestly, and I roll my eyes.

"But then you'd be more like a prostitute," Ella adds. "You'd be slutty, stripper, prostitute, Sarah."

"Guys, enough. I need to be serious now. What am I going to do tomorrow when I go to Ethan's office and..."

"And what?" Isabel says, peering at me.

"And he wonders why I'm looking differently because I am not looking like a mess?" I run my fingers through my hair. "My makeover is going to make me look different, I hope."

"Well, you're not going to have your contacts by tomorrow." Isabel shrugs. "And I don't really see any new clothes coming by tomorrow, seeing as it's the evening."

"Okay, fine. Then next week when I have my makeover and I'm looking all sexy. I don't want him to think I'm looking sexy because of him."

"You're doing it for you. Who cares if he thinks it's for him. When he sees all the other men fawning over you, he'll know it's not true." Ella grabs her phone. "Come on, let's do a personal ad, just for fun."

"I don't know. It doesn't sound like a great idea." I take another sip of sangria.

"But that hasn't stopped you before?" They both smile at me, and I shake my head.

"Fine, but I'm not calling myself Sexy Sarah, Slutty Sarah, or Sassy Sarah. My real name is not going to be a part of it, either."

"Fine. What about, 'Hot single female-seeking—'" Ella starts, and I cut her off.

"Nope. I don't want to show up on a date and the guy be like, 'I thought you said you were hot.'"

"But you are hot." Isabel nods toward my chest. "Men will see that."

"They will think I'm hotter than I am. They will

probably think I am Margot Robbie Barbie hot. I'm not Barbie hot and I'm not peroxiding my hair."

"Fine." Ella rolls her eyes. "What about, 'Young single female'?"

"But what if they think I'm *young* young. Like early twenties?"

"Okay. What about middle age?"

"No way. Mid-thirties is fine." I hiccup and then giggle. "I'm mid-thirties. Actually, I'm more early thirties, but let's say mid-thirties because I don't want them to think I'm super young because I'm not thirty or thirty-one."

"Okay, so mid-thirties, single female."

"Yeah, but I don't want them thinking I'm a normal female and then being like, 'Oh my gosh, she's a drama queen when they get to know me.'"

"I got it," Isabel shouts as an idea comes to her. "What about, 'Mid-thirties, slightly hot mess female'?"

"That makes me sound crazy. But it's also true." I giggle. "I am a little bit of a hot mess. So okay, that works."

"Yay!" Isabel pumps her fist in the air. "'Mid-thirties, slightly hot mess female seeking billionaire.'"

"Shouldn't I say millionaire?" I wrinkle my nose,

"No. Why settle for a millionaire when you can have a billionaire?"

"True. I should set my sights high." I raise my glass and then take another sip of my drink. I know I should stop, but I don't want to. "Are we drunk?"

"Most probably. And I love this about us." Ella taps her fingers against the table.

"I love this about us, as well. Though, I do think that we're being goofy."

"What's wrong with being goofy?" Isabel sings and starts moving her hands in the air. "Why don't you write a song about that, Sarah?"

"Okay. We're goofy. We're funny. We're all a little slutty," I sing and bite down on my lip.

"I thought you didn't like the word slutty?"

"Okay, fine. We're goofy. We're funny. We're all a little..." I pause.

"We're all a little what?" Isabel asks.

"Pretty?" Ella offers.

"Yeah, we're pretty, but that's not a fun enough song." I shake my head.

"We're a little dainty?" Isabel asks.

"Boring." I shake my head. "We're goofy. We're funny. We're all a little kinky," I say, and they both start clapping.

"I like. Are you going to put that in your ad?" Isabel's eyes are bright.

"Number one, I'm not actually writing an ad, and no way would I put that I'm kinky. Or maybe I would," I say, laughing. "If it was just for fun."

"You would get some really crazy men."

"I already get pretty crazy men."

"Okay, let's write a full ad."

"I'll write it." I grab my phone. "But just because it's fun, not because I would ever actually put such an ad out. Oh wait, hold on. I have a message here from Dave."

"Dave you work with?"

"Yeah. Let me see what he's saying." I read it quickly. "Oh, I guess the HR department just announced a company-wide intranet for suggestions to other departments. Boring," I say and close out of the app and rest my phone back on the table. "Okay, so what should I say? What do I start with?"

"Put the title at the top," Isabel suggests and grabs my phone. She starts to type, and I sip some more of my drink. "Mid-thirties, slightly hot mess female seeking billionaire," she says as she types. I take another sip of my drink and laugh. I love goofing off with my friends.

I know I'm being silly, and I know I'll never actually post a personal ad in the newspaper, but sometimes it's just fun to mess around and act stupid. That's what my friends and I love to do, and it's certainly better than me worrying and thinking about Ethan Rosser and how I'm going to impress him at work. It's definitely much more fun than thinking about how much money I'm going to have to spend to completely change my image so I can look like a bombshell. I have to remind myself that I'm not doing this for Ethan and that I'm doing it for myself.

Though I know, if I'm being completely honest, I am doing it for Ethan because of the way he makes me feel when I'm around him. He makes me feel warm and fuzzy inside. And he makes me laugh. More than any man has ever done before in my life. Though, I'm not going to question it. I know he would never date me. And I don't care, but it would be nice if we could somehow wind up as friends. It would be nice if he trusted me. It would be nice to spend more time with him, and I'm not going to question why I feel happy every time I'm around him. It is not lust. And it is not love. It's something in-between, and I'm not going to dwell on what it means.

10

Ethan

"Hey, Ethan. Have you seen the new intranet board recently?" Jackson's voice sounds like he's bemused as I answer the phone in the early hour of the morning.

"No. Why would I be looking at that? I'm doing actual work, not wasting my time online." I huff as I stare at the stack of papers on my desk. I have a million things to do, and I haven't been able to concentrate on any of them because of a certain young lady in copy-writing.

"Well, turns out one of your favorite employees has put a..."

"Who's one of my favorite employees?" I cut him off.

"You know."

"Are you talking about Edith?" I ask. "What has she done now?"

"Not Edith, your other favorite female at the company."

"I have no idea who you're talking about," I say, though my mind does flash to Sarah. But that's ridiculous because I don't even know her well. There's no way that she's a favorite employee of mine. I don't even know what her work ethic is like. I don't know if she's talented. I don't know anything. I know I like her, but there's no actual basis for my like.

"You know, that girl in copywriting."

"Sarah is not one of my favorite employees," I blurt out and instantly regret it.

"Oh, so you do remember her name." He chuckles.

"What is going on, Jackson?"

"I think you need to pull up the intranet."

"Why?"

"Because Sarah has posted something."

"She has?" I'm befuddled now. Didn't that just go up yesterday afternoon? What is she posting? I want to look but don't want to feel like I need to look. "What has she posted about?"

"I think you're going to want to read this for yourself," Jackson says, chuckling. "Or I can read it to you."

"I do not have time to play games right now, Jackson. I have work to do, and I'm pretty sure you have work to do, as well."

"Unlike you, Mr. Rosser, I know when to leave my work at home. Life is all about balance. You work as hard as you can, and then you play as hard as you can."

"Well, it doesn't sound like you're playing hard to me, right now, seeing as we're on the phone."

"I'll have you know that I just finished a date with a very beautiful supermodel who I'm not going to name."

"They're all very beautiful supermodels, Jackson."

"What are you saying? That I only date supermodels?"

"I'm not saying that. It just seems to be the case."

"I'd date Sarah," he says as if I want to hear that. "Do you know if she's seeing anyone?"

"What? What are you talking about?" The tone in my voice is steel-like, and I can feel my shoulders tense.

"Oh, actually, I'm pretty sure that she's not seeing someone." He laughs again. "Maybe she'll be up for a date with me."

"Jackson, what is going on? Why are you interested in Sarah, and how'd you know she's single?" I'm getting pissed off now.

"Why, are you interested if she's single?" he asks innocently. "What about the no-fraternization policy?"

"Jackson," I shout. "I do not have time for these games."

"Pull up the intranet, Ethan. Trust me, you're going to want to read this."

"I'm going to go. I..."

"Mid-thirties, slightly hot mess female seeking billionaire," he says loudly and then clears his throat.

"Huh?" I'm about to hang up, but now I'm confused. "What are you talking about?"

"That's the title of the post that little Miss Sarah Kahan just posted to the intranet at one twelve a.m."

"She posted what?" For a couple of seconds, I feel

disappointment. Is she a gold digger, after all? Did she see my article, and now she's trying to get her hooks into me? Because how many other billionaires work at Rosser International besides Jackson, and Jackson hasn't yet inherited his fortune. Though, he's still worth hundreds of millions of dollars from his trust. I sigh in disappointment at the thought that Sarah is like all the other women, after all.

"You want to hear more?" Jackson asks as if that's even in question.

"Go on, read it. Wait, let me get up from my desk and pour a stiff drink. I think I'm going to need it before I hear what this says."

"Oh, you're definitely going to need it," he says, chuckling. "It seems that little Miss Sarah is not so dowdy and innocent."

"What do you mean by innocent?" I think back to her dancing on the table. Those were not the dance moves of an innocent woman.

"I don't know. I figured, anyone that's coming to work with thick-ass glasses, hair in a bun, and looking like some sort of Great-Aunt Mildred that works in the library, isn't exactly trying to pull at work, right?"

"And what's wrong with that? Are you trying to say that she should be trying to pull? You know…"

"I know, Ethan. There's a no-fraternization policy at the company. That doesn't mean that women don't try and look good for men, and that doesn't mean there aren't lots of people banging in the office."

"Who is?"

"That's not important right now, Ethan. Do you or

do you not want to hear what little Miss Sarah has posted?"

"Fine," I say, stretching my legs and heading to my bar. I grab the crystal decanter of whiskey and pour it into a glass. I'm not even going to bother with ice. I have a feeling I don't need it. I take a sip. "Wait a second. Did she call herself a hot mess?"

"Yep," he says. "I guess if she's nothing, she's honest."

"Mid-thirties, slightly hot mess female seeking billionaire," I repeat the words over. "She's literally crazy. Does she want to get fired or something?"

"I don't know," he says, "but you might want to fire her after you hear exactly what is in the post, which you still haven't heard yet, and I'm not sure why you haven't wanted to hear yet. Is it because you're scared that..."

"I'm not scared of anything, Jackson. Go on. Tell me exactly what it says."

He clears his throat, and there's a long silence.

"Hello? Are you there?"

"I just want to make sure you're really ready for this."

"Jackson, you're getting on my nerves. Tell me what it says."

"Hold on, Ethan. Don't get your panties in a twist."

"Jackson, I will fire you if you do not tell me what it says right now."

"We both know that you're never going to fire me. We both know that you couldn't live without me. We both know that..."

"Jackson, you sound like a dick right now."

"Maybe that's because I am a dick," he says. "Or wait, maybe it's because I have a dick. You know what that supermodel asked me tonight?"

"What?" I groan as I jump up and head toward my computer. "If you don't tell me what it says, I will just pull it up and read it."

"She said to me she wanted to see if the rumors were true."

"Huh? What rumors?"

"About my twelve-inch cock," Jackson says, and I roll my eyes.

"Dude, you're like a brother. I love you. You do not have a twelve-inch cock."

"You don't know how big it is unless you've been peeking."

"Jackson."

"Yeah?"

"Read the rest of that post now," I say, "or I'll just find it myself and…"

"Fine," he says. "Okay, should I say it in my voice or in her voice?"

"What?" I'm exasperated now. I am about to go off on him.

"I could say it in a really high-pitched voice," he says, squeaking. "Mid-thirties, slightly hot mess female seeking billionaire. Maybe Ethan Rosser." He starts chortling. "Oh, my gosh. Was that too far? Tell me it was too far. No, it wasn't. It was…"

"Jackson. You know what, dude? I'm going to read

it myself. Thank you for letting me know. I am done with you and your bullshit."

"My bullshit? Why are you so upset? I thought you would be happy that I was letting you know that one of your top employees is soliciting for a billionaire on our company intranet."

"It was your idea to do the intranet."

"I know, and I thought it was a great idea."

"Are you going to tell me what it says or not?"

"Fine. Okay, are you listening to me?"

"I've been listening, Jackson." I'm infuriated now.

"To whom it may concern," he starts, "this is a long shot. I'm seeking a billionaire. I will also settle for a millionaire. Sorry, I'm not interested in any salesmen looking to sell me a time-share or part of their animal balloon company (been there, done that). I'm not a gold digger, though you may not believe that. I have references. Ask all my broke exes and my best friends.

"To be fair, I'm not a glamorous model, actress, or professional dancer. I do, however, take pole dancing lessons (for fun, of course, not dollar bills). I am an educated, (I still have the student loans to prove it), open-minded, (toy stores are fun and not for games), fairly cute (when I try), only a little curvy, (those last thirty pounds don't want to leave), single female. I want to be swept off my feet, wined, dined, and bedded in ways that make me forget my name. I have a job (that I hate) with a boss that makes me want to jump off a cliff. However, my friends make up for the day job. I'm ready for an adventure, and possibly a penthouse with a maid and a design budget. If interested, please respond before Monday morning so I don't have to go in to work. Love, Sultry Sassy Sarah." Jackson stops, and I'm dumbfounded and struggling to comprehend what I just heard. My heart is racing, and I almost want to laugh.

"You are not serious," I say finally. "This cannot be real."

"I'm one hundred percent serious," he says, chuckling like he's just left a Dave Chappelle show.

"I do not believe that she posted that on the company intranet. Is she out of her mind?"

"Are you upset because she said she hates her job and she has a boss that makes her want to jump off a cliff, or because she posted this?"

"I very much doubt she's talking about me." I pause. "Do you think she's talking about me?"

"I don't know, but possibly."

"You know what? I have to go," I say and hang up before he can answer. I bring up the company intranet and look at the message myself. I cannot believe that Sarah has posted this. I cannot believe she said she hates her job after I asked her to create a jingle. I've given her an amazing opportunity, and this is what she says?

I press my lips together. I want to find out her phone number, call her, and tell her off, but I know it is way too early to do such a thing. Instead, I log in to the HR files to find her company email address and send her a message.

Sarah, this is your boss, Ethan Rosser. We won't be able to meet tomorrow, but I would like to see you in my office first-thing Monday morning. Do not be late.

11

Sarah

Dear Diary,
I'm dead.
Seriously.
I cannot say more as my head is buried in the sand.
Shameful and Saddened Sarah

I wake up with a massive hangover and swear that I am never going to drink again.

I rub my pounding temples and let out a moan as Johnson jumps onto the bed to lick my face.

"It's moments like this that I wish I still lived at home," I whisper into the room. "Johnson, can you go and make me some eggs and a coffee?"

He just sits there and looks at me, batting his long eyelashes. I know he wants to go on a walk. There's no way that's happening right now though. I don't even think I can get out of bed.

"Oh, my head, how much did I drink last night?" I mumble as I think back to the night before, and memories come flooding in. Meeting up with Ella, hanging out with Isabel, dancing in the small little bar we'd gone to, drinking tequila shot after tequila shot, and then pitchers of sangria. We'd really gone to town. We'd been celebrating Ella's return to New York City, but maybe we'd gone a little bit hard for a weekday, especially considering the fact that I have an appointment with Ethan Rosser this morning.

My heart beats erratically as I think about him. Maybe he and I can be friends in some form of the word. I mean, I know we won't be *friends* friends. I am not on his level. He's my boss, and I know I can't hope for more. Sure, he kind of flirted with me, maybe, but there's a no-fraternization policy at the company that he instituted, and he made it pretty clear that there are thousands of women after him. And if there are thousands of women after him, he won't think twice about me.

My head feels like a hammer is banging against my skull, and I groan. "Oh, man, I don't feel good," I say as I try to sit up. I know I need to make some greasy eggs and drink plenty of water. "If I had a boyfriend or a husband, he could get them for me right now," I mumble, but that doesn't make me feel better because I have neither a boyfriend nor a husband. I've no potential ones on the horizon, either.

"Maybe one day I'll find myself a millionaire," I say, and then I freeze as I remember other things from the previous night.

"Wait, did I write a personal ad?" I groan, wondering if that's true. "Mid-thirties, slightly hot mess female seeking billionaire," I say out of repetition, and I groan. "I am going to kill Ella and I'm going to kill Isabel," I say. "I can't believe they had me writing that stupidness. I hope I didn't put it on a dating site anywhere." I reach over for my phone to see if I had posted it anywhere.

My heart immediately starts racing when I see a message from Ethan Rosser that had come in in the early hours of the morning. For a moment, I feel like maybe it's a drunk message. Maybe he's flirting with me. Maybe he does like me and wants to let me know that he's interested. Maybe he's even been trying to butt-dial me or was trying to get me to come over for a late-night booty call. I smile suddenly at the thought. I totally would have gone.

"That wouldn't even be a flattering message, Sarah," I chastise myself as I open the email. I don't know why I feel excited that he could be inviting me over for a late-night lovemaking session.

My heart drops immediately when I read what he has to say and the fact that he wants to see me on Monday. My jaw drops as he posts sentences from my personal ad. The private one that we'd messed around making last night.

"Ms. Kahan, please inform me as to why this was posted on the company intranet."

The words make my heart stop. What the hell is going on?

The fact that my personal ad, which was written as a joke, that was not meant to be seen by anyone, had likely been seen by everyone at Rosser International who logged in to the intranet, including Ethan, makes me want to curl up and die. How had my dumb ass posted it there? Then, I remember clicking on Dave's email and link and Isabel taking my phone and typing it up. She must have posted it by mistake.

"I hate you, sangria," I wail, thinking I'm about to pass out, throw up, or maybe both. That would just be my luck. I'd throw up and then pass out and wake up in my own puke. How disgusting, but maybe I deserve it.

I quickly call Isabel. She answers with a groan after three rings.

"You woke me up, Sarah. What's going on?" She sounds groggy and like she's also in the midst of a hangover, but I don't feel bad at all.

"I am going to kill you," I say, anger in my voice. But it's not just directed at her. It's also directed at myself.

"Okay. Can it wait until after I wake up?"

"No," I say. "Hold on. I'm calling Ella."

"Fine." She moans.

I place her on hold and do a three-way call. Ella answers almost immediately. "Hey, sunshine. How's it..."

"Don't sunshine me. Hold on." I press the button so we're all connected. "Isabel, you there?"

"I'm here," she says in a grunt.

"Ella, you there?"

"I'm here. Morning, Isabel."

"Oh, hey, Ella. How's it going?"

"Good. Are you hungover?"

"Yeah, I'm hungover. You're not?"

"Just a little bit," she says. "But Colton gave me this green juice that—"

"I don't want to hear it," I say. "I don't have a Colton. I don't have anyone. I'm hungover as shit, and guys, I hate you both."

"Oh, so it's not just me you hate," Isabel says.

Ella is silent.

"Don't you guys want to know why I hate you?"

"Well, I figure you were going to tell us," Ella says. "What did we do now? Is it because you're hungover, and is it because I have a man? I can have him bring you over some of the green juice that he…"

"It's got nothing to do with green juice. I don't care about green juice." I groan. "Though if he wants to send me over a bucket load of green juice and some eggs, I'm not going to say no."

"We can do that," Ella says. "You want some, as well, Isabel?"

"Hey, if it's on offer, I'm accepting," she says.

"Okay, hold on. Colton," Ella calls out to her boyfriend.

"Yes, dear." I hear mumbling in the background.

"Isabel and Sarah are also really hungover. Can you have your driver take them over some of those green juices that you ordered for me this morning, and then they most probably both need some greasy breakfast to suck up the alcohol?"

"Of course," he says sweetly, and my heart soars for a few seconds. While I'm very grateful to him, I'm also happy that Ella has a man who will treat her well and her friends well, as well.

"Okay," Ella says happily. "All done. Colton says that it should be there within forty-five minutes. Does that work?"

"Yeah, that's fine." I yawn. "Tell him thanks."

"Don't you have to leave for work though?" Isabel asks.

"I'm not going to work today," I say.

"You have to go to work," Ella says. "You have your meeting today with Ethan and..."

"I no longer have a meeting today with Ethan, guys," I say, waiting for them to ask me why. "Is no one going to ask me why?"

"We figure you're going to tell us." Isabel grunts.

"Fine. You know that stupid personal ad you guys made me write last night?"

"It wasn't stupid. It was so funny." Isabel laughs and then groans. "Ow, that hurt. I can't laugh. Don't make me laugh."

"Don't worry. I'm not trying to make anyone laugh because I'm sure not laughing right now," I say. "I am dead meat, guys. Seriously, dead meat."

"Oh, boy. What has happened?" Ella asks.

"Well, the personal ad that we wrote, mid-thirties, slightly hot mess female seeking billionaire."

"I thought that was such a cute title. We are amazing, and no wonder you're in copywriting because your ad was hilarious. Oh, my gosh. I want a billionaire who can put me up in a penthouse, as well." Isabel is obviously not picking up that I am upset.

"Guys, we posted it on my company intranet by mistake."

There's silence on the line. You could hear a pin drop as everyone processes what I have just said.

"Fuck," Isabel moans.

"Exactly. That's all I've been thinking since I've read Ethan's email. Ethan saw it and he emailed me at two-something this morning. I don't even want to look at the email again because I'm hella embarrassed. He told me that the meeting today is called off and he wants to see me in his office on Monday morning. Oh my God. I'm going to get fired. I'm totally going to get fired."

"Play it off," Ella says thoughtfully. "I mean, why would he cancel your meeting today?"

"I bet you it's because she said she didn't want to go in on Monday morning," Isabel adds. "He's most probably alluding to that."

"That's what I think, because he wants to fire me."

"Well, maybe play it off like a joke," Ella suggests.

"What do you mean, play it off as a joke?"

"I got an idea," Isabel says thoughtfully. "Why don't you say something like, oh, ha-ha should I bring some dollars, as well? Pretend like the whole thing was just one big joke and not a drunk post by mistake."

"You really think that will work?" I ask, wanting to believe it will work.

"Perhaps. I mean, what do you have to lose?"

"I guess." I grab my phone from my ear, and I press reply to Ethan's email. "So, what exactly should I say?"

"Just be like ha-ha, I'll be there on Monday as long as you have enough singles," Isabel suggests.

And even though I know it doesn't sound like a great idea, I type it because he does know I have a kooky sense of humor. And he does know that I'm slightly weird, so maybe if I act kooky and not like I am worried about his email, he will think this was just a really bad joke.

"Yeah, he might be like, 'oh, don't quit the day job. You're no Dave Chappelle' or something," I say as I hit send. "Right?"

"I don't know about that," Ella says quickly. "You know what, girl? Don't do it."

"What do you mean, don't do it? I already did it."

There's more silence.

"Oh, I don't know if that was the best idea you've ever had, Isabel." Ella sounds nervous. "I'm just saying, he might not find it a joke, and if he doesn't think it's a joke, he might think you're propositioning him."

"Oh my God, I'm going to die. That's it, guys. I will speak to you when I'm a spirit in heaven because, right now, my body is about to leave this earthly plane. I've got to go." I can feel my body tense, and I want to cry. I hang up and stare at the ceiling. This is possibly the worst day of my life.

My phone pings. I'm going to ignore it, but I know I can't.

It's a reply from Ethan. My heart races.

I'm not going to read it.

I'm too scared to even look at it.

I click it open. I need to know what he has to say.

12

Ethan

I stare at the email that Sarah sent me this morning and read it for the hundredth time. Each time I read it, I don't know what to think.

"Is this woman crazy?" I exclaim for what must be the tenth time.

"Did she seriously ask me if I was going to bring dollars to the meeting on Monday?"

I want to chuckle because it's kind of funny. But I know, as the boss, I can't just let it go. I just don't get her, and that is something that makes me uncomfortable. Normally, I know what a woman wants, especially from me. Normally, they want to win me over and bed me or try and catch me, as old-fashioned people would say, but Sarah Kahan, I have no clue what she's really after.

Does she want me for a night? Does she want me for life? Does she just not want me at all? Is she just a weirdo? It's looking very likely that she's a weirdo, but I just don't know. There's something about how her blue eyes twinkle when she's being sarcastic or angry and how the dimples in her cheek deepen when she laughs at something she thinks is funny.

It set off something in me when I saw those dimples; it made me feel proud that I brought them out and made her laugh. You wouldn't even know she had dimples half the time because she always seems so judgmental and annoyed. Though, that thought is a bit of a stretch because I don't know her very well, had never even noticed her before this week, so I don't know if that's how she always looks or conducts herself.

I stare at my response and wonder if she'll reply.

"Today's meeting is back on. Meet me at my home address at noon."

I don't know why I suggested that. It had been impetuous and impulsive, and a gut reaction to her stating that she was interested in knowing how many singles I was going to bring to the meeting on Monday.

I should meet her in my office; that's professional, but I feel like we've already crossed the line from professional. I feel like we're teetering on an invisible line of flirtation, hate, and animosity all in one.

I can tell we both aren't sure what to make of each other. I can also tell that she doesn't absolutely hate me. There was a little bit of flirtation on her side, as well, but I know that she was cautious. I know that she also thinks I'm an arrogant prick, which isn't surprising, as many women think that about me. In fact, it was a persona I craved, a way to keep the women at bay who believed they could break down my walls and get a sixth date with me.

I don't know how she's going to respond to my email. Maybe she'll say she's quitting. Maybe she'll say she's reporting me to HR for being too friendly. Though, that isn't very true, my email was anything but friendly, but maybe she thinks I'm trying to solicit her.

I don't know. It does make me slightly tense wondering what she's thinking. I am about to email her again when I see that she responded. I open it immediately.

"If I'm coming to your house, I need to know your address."

I smile widely, my heart racing. Fuck! What have I done?

"So, she's coming," I mutter. I jump out of my chair, head toward my large floor-to-ceiling windows, and stare at the skyline. I don't know why I've invited her to my place. I don't know what the conversation will be about. I don't know how to ask her about the personal ad and why she did it or her response about the money. I don't know what she wants or what she's expecting. All I know is that I want to see her. I want to talk to her, and I want it to be in an environment that isn't one hundred percent work-related, which is weird because our conversation will be one hundred percent work-related.

I know I have no other option other than to be professional.

I'm not going to flirt with her any more than I

already have. Perhaps this will be a test to see if the ad was truly a mistake or not.

Maybe she was testing the waters to see if I'd bite. So maybe I'll test the waters to see if she's trying to test me. Maybe this is a way for me to figure out if she's just trying to catch herself a billionaire whose name is Ethan Rosser or not.

She most probably saw the article. In fact, hadn't she told me she'd seen the article?

Interesting.

Maybe she thinks I'll be the one to provide her the penthouse, which is definitely not going to happen. I don't even live in a penthouse, though I could if I wanted to. I feel like it's pretentious, and I am not pretentious. Well, not about most things. There is a certain element of pretentiousness that comes along with being the CEO of a Fortune 500 company and having a Harvard MBA, but that is because of other people's perception, not because of who I am. At least, that's what I hope.

I text her my address and stand there for a few minutes. If she's on time, she'll be here soon. I need a shower. I need to have some coffee so my brain is switched on right, and I need to figure out why the hell I invited her to my place and what I'm going to talk about. I know I'm crossing a million ethical lines, and I know if anyone else in my company were to even suggest such a thing to one of my employees, I'd have HR fire them on the spot. But then again, I am the company.

I make the rules.

"You should abide by the rules you set, Ethan," I mumble, trying to remind myself that I can't cross the line. If my employees can't cross the line, then I can't cross the line. I pride myself on one rule for everyone at the company, one policy for all, open door talks, etc.

It's just a different door that's open now. I chuckle to myself and shake my head. I have no idea what I'm doing, but I figure I have... I look at my watch for a second... fifty-eight minutes to figure it out. Fifty-eight minutes to find a reason to have invited Sarah Kahan to my apartment. Fifty-eight minutes to find out everything I can about her online and in her HR file. Fifty-eight minutes to figure out if this woman is trying to pull my leg or if she's just the biggest goofball. I think about the jingle we have to write for Lord Chambers and the conversation that we will have.

I can make the meeting about the jingle.

I can make the jingle part of the marketing plan for the new home renovation stores we're about to open, which will sell ninety-five percent of our products. Many people in the company, including Sarah, don't yet know about this launch.

However, maybe that's the reason I can give her to having her come to my home instead of the office.

"You got it, boy." I smile to myself as I head to my bathroom to shower.

I pull off my shirt and boxer shorts, turn on the water, and wait for it to get hot. I step in and take a big, deep breath as the hot water cascades down my body. I grab the shampoo, squeeze it into my palm, rub it into my hair, and close my eyes. All I can think about is

Sarah in there with me, naked except for a thong and maybe some heels, dancing, grinding on me, taking her bun down and shaking out her hair, taking off her glasses and batting her big blue eyes, and then dropping to her knees and taking my cock in her mouth.

"Fuck," I say as my palm finds my cock and starts moving back and forth. The last thing I need is to have a dirty fantasy about the woman that's going to be in my apartment within an hour or so, but I can't stop myself. I don't even know what she looks like naked, but I've seen her shape through her clothes. She looks like she's got a beautiful, curvy body, just the way I like; big boobs and a big ass. Fuck, I could fuck her so hard and so fast. I'd love to hear her screaming out in pleasure. I'd love to hear her calling out my name. I'd love to hear her begging me.

"Oh, hell," I say as my hand starts moving faster and faster. "You're in trouble, Ethan," I mumble as I explode into the shower, and my cum goes down the drain. I know it's better for me to release my pent-up sexual desire for this woman now rather than when she arrives. The last thing I need is to suggest that she earn those singles today while grinding on my lap because, even if I'm joking, I don't know what will happen.

There's a part of me that feels like she'll slap me across the face and tell me off, and another part of me feels like she'll be delighted by the offer and give me the lap dance of my life. I already know she's got the moves. I've already seen her swinging her hips. I've seen her parted lips and sweaty brow. It would be very hard to stop her if anything got going.

It would be even harder to stop me. In fact, I know there would be no stopping me. The last thing in the world I need right now is a lap dance from Sarah Kahan, because I don't know what would come after that.

Or maybe the problem is, I do know. Maybe the problem is that I kind of want it to happen. I know it can't. She knows it can't. I cannot cross that line. No matter how badly I want to. I don't even know how I'd tell her about my five-night rule. Though, I know I'd enjoy each and every one of those nights. I'd savor them. I'd have her coming so hard, that she'd realize she's never had an orgasm before me.

But I know I can't go down that road. Not at all. It would be bad news. I have to focus on work. Like always. Work is what is important.

13

Sarah

Dear Diary,

I know anyone reading this diary will wonder what caused my last entry. But I do not have time to dish on that right now because I have more important news to tell you about. Your girl had an O today. Yes, a capital O.

I know you want to know who, what, why, when, and where. But a true lady never reveals her secrets.

Lucky for you, I'm not a true lady, hehe.

Sexy Slamming Sarah

My phone screen flashes on and off, and I see it's now noon. I've been standing outside Ethan's building for the last hour and ten minutes. I got here far too early, and I'm not sure if it's due to eagerness or nerves. I have no idea why he wants to see me in his home. This is not a typical request from the CEO of any company. Aside from maybe the company Christian Grey ran, and it's been so long that I can't even remember the name. Not that I'm an innocent college student about to fall into Ethan Rosser's dominant trap. I'm totally not into that sort of stuff. Not that it's ever been offered to me before.

"Not like it's going to be offered to you now, dumbass," I mumble under my breath as I enter the building and head toward the elevator. I'm surprised Ethan doesn't live in a building with a doorman. I thought every rich person in Manhattan would do so. I guess that means Ethan is not like every other rich person, but I know inside, a part of me already knew that. Even though I don't know any other rich people other than Colton Hart, Ella's boyfriend, and if I'm being honest, I barely know him.

I push the button and wait for the elevator to arrive. My entire body is vibrating, and I ponder running out of the building and heading home. I can bury myself under the sheets, watch TV, and pretend that none of this is happening. I look back to the entrance and am about to leave when the elevator doors open, so I walk inside slowly. So slowly that if I were having a race with a tortoise, I would lose. I'm nervous. Really, really nervous. I have no idea what is about to happen.

I could be fired. I could be asked to strip. I could be told to cook him lunch from scrap meats, though that is very unlikely. The only reason it popped to mind is that I'd been watching *Chopped* before I left my apartment to head over here. There is no way that Ethan is going to give me a selection of random foods and tell me to come up with a meal. Though, maybe he's expecting to hear a jingle.

I tap my fingers against the wall and try to think of a cool beat. "Da dum, da da da, da dum," I sing in a high C octave. "Da dum, da, da, da, da dum," I hum again. "Get your lights, make it bright, treat your guests to a multi-fest, make it shine, treat them right. They are royalty," I sing and tap my foot to the beat. "Not bad," I mumble. "Not perfect, but not bad." I take a deep breath. My mind wanders to Ethan and his seriously handsome face. I wonder how many women would kill to be where I am right now. I can't believe that I'm about to see his home.

What is this life?

A week ago, I was bitching that he didn't even know I existed, and now I'm about to have a one-on-one with him about who knows what? I quickly pull out my phone and text Isabel and Ella. Even though I am mad at them, I want them to know where I am. Just in case anything crazy goes down. I've watched enough *Dateline* to know you can't trust anyone. The elevator dings when it reaches the floor, and I step out hesitantly. My heart is racing now, and I feel both hot and cold at the same time. I pause as I exit and take a breath. I'm feeling slightly faint.

Am I making a mistake going to his home? Not that it really matters if I do think it's a mistake because lord knows I'm not going back home now. I am going to see this thing through. I head toward his front door and am about to knock when it opens. Ethan is standing there with a towel around his shoulders. He's wearing loose black shorts and a baggy gray shirt. His hair appears damp, and I wonder if he just got done working out.

"You're late," he says as he steps to the side to let me in. I walk in, and he slams the door closed behind me. My heart races as I stand there. Why did the door slamming sound so final? He is going to let me leave, isn't he? A part of my brain is hardwired to think that he's going to lock me up in a dungeon and keep me as a sex slave, but that may be due to all the dark romance TikTok videos I've been watching.

"It's noon."

"It's twelve oh five," he corrects me with an attitude, like those five minutes are five hours.

"I was here at noon." I think, earlier than that, but I'm not going to tell him that.

"Yet, you're only now inside of my house at twelve oh five."

"The elevator isn't a space shuttle, you know. It doesn't go from zero to one hundred in one second."

"Then you should have accounted for the elevator time when you made your way over here." Ethan is getting on my nerves, and I don't respond as I follow him into a large, open space. His apartment is gorgeous, with a large kitchen to the left and an even larger living room opposite. He opens the fridge, pulls out a pitcher, and nods toward it. "Would you like some water?"

"Yes, please," I say, even though I don't want any. But it gives me an excuse to hold on to something and not play with my hair, which I often do when I'm nervous.

"Lemon slice?" he asks as he opens a cupboard door and takes out two tall glasses. He places them on his white marble countertops, then opens his sparkly white fridge again and takes out a lemon. I nod my assent, and he grabs a knife from a butcher block and a small wooden cutting board and cuts the lemon in half. His fingers are deft and fast, and I wonder if he likes cooking and if that's something he does to show off to his female guests. If I find out he has culinary skills, as well, I will scream. Does the man have everything going for him? "So, you're seeking a billionaire, are you?" he asks casually as he hands me a glass, and I stifle a groan.

I should have known he was going to bring this up right away. I'm not ready for this conversation. How do I explain everything without sounding like an idiot?

"You really do have a beautiful home," I say to Ethan, trying to be polite while changing the subject. He stares at me for a few seconds and I think he's going to tell me to just acknowledge the bear in the room, and I brace myself for the response. He can't really think I wrote it on purpose or with hopes of reeling him in, can he?

"Thank you," he says with a thoughtful nod. He takes another step toward me, and there's a supercilious smile on his face. He reminds me of a wolf sizing up its prey. I shiver at the thought that I'm his prey. I'm not going to lie; I quite like the feeling of him sizing me up. "I guess you finally get to see it, huh?" Like I've been itching for years to get into his home. Pompous jerk.

"What does that mean?" I ask him, frowning. Just because I'm attracted to him doesn't mean I'm going to allow him to talk to me like some desperado doing anything she can to get into his home. He's lucky I showed up.

"I mean, it sounds like you've wanted to see my place or a billionaire's place for a while," he states like that's a fact that can't be disputed. Like he's a reporter on CNN shelling out facts that everyone agrees upon.

"How dare you!" My voice is sharp, and I try to calm myself down. *You catch more flies with honey, Sarah.* "I had and still have no interest in seeing your place. You're the one who told me to come over. I thought we had a meeting in your office today, which I was prepared for. It's not my fault you canceled the meeting." I bite down on my lower lip as I realize I've walked into his trap. Or maybe I trapped myself. I don't know. "I guess we should address the elephant in the room before we go any further." I lick my lips nervously and then take a sip of the lemon water. Why does rich people's water taste better than mine?

"There's an elephant in the room?" he asks, his eyes wide as he looks around. There's an alarmed look on his face, and I want to tell him that he's a pitiful actor. "Shit, where is it? How do we get rid of it? I hope it doesn't destroy my furniture." He paces around, and I roll my eyes as he opens a drawer and grabs a rolling pin.

"Very funny." I suppress a giggle. He really is a goof.

"What?" he says. "You don't have a sense of humor?"

"Let's just say I'm not suggesting you quit your day job anytime soon and go into comedy."

"I'll have you know that I'm a fine comedian and a fine roaster. Just ask Jackson Pruitt."

"Why, have you roasted him?"

"Yep, when we were back at Harvard." He grins. "Those were the days."

"I didn't realize you guys have known each other so long," I say, considering what I know about them. It makes sense that they are old friends though. They are always together. Everyone knows that Jackson is Ethan's right-hand man.

"Yeah. We've been best friends for a while." He nods as he puts the rolling pin on the countertop. "So, you said you wanted to address the elephant in the room?"

"Well, I think it's an African elephant," I say, smiling, and he chuckles.

"So, about that post." His face turns stern, and he crosses his arms. "What was that about, exactly?"

"Is that why I'm here?" I ask, wondering why this conversation couldn't have taken place in the office. "You want to fire me because I accidentally made a joke post? I thought you had a sense of humor."

"We both know that post wasn't a joke. Give me some credit, Sarah. I'm a CEO. I went to Harvard. I've got brains. There's no way you decided to write a post at one-something in the morning as a joke. For what? What would be the purpose?"

"I don't know. Just to test out the intranet system and..." I sigh loudly, knowing it sounds false. "Fine. It wasn't a joke. I mean, it was a joke, but not posted as a joke. Does that even make sense?" I start playing with my fingernails because I know I'm not making sense. But I'm nervous, and I start to ramble.

"No," he says, shaking his head with his brows furrowed. His blue eyes are keen as they observe my face, and I feel like he can see inside my head. He's unnerving, and for some reason, butterflies in my stomach are doing somersaults. "Come on, let's have a seat." He heads toward the living room and takes a seat on a large black leather couch. He sits back and rests his arms across the back. There's an empty spot next to him, and I debate sitting there. My eyes move to his muscular legs and his gym shorts, and I swallow hard. The man has a body that could be in *GQ*.

I'm about to sit next to him when I notice a recliner to the right and decide to sit there. I don't want to sit on a black couch next to Ethan Rosser. I don't know what could go down. My fingers want to touch him, and I don't trust myself to not run my fingers accidentally against his thighs.

"So, you were saying?" He turns toward me and leans forward, sporting a little smirk on his face. I wonder if he knows why I took a different chair.

"I was hanging out with my friends," I say quickly in explanation. "One of my best friends, Ella, just got back from Europe. Her fiancé or boyfriend or whatever decided to take her on their first date and they just got back."

"What?" He frowns, confusion apparent in his expression. "Okay, this story sounds like a lie already. I'm sorry, Sarah, but I'm afraid you're not exactly Hemingway here."

"No, it's not a lie. I know it sounds weird." I ignore his comment about Hemingway. I'm not going to take it personally because I know the story sounds fake, but as they always say, truth is stranger than fiction.

"Yeah, it does sound weird that someone's fiancé would take them to Europe on a first date." He pauses. "Like, how are they engaged if they've never been on a date? Unless you're saying it's some sort of arranged marriage? Or was she on that dating show, *Married at First Sight* or whatever?"

"No." I sigh, though I find it quite funny that he's talking about *Married at First Sight*. I'm shocked he's even heard of the show. "She's not been on a dating show, though maybe that would have been less dramatic." I don't really want to get into all this, but I suppose I have to, to have it all make sense. "Let me explain a bit better. My best friend, Ella, is now dating her brother's best friend. She's known him for a long time. And while they were hooking up and stuff already, they also fell for each other, but they'd never really been on an official first date, nothing romantic, you know? So, Colton wanted to take her to Paris and London and wherever else they went, if that makes sense."

"I guess so. So, you're saying the friends with benefits became more?" He recoils as if the thought makes him nauseous. I guess he's not someone who will find himself in that position. I'm not sure why that realization upsets me. It's not like he and I are friends with benefits. Though, I know I wouldn't even have to be friends with him to enjoy the benefit of his big hands. *Stop it, Sarah. Focus!*

"Yeah, you could say that, though they weren't technically friends with benefits, but... Oh, you know what I mean."

He shakes his head. "Not really. I sure hope their story doesn't get around the city, because I would hate to think any woman that I'm sleeping with thinks that there's a possible engagement coming at the end." He shudders.

"Okay, point taken," I say, shrugging. "If I meet any of your women, I'll be sure to let them know."

"Thanks."

"Lucky ladies." I roll my eyes.

"Lucky them, indeed," he says, winking. "So, continue, your friend came back from Europe?"

"Yeah, and we were drinking and having fun to celebrate her being back in the city. Us girls love to get together weekly and just let loose." I shrug. "I mean, I'm sure you and your boys do the same weekly or nightly?"

"Rarely."

"Uh-huh."

"I'm guessing your other friend was there, as well, the one from the bar that night?"

"Yeah, Isabel was there." I nod my head. "So, it was Ella, Isabel, and me, and we were drinking tequila shots and—"

"Maybe you guys need to stop drinking. First night you were drinking, I see you dancing on tabletops, pretending you're a stripper called Slutty Sarah."

"It was Slutty Stripper, actually, and please don't call me that again." I want to gag at the name. Yet again.

"Sorry, I won't say it again. So, one night you're

dancing on tabletops. And now you go drinking and you're sending inappropriate messages to the company website."

"Intranet," I say, correcting him because his words are making me sound and feel like a lush. There's no way he's going to believe I haven't had alcohol in a while before those two nights.

"I know it's an intranet," he says. "But what you did was inappropriate, Sarah. Do I need to sign you up for Alcoholics Anonymous?"

"No." I let out a deep sigh. "I'm sorry. I really am sorry. It was a horrible lapse of judgment in both instances. Though, technically, I was dancing on the tabletop on my own time, and it was none of your business. I did that because I wanted to have fun and let loose." I don't want to explain why I wanted the attention that night, so I move on quickly. "But anyway, that doesn't matter right now. Last night, I wasn't even the one typing up the message. There's no way I ever would've posted something like that. I'm not that sort of woman." I feel indignant now. Granted, he doesn't know me well, but does he really think I would post something like that on purpose?

"So, who posted it?" The disbelieving tone is there again. He's so smug, it's infuriating.

"So, I got an email from Dave. You know my coworker in copywriting."

"I know him." He nods and hums a show tune, and we smile at each other for a few seconds.

"Basically, he sent me an email with a link to show me that the company intranet was up. So, I guess I opened it and I didn't close out of the site properly. And then, Isabel grabbed my phone and we were all joking around that I was going to make a personal ad because I'm single," I cringe slightly inside, "and I'm ready to mingle." I cringe even harder at my honesty. I wonder what Ethan is thinking about my comments. I wonder if he's wondering what I mean by ready to mingle. My gosh, he's going to think I'm trying to get laid.

"Well, we thought it would be fun to write something goofy. I was never going to place the ad in the papers or anything. And I certainly was not going to post it on an online dating site, and I did not intend to put it on the intranet. Why would I do such a thing? I don't even really know how it happened. Isabel doesn't, either. I think she must've been super drunk, as well, and not noticing where she was typing, and I don't know how it ended up getting posted." I pause. "I feel absolutely awful, Ethan. I really do. You must think I'm an idiot, an even bigger idiot than you already thought I was." My skin is burning up, and I feel like I'm going to cry. I don't want this man to think I'm a dumbass.

"I don't think you're an idiot." He shakes his head. "Would I have hired an idiot to write a jingle for me?"

"I don't know. Maybe if it was a jingle for idiots."

"It's not," he says as he jumps up from his seat on the couch and heads toward me. He leans down, grabs my hand, and pulls me out of the chair. "Come on, I want to show you something."

"Oh?" I stand up. What does he want to show me? Has he forgiven me? Does he believe me? The story was true, but I know how unbelievable it sounds. I hope he's not taking me to his office for us to reread the ad as some sort of learning experience. That would be so demeaning. This entire conversation makes me feel like a little kid explaining why they painted on the wall by mistake or something.

"I want to show you my art studio," he says as he heads down the hall. There's an uncertain look on his face, as though he's not sure if he wants to show it to me or not.

"Your art studio?" I ask him, surprised. He's an artist? Is he going to ask me to pose for him? Or is his art studio really a dungeon? Is this the kinky part? Would I care? A certain part of me would quite like for him to have his wicked way with me. I must be crazy. Or just sex-starved. Or just really into him,

"Yes." He nods. "Come and see."

He takes me down a long hallway, and then we walk into a room. He turns on the light, and I'm surprised as I see several easels with canvases, some half-painted, some completed. I look around at the walls that are full of different oil paintings. I feel like I'm at the Louvre.

"Did you paint all these?" I ask in astonishment. There's no way, is there? If he did paint these, he's super-talented. How has no one at Rosser International talked about his artistic talent?

"I did. I hope you like them." He smiles modestly. "I like to paint to relieve stress."

"You're really good. Wow."

I walk up to a painting of Central Park at night. There's a couple sitting on a bench, looking like they're in a very intense conversation. The faces of the couple look so realistic. A discarded bouquet of flowers on the bench is falling to the ground, and the petals look so real.

"You're really talented," I say, unable to think of anything else that can express how blown away I feel by seeing these paintings.

"I'm okay." He shrugs and grabs my elbow. "I brought you in here to show you that this is my safe space. This is where I come when I'm stressed or need to think." He turns to me and smiles. "And sometimes I get drunk in here."

"Okay." I have no idea why he's telling me this. His painting to relieve stress has nothing to do with me going to bars and doing idiotic things with my friends.

"Sometimes, when I paint and I drink, I do stupid stuff," he says, laughing, obviously thinking about one of those instances. "I'm going to show you something."

"Okay." My eyes follow him as he walks over to a stack of canvases that are leaning against the wall. He sorts through them carefully and then picks one out of the pile. He heads back over to me and holds it up to show it to me. My jaw drops and my eyes go wide as I see the painting.

I'm pretty sure it's a self-portrait of him in the nude.

"Um..." I swallow hard, trying to keep my eyes off of his engorged penis, but I'm finding it very hard to look away. Very hard, indeed. *Stop blushing, Sarah.*

"I did this one night a couple of months ago." He chuckles as my eyes go wider and wider. Is he really that big? Should I be staring so hard at his cock? Granted, it's a painting, but it seems so real.

"It looks very real." I nod. "The reason you're showing me this is because, what?"

"Because I don't do nudes, and I certainly don't do nudes of myself." He laughs, staring at the painting critically. "But one night, I stripped off my clothes, and I took a photo, I printed it out, and I painted myself naked. This is not the sort of painting I ever do or want to do, and you're the only person, I think, in my life I will ever show this to." His eyes take me in, and a feeling passes between us. I don't even know what it is. An understanding. A mutual respect. A trust. Something unique, and I can feel my entire body warming in happiness.

At this moment, a certain amount of pleasure and pride passes through me. I don't know why he's showing me his art or if that means he trusts me, but I like that we have shared this moment. I like that he's sharing something he's never shared with anyone else. It makes me feel special. It makes me feel that we have a bond, even though I know that we don't. I realize that a part of the reason he's let his guard down is so that I don't feel so badly about what happened. I find that touching. It shows that he's compassionate toward others, including me. It makes me feel differently about him, as well. Does that mean that I am now also drinking the Kool-Aid?

"It's really good. I see nudes... I mean, paintings of nude models all the time at museums. I'm not an art nerd or historian or anything, but I love spending a lazy afternoon walking around a museum and then going to the cafe for some tea or coffee and buying souvenirs," I admit with a blush.

"But do you really see nudes that artists have painted of themselves?"

"No, I guess not. That's very true." I laugh at his self-satisfied smirk. "You have me there."

"Anyway, my point is that I understand what it is to want to let out steam and end up doing things that are stupid and not really processing what you're doing. But," he says as he puts the painting back down, "you're going to have to make sure this doesn't happen again, Sarah. You cannot post personal ads to the company intranet again, drunken night out or not. You do realize I'm going to have to have HR send out a memo to all employees. And while we won't name you, it will be pretty obvious to anyone who has seen the memo, what you've done."

"I understand," I say, gulping. I wonder if Dave or Ginger saw the memo. I'm pretty sure they didn't because I haven't heard from either of them this morning. They are such gossips that I know I would have woken up to a plethora of texts and calls from them if they had seen or heard anything.

"But here's one thing, and that should make you happy."

"Yeah?" I ask, looking down at the ground, feeling very embarrassed. Nothing about this situation is making me happy, besides seeing a painting of a naked Ethan. That had been pretty tantalizing and satisfying. I wonder if it's true to life.

"Less than ten people saw the memo."

"What?" I blink at him in surprise. "But you have tens of thousands of people that work for you at Rosser International."

"I do," he says, "but you're lucky that you sent it at one-something in the morning. I saw it, Jackson saw it, a couple of other people saw it and then I took it down."

"Oh, I didn't realize that."

"Of course," he says, "it's not like I could leave that up for the entire company to see. I don't want to give people ideas." He chuckles, though there's a pained expression on his face. "Plus, if that was your way of trying to get with me—"

"I know it failed," I say, cutting him off. "Not that that was my way, of course. But if it were, it would've failed." I blush. I'm just making it worse for myself. Why did I say anything about it failing? He's totally going to think that was my plan all along now.

"You are one hundred percent certain that's not what you were trying to do, right?" His eyes are searching, and a thoughtful expression crosses his face.

"I am positive. I swear, Ethan. I was not coming on to you. I was not trying to get you to buy me clothes or get me a penthouse or anything."

"I guess that's true because the reality of the situation is that you don't even want to be around me, do you?"

"Huh?" I ask, swallowing the lump that has formed in my throat due to the topic at hand. Will we ever stop talking about this awful post?

"You didn't want to come in to work on Monday morning, right?"

"It was just a joke. I—"

"And you think I'm an arrogant prick or whatever it was you said?"

"I mean, not always."

"Fine. I'll take you at your word." He taps his leg a couple of times and then nods. "Why don't we get to work?"

"Sure," I say, surprised that he's changed the subject so quickly. "So, are we done with the personal ad or..."

"I'm done if you're done," he says, shrugging as if he wasn't the one who made it a big deal in the first place.

I nod enthusiastically, like a puppy that's just been asked if it wants to go on a walk to the park. "Trust me when I say, I'm sure. In fact, I am one hundred percent certain that I'm done talking about this with you for the rest of my life. So, just to be clear, you're not going to fire me, right?" I don't know why I ask again. I don't even know why I'm putting it in his mind. He hasn't even mentioned firing me.

"Not now." He smirks, knowing he's not putting me at ease. "Especially not if you write me the best jingle known to man."

"Okay." I lick my lips nervously. "That's a tall order."

"Well, have you been working on it or not?"

"A little bit. You didn't exactly give me the full information about the product. However, I have come up with a couple of things," I say quickly, just in case he thinks I'm not up to the job. If there's one thing in life

I'm good at, it's my job. Even if it is boring and I'm being underutilized by the company. "If you want to hear what I've got, I could show you, if you want, of course?" I'm nervous again. I've never presented my work, especially partial work, to the CEO of a company before. I want to impress him. I want him to think I'm talented. I want him to be happy that I'm a part of his organization.

"Of course. Let's go into my office. Because, to be fair, one of the reasons I called you here today wasn't just to talk about the personal ad. It was also because I need a theme song created for a new department store that we're opening, that focuses only on home renovation products."

"We're opening a home renovation store?" I wrinkle my nose in surprise. "What? Since when? I never heard of that from anyone. It hasn't been in any of the company newsletter updates."

"I know," he says, a devious glint in his eyes. "It hasn't been announced yet because we're under contract to launch a new line with several external department stores. Our own stores are being kept hush-hush right now."

"But why?" I don't get it. Why wouldn't we be blasting that information everywhere?

"Because we've just signed a major deal with Home Shop Depot and part of that deal includes a clause that says nothing can be announced until products have been at Home Shop Depot for at least a month." He rubs his fingers together. "They are the number one home supply store in the country. It is important to keep them happy. They are making a big deal of this collaboration. It is worth a potential two billion dollars a year to Rosser International. Something we do not project to make with our own stores."

"I see." I nod as I think about what he's said. Two billion dollars is a lot of money. "I guess it makes sense that they don't want people buying our products at our own stores, instead of Home Shop Depot. They might just back out."

"Exactly." He points at me. "You get it. Is this why you're trying to get into business?"

"Me?" I point at myself then and laugh. "Not at all. I would make a horrible businesswoman." I try to control my giggles. "But it seems to be the logical reason why you wouldn't announce anything."

"Smart. That is why, but we are getting ready for a huge launch behind the scenes, and I feel like a great jingle will help get people into the store once it opens."

"Really? I suppose that could be true. What's the store name?"

"Ah," he says, a twinkle in his eye. "Why don't you see if you can guess?"

"What? How am I supposed to guess?"

"I don't know. Tell me what you think it would be?"

"Rosser Home Goods," I say without a pause. I don't think I'm right, as it's very unimaginative, but I have no other guesses.

His eyes widen, and he bursts out laughing. "Well, well, well, you are a genius."

"No way. It's not really Rosser Home Goods, is it?" I try not to make a face. *Boring*.

"It is, indeed." He smiles as he takes in my not-so-good poker face. "Maybe not the most original, but it fits with our brand."

"Sure, it definitely fits. So, you want me to create a jingle that goes with Rosser Home Goods?"

"I do, as well as a jingle for Lord Chambers' Lighting brand."

"I have a question," I say as I put on my work brain. "So, is this jingle specifically for Lord Chambers or is it for the Royal Lighting line as a whole?"

"It was specifically for Lord Chambers," he says, pausing. He thinks for a moment and then continues. "But maybe, just maybe, we can do it for the lighting line and just throw in his name as part of the jingle so he feels acknowledged. You know how these royals are."

"Not really," I say, shaking my head. "I've never met a member of royalty before in my life."

"I see," he says. "Would you like to?"

"What? Meet a member of royalty, like the king or something?"

"The king?" He raises an eyebrow.

"You know, King Charles or that new King of Denmark that has all this drama with his wife." I pause. I don't want to admit to reading gossip websites.

"No, Sarah, I'm talking about Lord Chambers."

"Oh." I feel like a bit of a fool, then, because, obviously, he'd be talking about Lord Chambers. Why on earth would we go from talking about Lord Chambers to talking about King Charles of England? It's very unlikely that he's designing a light to be sold at Rosser Home Goods. And when I say very unlikely, I mean hell would most probably freeze over, and dinosaurs would be back on Earth before it happened.

"You know what, Sarah?" Ethan says as we walk down the hallway to another room. I watch as he opens the door to a large study and walks inside.

"What?" I ask as I follow him into the room.

"I believe you."

"You believe me about what?"

"I believe that you didn't write that personal ad to try to garner my attention and win me over into your wicked ways of lovemaking and—"

"What?" I say loudly. "Lovemaking, what?"

He chuckles. "Well, you know, your black widow web. Trying to catch me with your lovemaking skills."

"I already told you I didn't attempt to do that."

"I know, but I still wasn't sure. But I do believe you. I don't think you're that sort of woman." He smiles and then bursts out laughing. "You're just very open and a little gullible. I can't believe you thought I could introduce you to King Charles."

"I mean, now that I think of it, I know how stupid that sounds," I admit, and I can't stop myself from giggling.

"Not stupid." He shakes his head. "Just innocent. Like you."

"Oh, trust me, I'm far from innocent," I shoot back before thinking, and I want to groan as he gives me a knowing look. Why does my big mouth always get me into trouble?

14

Ethan

I can't believe that I've shown Sarah my art studio. My safe space. My sanctuary.

Sarah is the only woman who has ever seen it and only the fifth person in my life who knows that I paint —the others being my grandparents, my parents, and Jackson. I'm not sure why I decided to show her the painting, especially because I'm nude in it.

It certainly wasn't because I wanted to get a reaction. Which she did give me.

I think it's because I wanted to show her that she isn't the only one who sometimes does inappropriate things when drunk. I wanted to take away her embarrassment, which I think I did. Now, we've moved past that, but she still seems slightly embarrassed.

And she's not drunk right now. I know it's because she just told me she's far from innocent... in a way that tells me she is, indeed, far from innocent.

As I stare at her blushing, I know she's telling the

truth about many things today. I know she was on a girls' night out, having fun, and the personal ad was accidentally posted. I don't understand how it was accidentally posted, but I know she didn't do it intentionally. She's not that sort of lady. And I don't think she's trying to manipulate me to make me fall for her.

That doesn't mean I don't feel the chemistry. There's an attraction between us; there's no denying it. Even as I stare at her now, I want her. And I can tell from the furtive glances that she's giving me, she wants me. I can still see her licking her lips as she checked out every single inch of my painting, and I feel hard again. I want that tongue on my cock, for real.

It's nice to be around Sarah. She's not trying too hard. Usually, women who like or want me are overtly sexual about it or try to come on to me. I don't know why they think that will work. I don't fall for women just because they offer themselves up on a platter. Half the time, they don't even really want me. It's usually all about the money and the luxury goods they think I can buy them. I know that whatever is happening between Sarah and me is not about the money in my bank account.

"Is everything okay, Mr. Rosser?" she asks me, her voice sweet and nervous. "I didn't mean I'm not innocent, like a whore or anything. I was just..." She pauses as she giggles nervously. I don't know what it is about the tone of her voice, but it's so beautiful. It sends shivers down my spine every time I hear it.

"I'm fine," I say, stepping toward her. "I was just thinking about the jingles and your request. And, of course, if I can get King Charles to design a light for our collection, it will send sales through the roof."

"You know King Charles?" she asks, shocked.

"No, I don't. Aside from on TV. Plus, he has most of the money in the world, thanks to plundering. Well, maybe not more than the Royal family in Saudi Arabia. So, I very much doubt that he needs to design a gold pendant light for the Royal Collection." I laugh, change the subject, and don't dwell on her innocent comment. I'm not sure either of us is ready to walk down that path yet. Though, I feel very ready inside.

"So, can I hear what you got?" I ask her, cocking my head to the side. This will be the real test of her skills.

"Now?" she asks, blinking rapidly.

"Now is as good a time as any, right? Also, if you would like to play any instruments"—I wave around—"I have several I can show you and lend you to play."

"Oh! Really?" She glances up in surprise. "I didn't know that you played anything."

"Private school." I shrug. "You had to take music lessons. I played piano, wanted to learn guitar. Taught myself a couple of chords. I'm no good though."

"Oh, I could teach you, if you want." She pauses. "Not that you'd want, of course. I mean, I can't teach anyone, I'm not that good, but—"

"You play guitar?" I ask her, surprised.

"Yeah," she says, smiling weakly. "I'm not good or anything, but I do know how to play."

"Why do you think you're not good?" I ask, and she blushes nervously.

"Because I work as a junior copywriter at Rosser

International and don't have much time to practice. Plus, I'm not on tour right now." She giggles.

"Okay, but there are plenty of good artists that aren't on tour right now." I wonder how serious she is about being a musician and if she's any good. She's radiant and cute, so I have no doubt that people would be drawn to her.

"True, I just don't know that I'm one of them. I... Never mind. It doesn't matter. I'm not really an artist. Like, I just play for fun, you know? I don't want to be Taylor Swift or Ed Sheeran." She whispers something under her breath, but I can't understand what she's saying.

"Well, you couldn't be Ed Sheeran because he's a man. And you're a woman." I stare at her shapely body and suddenly feel hot and bothered. "Though, I guess, nowadays, you could be, if you got a sex change and transitioned."

"I don't want a sex change, thank you very much. But I do love Ed Sheeran, I think he's great. He's one of my favorites. Him, Passenger, David Berkeley, and James Bay." She sounds excited now. "In fact, my favorite artist right now is this guy called Noah Kahan. Have you heard any of his songs?"

"Never heard of him." I think for a moment as my brain processes the name she just told me. "Wait, isn't your last name Kahan, as well? Is he, like, a relative of yours or something?"

"No, I wish. And yes, that is my last name. Good memory."

"I like to think my memory is pretty good. So,

there's a young man with the same last name as you. I mean, I'm guessing young, he could be old."

"He's young," she says. "He's, like, twenty-seven, I think. Anyway, he has a beautiful voice. Mainly folk-rock, bluesy songs. He's this indie artist, and I just love him, and we have a very similar style."

"Could you play one of your songs for me?" I ask her, wanting to hear an original. I surprise myself by asking because I normally don't have patience for people who wish to show me their random skills.

"Oh, no, no, no," she shakes her head quickly, "I am not talented. There's no way."

"But you will play the jingle you created for me?"

"I mean, sure, I'll play part of the jingle that I thought up. It's not great or anything, because I didn't know, really, anything about what you wanted. I figured you would give me more of a brief in our first official meeting." She smiles sweetly. "But if you have a guitar you can lend me, I will play you what I've come up with, so far."

"Let me get a guitar for you," I say as I head out of the study toward my bedroom. "I'll be right back!" I shout as I jog down the corridor. I open the door, and for a few moments, I consider calling her to follow me. I stare at my welcoming bed and how badly I want to see her on it, but I don't want to make her feel like I invited her over for one purpose and one purpose alone.

If I'm being honest with myself, I would love to kiss her. I would love to touch her. I would love to be with her. I want to look down into her eyes, brightly shining up at me from the bed. And then kiss and devour her. But I cannot let her know this. I cannot let her know that I want her. That would be highly inappropriate and unprofessional and go against everything I stand for as the CEO of Rosser International. I cannot be a hypocrite. I can't tell employees that there's a no-fraternization policy at the company and then hook up with one of my employees. Technically, I can because I'm a CEO, and I make the rules and can break them if I want.

Would she even want to hook up? And if she did, how would she feel at the end of our time together? Would we be able to interact afterward? *Stop thinking about it*, I lecture myself. It's never going to happen. I sigh as I open my custom cabinet and grab one of my Fender acoustic guitars. I hold it to me, and then pick up one of my other guitars. If the jingle she's created is simple enough, I might be able to play along with her. I carry both guitars back to the studio and stand at the door, watching her. She's looking out of the floor-to-ceiling window and staring outside. It is a beautiful view. And it's a nice day.

That's one thing I have in every office that I work in. A great view. It's the only way I can stay and live in the city. Sometimes, my mind drifts, and I like to think, and I'm always motivated and inspired by looking at the skyline. Sometimes, I think I should move to Seattle or Portland and be able to look out at the trees and mountains. What further inspiration would come from being in nature? Maybe one of these days I'll do it, but not anytime soon.

"Hey! I have the guitars," I say as I finally walk into the room. She turns back to look at me with a small smile on her face.

"Thanks," she says. She's got on her big, wide glasses, and her hair is in a loose bun again, but I see past that. All I can see are her delicate features and her friendly eyes. Her generous smile. She is light, happy, and full of goodness—she's beautiful. She is absolutely beautiful. Whether her hair is up or down and whether or not she has glasses on. I can't believe I haven't noticed it before. She appears timid as she comes toward me. Does she know I'm thinking of pulling that hairband out and taking off her clothes?

"Two guitars? I'm guessing, one for you?"

"I figure if the tune is easy enough, I'll strum along, if you don't mind."

"Oh, it's plenty easy," she says eagerly. "Very, very easy."

She takes the proffered guitar and takes a seat on one of the black leather chairs. I sit in the chair next to her and look over at her.

"So, what chord are you thinking?"

"For the jingle or for Rosser Home Goods?" she asks.

"Well, I just told you about Rosser Home Goods, so I'd be shocked if you had anything prepared for that."

"Oh, I actually came up with something just now," she says, laughing and throwing her hair back. She strums the C chord and then makes some adjustments to tune the guitar.

"Sorry," I apologize for the sound. "I haven't played it in a while."

"No worries, I can tune yours, as well, if you want me to."

"I normally use an electric tuner that I left in my room, so I would be grateful."

"Of course," she says. She gets to work tuning her guitar, then places it at the side of her chair and takes the guitar from me. As she takes my guitar, our fingers touch and I feel a frisson of electricity pass between us. I know she feels it, as well, because she gasps slightly, and her lips part. I try not to stare at the pinkness of her plump lips. I try not to breathe in her heady, fragrant scent. I'm not sure how much longer I can ignore how she's making me feel.

"So... We can start with the jingle," she says, strumming some more notes, "because that's probably more pressing, right?"

"Yeah, it is. I think Lord Chambers would be delighted to hear something very soon."

"When you say very soon, how soon do you mean?" she asks.

"I mean, within the next couple of days."

"The next couple of days?" She looks shocked by my revelation. "What? I don't know—"

"If we spend a couple of late nights working on it, we should be able to come up with something." I shrug, staring at her, pretending that her eyes didn't fall to my crotch for a few seconds as I talked about nights.

"I mean, I guess, but I have to go home, and I have

to feed my dog, Johnson, and take him on a walk and—"

"Bring him over here," I say. "You can work all day and night, and I'll feed him and walk him so you can concentrate."

"What?" she says, surprised. "No, I can't do that. He would tear up your place." She laughs. "But thank you for the offer. We'll start, and then I'll go home, and I'll work at home and—"

"But I would like to hear the different iterations along the way. I'd love to see your creative process," I say as though that's a normal request. And even though that's not a hundred percent true about everything that goes on at the company, it is with her. I want to see how she works. I want to see this jingle come to life through her eyes. I know that I just want to be around her, and this is as good of an excuse as any. I'm not even going to question it right now.

"I just..." She seems to struggle for an answer, and I can tell she's nervous.

"You just what?" I say, leaning closer toward her. A tendril of her hair falls out of her bun and in front of her face. I reach up and tuck it behind her ear.

"Oh. Thanks," she says, blinking rapidly as she touches her ear and strokes her hair back.

I reach up, take her glasses off, hold them in my hand, and stare into her wide eyes.

"Can you see me?" I ask her softly, wondering just how bad her eyesight truly is. Hopefully, she's not blind as a bat. That would be unfortunate.

"Yes." She nods, blinking even more rapidly now. "I

can see people who are close to me; I just can't see when it's far away. It's blurry."

"I see." I smile and move my face closer so she can see into my eyes.

"I'm getting contacts soon though," she says, then shakes her head. "I mean, not that you care about that or anything. I just... wait, why did you take my glasses off?" She looks at me with rounded eyes and lips, and I can't resist.

"Because I wanted to do this," I say as I press my lips to hers. After her initial hesitance when my lips made contact, she kisses me back. I know this is the worst thing I could be doing, but I can no longer resist her and how she makes me feel. My right hand reaches up, tugs on her hairband, and pulls it out so that her hair falls, cascading down her shoulders.

I run my fingers through her locks, and she gasps as she reaches up and touches the side of my face. I deepen our kiss. My tongue slips into her mouth, and she kisses me back eagerly, her tongue dancing a waltz with mine. I hear the guitar fall to the side, but I don't care. I pull her up off her chair and lift her onto my lap. She moans but doesn't resist. My fingers skim down her back and toward the side of her body, coming up and caressing her breast. She presses herself into me, and I groan. There's no stopping this moment now. No matter what my subconscious screams at me about fraternization policies and work relationships. Sometimes, rules are made to be broken.

15

Sarah

Dear Diary,

I know I promised to give you more information about my O, but I'm not the sort of girl who kisses and tells on the very same day. Okay, maybe that's not quite true. Maybe I do kiss and tell on the very same day. Maybe I do kiss and tell in the very same hour, but this was special. And when I say special, I don't mean cue the violinist and hundreds of white doves. I mean, it was hot, and when I say hot, I mean HOT. And yeah, I am also a little bit pissed off, which I didn't want to inform you of the other day. I'm sure you're wondering why. Don't worry, I'll tell you. Do I have any secrets from you?

Love always,
Shameful and Sassy Sarah

Oh my gosh. Oh my gosh. Oh my gosh.

That is all I can think inside my brain as I kiss Ethan Rosser.

I am kissing Ethan Rosser. I am too old to be this giddy, but this is something I did add to my yearly lottery list.

Ethan's lips are pressed against mine firmly, and I can't stop myself from melting into him. I still can't quite believe how easily he lifted me and put me on his lap. We've gone from zero to fifty within seconds. I was just about to play the guitar, for heaven's sake, and now I'm here with my fingers strumming down the side of his face as opposed to the wire strings. His fingers are in my hair, and I'm feeling hardness beneath my bum cheeks. I'm trying my very hardest not to rub back and forth. His tongue is inside my mouth. I'm sucking it, and it tastes like toothpaste. I giggle at the thought. I know what Ethan Rosser's toothpaste tastes like.

"What's so funny?" he asks as he pulls away, a frown on his perfect face.

I try not to pout because I miss the taste of him in my mouth. "What do you mean, what's so funny?" I ask, knowing I'm blinking rapidly but unable to stop myself.

"You giggled just now as we were kissing. I didn't even know that was possible."

"Oh, I was just thinking that your tongue tastes very minty."

"Oh." He chuckles. "Aquafresh."

"Aquafresh?" I stare at him dumbly for a couple of seconds, and then it dawns on me. "Oh, that's the name of your toothpaste."

"Yeah," he says. I'm still on his lap, and now he has

his arm around my waist, and he's pulling me in closer. "Your mouth tastes like strawberry wine. So delicate and sweet. I wonder what other places on your body taste like." It's like he's hit a button with his words, and my entire body is now buzzing. I shift slightly on his lap and feel his hardness pressing into me.

I take a deep breath. "We shouldn't be doing this."

"I know," he says. "But I guess we've already started, so there's that." I attempt to get up, but he grabs me again and keeps me still in his lap. "I haven't finished kissing you yet, Sarah Kahan," he says before he presses his lips against mine again.

I don't resist. I can't. Who am I? I don't want this moment to end.

I'm just a junior copywriter, and if the gorgeous and delectable Ethan Rosser wants to kiss me, he can. He can have his wicked way with me because no matter how many times I've called him a jerk or a pompous prick or any other horrible thing, I can't deny the fact that I think he is the hottest man I have ever seen in my life.

HOTTEST!

He could give Brad Pitt and Bradley Cooper a run for their money. In fact, I would likely turn them down for Ethan. Not that I would admit that to anyone. Ethan is sexiness at its highest peak. He is the pinnacle of everything a hot alpha male should be, and I am really into alpha men. I grab his face and deepen the kiss. To hell with it. If this is going down, I'm going to enjoy every moment.

Every single moment.

He groans as he shifts his body and holds me tightly to him as he leans back in his chair. I shift so that I'm now straddling him. His cock is now positioned between my legs, and I feel like the dam that is Sarah Kahan is going to burst right then and there. Especially if he keeps moving me back and forth like this. I haven't dry-humped like this in a long time, and I wonder why not. This is even hotter than sex. *Kinda*.

"Fuck, this is hot," Ethan says as his hand slips up my shirt, and I feel him rubbing his palm against my warm back.

I wonder if he's going to take off my bra. Do I want him to take off my bra? I'm not going to stop him if he wants to, but we might be moving a little bit quickly. I'm loving it, but I'm not sure if I'm out of my mind. He runs his fingers over my bra strap, and I still, waiting to see if he's going to unclasp it. He doesn't. A twinge of disappointment runs through me, but I dismiss it. How can you be disappointed when you're kissing the most gorgeous man on Earth? This is like a dream. He moves his hand to the front of my top, and I feel him cupping my breasts again. I press my body even closer to his as he slips his fingers inside and plays with one of my nipples.

My panties grow moist immediately. *Moister*.

This is fucking hot. I reach down and run my fingers along the front of his pants. He grunts loudly as I gently rub over his crotch.

"Play with fire and you're going to get burned,

Sarah." His voice is deep and gravelly as he kisses the side of my face.

I stare into his dazzling blue eyes, and I grin. "Who knows? Maybe I like being burned?" I am not sure why I say that. It's not even true, and I have no idea what he has taken from me saying that. I don't even know what I would take from that.

"Oh." There's a light in his eyes as he raises a single eyebrow. "What do you mean by that?"

"Well, you know," I say, looking down and only raising my eyes to him. I'm nervous but also trying to flirt, but I'm not sure if I'm sounding like an idiot. Or just super horny and out of my mind. Most probably the latter because that's what's true at this moment.

"Tell me."

"A little candle wax here, a little whipped cream there, a little syrup," I say, moaning as his finger continues to play with my nipple.

"Fuck, that's hot," he says. "So, you're into a little S and M?"

"Yeah," I lie. I've never participated in any S and M before in my life. I quickly shake my head. "Actually, that's not quite true."

"Oh." He frowns. "What'd you mean?"

"I mean, I've never done any S and M. I don't know why I said that. I was just trying to sound sexy," I admit.

"It's fine," he says. He stands, picks me up in his arms, and steadies himself.

"What are you doing?" I ask as I wrap my arms around his neck. I'm disappointed that we're moving. I was enjoying being on his lap.

"Taking us to a more comfortable spot." He steps over one of the guitars and carries me out of the room.

"Oh, you can put me down. I can walk. I..."

"Maybe I like carrying you," he says. "Do you mind?"

"No." I shake my head because it's quite flattering to be carried by a strong, muscular man, especially when you're not skinny. It makes me feel like I'm light as a feather, even though I know I'm not.

He heads down the hallway to an open door and walks inside. I'm in awe as I look around. We're in his bedroom, and it's the most masculine bedroom I've ever been in. His walls are dark charcoal, and there's a huge king-size bed in the middle of two dark night tables. Two brass light sconces give a warm hue to the room. He drops me unceremoniously onto the bed and then climbs up beside me. He reaches down, and I feel his fingers running down my calf toward my shoes. He takes off my pumps and drops them onto the ground. His fingers are nimble and soft, and I shiver at his touch.

"Feeling comfortable?" he asks, and I nod slowly. I'm comfortable but super out of my element. Is this really going down?

"What are we doing?" I ask him, even though that's the stupidest question I've ever asked. It's quite obvious what we're about to do. I just don't know if we should be doing this. And when I say we, I mean I. Do I really want to hook up with my boss?

A voice in my head starts laughing, as if that's the stupidest question I've ever asked myself. Of course, I want to hook up with him. I have since the first time I ever saw him.

"What do you mean?" He stares at me like I'm crazy. He looks around the room and then at me. "We're in my bedroom, on my bed."

"Well, don't you have a no-fraternization policy at the company?" I ask softly. I hate to bring it up, but it's his rule, and I don't know if he'll be upset with me if he breaks it.

"Well, I think, technically, we're okay. The no-fraternization policy is technically about people dating." He smirks. "We're not dating. We're just having some fun."

"Okay," I say, nodding slowly because nothing he said is a lie. It doesn't feel great to hear that we're not dating or that he doesn't want to date me, which is what I assume he means, but it's not like I want to date him, either. I barely know him. At least, that's what I tell myself, so it doesn't hurt quite so badly.

"Plus, I think we both know that lots of people hook up at the company, right?"

I stare at him with wide eyes. "I don't know." I hope he's not trying to get me to snitch. That's the last thing I want to do to my fellow coworkers.

"Don't worry," he says, laughing. "I'm not going to ask you who at the company is hooking up. We both know that it happens."

"I mean, I've heard that perhaps it happens."

"It doesn't matter," he says. "The point is, hooking up is fine, and even if it's not, I don't care because I'm the boss, and I can do whatever I want."

"You are going to drive me crazy with your I'm the boss shit," I say, not knowing how to respond.

"I'm going to drive you crazy?" he asks. "What do you mean by that?"

"I mean, this is kind of weird, right? That we're here, I'm in your room, it's a workday, and..."

"Shush," he says, pressing a finger on my lips. "I think we can both agree that this is something that's been on our minds for a while."

"What do you mean?"

"I mean, our sexual chemistry." He reaches up and starts undoing the buttons on my shirt. I stare at him and nod slowly. I'm glad to hear that he has felt it, too, and it isn't just in my head.

"You barely noticed me this week though. You didn't even know who I was before."

"As soon as I saw you in that bar and we made eye contact, I haven't been able to get you out of my mind." He pulls off my shirt and stares at me in my bra. My heart is racing so rapidly that it may pop out of my chest.

I watch his eyes turn dark and stormy as he looks me over, and I try to push my breasts forward and suck my stomach in.

"You're fucking hot," he says as he reaches over and grabs the back of my neck and pulls me closer to him. It's hot and powerful, and I love that he's taking charge.

I reach over, touch the side of his arm, and squeeze his muscles. He leans down and kisses me again; this time, his fingers run up and down the side of my body.

He then pulls my bra straps down and slips them off, my nipples pebbling in the cool air. His lips move to my neck, and he kisses down toward my breasts before taking one of my hardened nipples in his mouth and sucking. It's my turn now, and I reach up and start unbuttoning his shirt.

If I'm going to have no top on, he is definitely going to have no top on. I can barely process what's happening, but I know I don't want it to stop. My fingers fumble around on his shirt until I finally get all the buttons open. He leans back a little to give himself enough room to maneuver, pulls his shirt off, and throws it to the ground. I'm in awe as I stare at his tan, muscular chest. There's a sprinkling of hair, but it just makes him even sexier. He licks his lips and then reaches for my skirt. He grabs it and pulls it down swiftly, tossing it to the ground so that I'm now lying there in only my panties.

"If I'm only going to be in my panties..." I trail off, raising a questioning brow toward his pants. I watch him pull them off, and my mouth goes dry as I stare at him in a pair of black briefs that cling to his body. He's hard, and I can see the outline of his cock in the material. From what I can see, it's big. Really, really big. He smirks as he leans back down and runs his fingers between the valley of my breasts toward my belly button. I think he's about to stop, but his fingers keep on going straight down into my panties. My eyes close of their own accord at the sensation as he slips his fingers in and rubs against my clit. He can feel that I'm already wet, and he growls slightly before pulling his fingers out and sucking on them.

Holy hell, it's the hottest thing I've ever seen.

"You taste sweet, just like I knew you would. Sweeter than strawberry wine. I could lick that pussy dry and still thirst for more." He growls, and my stomach flips.

I wet my lips, which, along with my mouth, have become ridiculously dry. I'm sweating, and my heart is racing at the enormity of what's happening. Is this moment real?

I'm freaking out inside. I know that neither Ella nor Isabel will believe what's happening. I can barely believe what's happening, myself. I can't wait to tell them. I know it's a weird thought to have at this moment, while I'm here practically naked with the CEO of the company I work at, but I know my friends will not believe what is happening right now.

"Well, you can quench your thirst now, if you want." I look up at him, batting my eyelashes and spreading my legs slightly.

Before I know what's happening, he's pulling my panties off.

"Whoa, big boy," I say, giggling again. I don't know where this confident banter has come from, but I'm not hating it. Being around him makes me feel powerful and confident.

"You're so fucking hot," he says as he stares down at my pussy. "Fuck, I'm going to eat you so good right now." He buries his face between my legs, and I throw my head back and make indiscernible noises out loud as he starts licking and sucking. All I can think is that my grumpy-ass, arrogant boss is going down on me, and it's amazing.

I reach down, grab his hair, run my fingers through his silky tresses, and close my eyes. My body is vibrating with lust and passion, and I can barely stop myself from trembling. He reaches up and plays with my nipples before spreading my legs even wider. I feel his tongue enter me, and my body starts bucking as he fucks me with his tongue hard and fast.

I'm close to orgasming already, and it feels incredible. Better than amazing. I hear a scream and realize it's coming from me. I can barely take how amazing this feels. I understand now why wars have begun with love affairs. I'd go to war to experience a pleasure like this again.

"You like this, do you?" he asks, looking up at me from his position between my legs. His eyes are full of desire, and I can't form the words to answer, so I nod my head ever so slightly. "Good," he says and inserts his tongue back inside of me. He alternates between sucking on my clit and fucking me with his tongue. Before I know what's happening, my body is exploding, and he's still going, continuing to lick me through my orgasm, even as I explode on his face.

"And another." He grunts as he continues sucking and licking. He wants to give me another orgasm, and I know that I can barely handle the first one.

I feel the second orgasm coming. "Oh, Ethan!" I shout, and my body explodes with intense pleasure. He growls, and I see that there's a broad smile on his face as he kisses up my body and looks down at my lips.

"That was fucking hot," he says as he presses his lips against mine. "You're even sweeter than you look."

He grabs my face and I just lick my lips wickedly and push him back. "I like to think so, now shh, for a moment, because it's my turn to taste how sweet you are."

16

Ethan

I can still taste Sarah on my lips. She's sweet and fragrant, and I want to bury my head back in her pussy, but I know that I can't. She's looking at me with big, wide, sultry eyes, and her lips are still parted. The way she screamed my name made me harder than I've ever felt in my life, and I know I need a release.

"What would you like me to do, sir?" she says in a teasing voice, and I narrow my eyes at her, wondering if she knows just how sexy she is at this moment. This is a side of her I never expected to see, and I love how she surprises me.

"I think you know what I want you to do," I say, nodding toward my crotch, and then I pause. "If you want, of course."

"Oh, I want. Very much." She giggles slightly and shifts so that she can grab the front of my briefs. I think she's about to pull them down, but instead, her fingernails trace right along the length of my cock, not too rough, but rough enough so that I can feel it. "You are going to drive me crazy, my sassy Sarah." I grab my briefs, pull them down, and have them join my pants on the ground. She gasps as my cock springs free and straight up into the air. I can't help but smile as she looks at it, all seven and a half inches, thick and juicy. I know she's impressed. Most women are. Though, the way she's gazing at me makes me feel proud. She eyes me for a few moments; her face is glistening, and she's smiling widely. Not playing sultry games. My heart twists for a second, and she winks. I wonder if she knows what she's doing to me. There's no way she can know because I barely even understand the emotions I'm feeling.

"Whoa," she says, licking her lips. Her fingers find my girth and she moves them up and down.

"Oh, fuck," I say, as her cool palm encloses on my skin, and she squeezes slightly.

"Do you like this, sir?"

"Don't call me sir," I bark at her as I look down. "I'm Ethan." Little does she know, I've been intrigued by S and M and dominance, and I have a particular fantasy of being a schoolmaster. Although, I'm not about to admit that right now.

"What if I want to call you sir, Mr. Rosser?"

"Do you get off on that?" I ask her, wondering if she'd dress up in a short skirt and tight top. "Do you get off on the fact that your boss just made you orgasm?" Would she like me to take her over my lap and spank her?

"Well, I don't know if I get off on the fact that my boss made me orgasm, but I did get off, so there's that." She watches her hand moving on my cock for a minute. "Now, you can get off with your employee making you orgasm."

I study her for a couple of seconds, then her lips move down, and I feel them on the tip of my cock, sucking gently. Her tongue licks the pre-cum off my tip, and I know that whatever happens next is going to be amazing. She pushes me back so that I'm lying flat back on the mattress. I stare up at her as she runs her fingers across my chest and plays with my nipples. My cock's not getting the attention it was before, but I know it's coming.

Her hair hangs down by the side of her face, and I reach up again and touch the side of her cheek softly. She looks at me in surprise, and I shake my head. Her lips are pink and parted, and I watch as she kisses down my chest toward my cock again and then takes me in her mouth. She's bopping up and down, her breasts jiggling underneath her, and I know that I'm not going to last very long. She takes me deep into her throat until she's almost gagging, and I reach back and grab her hair and pull it away so that I can see her face. Her eyes are concentrating on her task at hand, but I can tell she's enjoying it from the way she's moaning.

"Stop," I say as she continues her up-and-down motion, taking all of me into her throat, and that's when I feel it building. I grow even harder, and I know I'm about to explode. I try to push her away before I come, not knowing if she wants to swallow or not. It seems that she doesn't care because she doesn't stop, and then I feel myself exploding hard and fast. I groan and grunt, and she seems to love it because she continues bobbing her head up and down, taking every drop of my cum into her mouth. She continues for a couple of seconds and then looks up at me, licking her lips. "Didn't realize I was so hungry," she says, and I growl as she winks at me. "I may look like a dowdy librarian, but that doesn't mean I am one."

"Fuck," I say, glancing at her. "That was hot."

"I know," she says. "It was hot for me, as well."

I pull her up toward me and kiss her on the lips. She presses her body down against mine, her breasts against my chest, her leg curved over my leg. I reach down and caress her back and squeeze her ass cheek, my fingers going down toward her pussy and her thigh. I can feel she's trembling, and my cock begins to stir again beneath her stomach. "You're fucking hot, you know that?"

"You said that to me multiple times, and I have to say, I do appreciate it." She grins. "You're not so bad yourself, Ethan."

"Oh, so now you call me Ethan?"

"I mean, I can go back to sir, if you want me to."

"You can call me whatever you fucking want," I say, kissing her hard. "So, what's that jingle you've been working on?" I ask her as I push her onto her back and run my fingers down her stomach, toward her pussy again. She looks at me in surprise.

"We're talking about work now?"

"We can fuck and talk about work. My two favorite things."

"Fuck?" She blushes. "But we've both come already."

"Oh, we're just getting started, honey." I grunt because there's no way that I'm not going to fuck her. I just need a little time to get hard again so that I can last and give her the fucking of her life. Because now that I've heard her scream once, I want to hear it over and over again. She blinks, and I can tell she's not sure what's going to happen. "Let me hear the jingle."

She stares at me for a couple of seconds and then nods. "So, this is something that was in my head for the Rosser Home Goods jingle," she starts and then pauses.

"Okay, I'm listening." My fingers trail up and down her stomach, and I reach over and kiss her collarbone.

She starts singing, "Rosser Home Store. Rosser Home Goods is the store for all your needs. We got lights, very bright. We got nails, don't catch it in your tail. We got floors, for even outdoors, and we got grass for your ass." She laughs, and I am bemused.

"That was cute," I say. Then, because I feel she should know, I tell her how beautiful her voice is. "You've got talent," I say. "You can carry a tune." I don't know why I'm so surprised, but her voice is melodic and beautiful.

"Carrying a tune doesn't mean you have so much talent that you'll make it as a star." She sounds rueful, and I realize that this is important to her. I also realize she lacks self-confidence, which makes me sad. "It just means that you took a couple of voice lessons, and—"

"Don't put yourself down. You've got a nice voice. Have you ever written anything else?" I ask her, and she blushes.

"I've written a few songs, maybe." She looks away and looks down. "Or maybe a couple hundred, but trust me, they aren't all that."

I grab her chin and turn her face toward me again. "You don't have to be embarrassed. I showed you my art. I'm no Picasso."

"You're pretty close though." Her eyes light up. "You're really good."

"I'm okay, but my point is that just because I'm not Picasso doesn't mean I don't have any talent. Or that I couldn't sell some art to someone. You might not be at the level of a major pop star right now, but you're still amazing. I'd love to hear one of your songs, if you'd like to share it with me."

"I mean, I guess. Ella and Isabel are always saying that if I want to become a singer-songwriter, I should share more. I think they were talking about karaoke nights and stuff, but..." Her voice trails off, and I can see she's debating whether or not to share with me. I hope she trusts me enough to share one of her pieces.

"But I'm here, and I'm as good as any karaoke night," I say to her, hoping she will sing one of her songs because I really want to hear it. More than should be legal.

"Okay." She nods slowly. "But I'm a little bit nervous, so I might close my eyes and pretend you're not here, if you don't mind."

"It's okay, as long as you don't mind me doing this,"

I say as I slip my fingers between her legs and gently rub her clit.

"Mmm," she moans. "I think that might be distracting." She whimpers, and her legs widen. I grin as I slip a finger inside of her. Her body shakes as I add another finger. I love the effect I have on her. My thumb rubs her clit, and she moans. "I'm not going to be able to concentrate if you do that." She can barely talk through her moans.

"Oh?" I say, moving slightly, so now I'm hovering over her. I grab my cock and rub it against her clit, and she moans again. "What about if I move my thumb, and it's just this?" I say as I pull my fingers out.

"I don't know," she moans. "Oh, fuck, Ethan."

I grin as I glance down at her; her blue eyes are practically begging me to take her, and I want her. I could thrust into her right now, but I want to hear her sing. "What do you want?" I ask softly.

"Fuck me," she says. "Just fucking fuck me."

"I will if you sing for me," I say, nudging the tip of my cock slightly into her opening.

"You better never call me a tease," she says, shaking her head. "You're the tease."

"No, not right now. I'm not. Let me hear your song."

"Fine," she says, and she closes her eyes. She hums slightly, and I listen to the melody, nodding my head to the beat. "Swim in the ocean," she sings. "That's what you told me to do, swim in the ocean, and you said I'd be coming home to you. But what you didn't tell me is that the nights will stay long, and the water is cold, and you are still gone. Sometimes, I swim in the ocean, and I think of you, but there's not really anything else I can do."

She pauses, and all I can do is clap. "That's beautiful," I say. She slowly opens her eyes and looks at me. I can see she's trying to figure out if I am being honest and sincere, and I am. "That was really touching." I press my finger to her lips, then lean down and kiss her again. "You've really got a beautiful voice. You're really talented."

"Oh, it's just something I do for fun. It's not like I expect to be a singer-songwriter or anything," she says, and I realize that's exactly what she wants, and I know she has the talent to make it. I wonder if I should tell her about the entertainment section of the company we're about to open. I wonder if I should tell her I would love to sign her, though a part of me would be sad because I know she can make it. I know she's got the talent, and she's beautiful, but if she makes it, she'll leave Rosser International. She'll leave the copywriting department. She'll most probably go on tour and travel the world, and then I'll never get to see her.

"So, are you going to fuck me yet?" she asks, interrupting my thoughts.

I blink as I look down at her. She has no idea what I've been thinking. "You really want this, huh?"

"As long as it's not breaking any policies," she says, and I know neither one of us cares about that anymore. "Seeing as we're not dating or anything."

"We're not dating," I say as I adjust my cock and bring it to her opening again. "We're not fucking dating at all," I say as I thrust into her. She cries out as I move in and out of her. She's wet and tight and feels like fucking heaven. I know that I'm making a huge mistake. I know that this is the last thing I should be doing. I know, dating or not, this is definitely breaking the no-fraternization policy at the company, and I don't give two fucks. More importantly, I feel like I'm fucking someone I like, which might be even more dangerous.

I watch her breasts as they bounce back and forth, and she wraps her legs around my waist. "Fuck, yeah," I say as I pump into her. "Oh, fuck," I shout, "just so you know..."

"Yes, Ethan?" she gasps, holding on to my shoulders tightly, her fingernails digging into my back as I continue to slam into her.

"This is not going to happen more than five times," I say, and surprisingly, she starts laughing. The sound makes me smile, and I pause, cock deep inside of her. "What's so funny?" I ask as I lean down and kiss her on the lips.

"Who says I want it to happen five times, Ethan?" she says, shaking her head. "Once is good enough for me."

"That's what you think," I say, growling as I thrust into her harder and faster. I grab her ankles, pull them up over my shoulders, and pull her down so that her ass is against my upper thighs. I pull out, and she whimpers at the loss of me, and then I slam back into her. Her pussy is wetter than it was when I was eating her out, and I know that neither one of us is going to be able to recover from this anytime soon. "If you don't think you'll want it more than once, we don't even have to do it," I say as I pull out again and rest the tip of my cock against her clit.

"Shut up," she says, "and fuck me."

"I love it when you talk dirty to me, Sarah."

"And I love it when you fuck me, Ethan. And please don't worry, I'm not expecting anything from this," she says, shaking her head. "Except another orgasm."

"Coming right up." I growl as I grab her ankles and thrust into her hard and fast.

17

Sarah

Dear Diary.

Yes, I slept with Ethan Rosser. And yes, Ethan Rosser is hot. And yes, he has a big cock, and knows how to work it. And yes, I don't regret it, but I'm just not sure where we go from here. What am I going to do?

Confused and concerned Sarah.

We're sitting in Ethan's home office, and I'm wearing a pair of his boxer shorts and an oversized T-shirt. He's wearing a pair of boxers and no top. I'm playing the guitar, trying to come up with a cool tune for the jingle that we're going to use for Rosser Home Goods, but I'm finding it very hard to concentrate. My legs and my pussy are aching, and my entire body is sore, in the very best way. I feel like I'm in a movie, some sort of surrealist picture filmed in Italy or France, because I can't quite believe that I'm here, sitting in his boxers and T-shirt, and we've already had sex twice. I don't know what it means. It most probably means nothing. He already told me it wasn't going to happen more than five times, and I don't want it to happen ever again after today because it would be weird and awkward and... Oh, who am I kidding? I definitely want to fuck him again.

"Oh, I like that," he says as I strum randomly, not even thinking about the notes I'm playing.

"Oh," I say and continue strumming. My fingers move across the strings, imagining they are gliding across his body.

"Yes, that sounds great. Da da dum. Da da dum." He's humming along to my beat. His face is serious now. He's back in work mode, and a part of me wonders if I can get him out of work mode—again. A part of me wonders if I can seduce him and have him put the guitar down and come and take me yet again. But I don't want to try it. I don't want to risk it because, what if he says no? What if he says he needs to focus and concentrate? That will make me feel like shit. That will make me feel like I'm not the seductress I think I am. I don't even know who I was when I was saying half the things I was saying in his bed. I blush, thinking about how I told him to, "fuck me now." Who says that to their boss? Fuck me now? I have never said that before to anyone in my life. But it had felt right at the moment.

"So, was the balloon salesman thing true?" he asks as he stops humming, and I gaze at him in confusion.

"Huh?" I put the guitar down.

"You said you dated a balloon salesman before or something? Or was it a time-share person?"

"Oh, you mean from the ad?"

"Yeah, from the ad." He sits next to me. "I was just curious."

"So, I did date a guy, he used to make animal balloons for kids' birthday parties," I say, making a face, thinking of Shamus.

"Oh, cool. And he was good?"

"No, he sucked. He couldn't make any animals."

"Wait, what?" He glances at me and lays his palm on my thigh gently. "What do you mean?"

"I mean, he was a con artist. He had ads that said he could make all these different types of balloon animals from photos he took off Google. And then, when he would get to the party, he would have all these balloons and then he couldn't make any animals. But then he'd start singing and dancing and doing all sorts of stuff to try to get the kids' attention onto something else."

"Wait, what?" Ethan scratches his forehead. "So, he was an animal balloon party con man?"

"Yeah. He was a jackass, and yet I still dated him." I shake my head to rid myself of the memories. "My radar was off that day."

"Please tell me you didn't know he was an animal balloon party con man when you first started dating him."

I press my lips together. "Can I plead the fifth?"

"Oh, please, tell me you did not know." He looks shocked.

"Let's just say I was at a birthday party for a friend's kid that I went to because she begged me to attend. I hadn't even wanted to attend because it was going to be boring with a bunch of snotty spoiled kids in Connecticut. But I digress. There I was, at this party, and there he was. Standing there, looking like a tall, skinny hunk. He was supposed to be making giraffe balloons, yet he wasn't. And I did kind of notice he wasn't making them, but I told myself he was distracted because he was attracted to me and the reason why he'd been unable to make them was because he was too busy trying to flirt with me." I pause. "Anyway, long story short, we dated for a couple of weeks."

"Oh, wow, long time." He laughs as I stick my tongue out at him. "Why did you break up?"

"Because he told people that I was a trapeze artist."

"What?" He looks astounded.

"Don't ask. Basically, he told people we met working at a circus and I was a trapeze artist. And lo and behold, he was getting money for me to do a trapeze act in Central Park at some party. Me, who can barely walk a straight line on the ground," I say, thinking back to that embarrassing day. "Yeah. So that was great."

"He sounds like a winner," Ethan says sarcastically.

"Total winner."

"Was he at least good in bed?" he asks me.

"I know you didn't just ask me that, Ethan." I'm appalled that he would go there with his questions.

"I mean, was he as good as me?"

"I'm not answering that," I say, shaking my head. I'm not going to tell him that I never slept with Shamus because all he seemed to want to talk about was the different parties he was going to be performing at and how he was going to be a big star.

"And what about the time-share salesman?"

"Oh, you don't want to hear about him."

"I do," he says. "You did post it. I want to hear more."

"Basically, my friend and I won a trip on a cruise."

"Oh, that sounds fun."

"Well, the story isn't that fun. We got a letter in the mail, basically saying we won this cruise for a week to The Bahamas for ninety-nine dollars."

"Okay," he says. "So, not exactly free."

"Anyway, we have to call the number to get the details."

"Sounds pretty normal, so far."

"I call the number, and this guy says, 'Congratulations, come down to the office.' So, I go down to the office, and it's this really hot guy that looks like Jason Momoa, and he's from Hawaii," I say, thinking back to the first time I saw Walker.

"Ooh, so you like Jason Momoa?" Ethan says. "He looks very different than me."

"I mean, I wouldn't say no if..." I pause, and he lifts an eyebrow.

"If he what?"

"Nothing," I say. I'm not going to tell my boss, the man I just hooked up with, that Jason Momoa would be my hall pass if I had one. "Anyway, the guy, Walker, starts trying to sell me some hotel vacation in the British Virgin Islands, and I'm just like, 'No, I just came for my free cruise for the ninety-nine dollars for the taxes.' Long story short, he takes me out to lunch, or at least I thought he was taking me out to lunch, but it was basically a sales pitch."

"Please, tell me you didn't date him, too."

"Let's just say that we went on a couple of dates, and it didn't work out."

"And are you going to tell me why it didn't work out?"

"Let's just say that we were in bed for the first time, and he says to me, 'So can I get your contract on the paperwork before we bang?'"

"No, he didn't." Ethan is laughing now. "Please tell me you didn't bang him."

"No, I didn't bang him. I grabbed my jacket, pulled it on, and left." I frown. "And no, I didn't see him again. I'm not that stupid, even though he did try calling me multiple times from several different phone numbers."

"Sounds like that dude really wanted the commission."

"Yeah, he did. So, you can see now why I'm kind of not interested in dating broke-ass men." When I look at him to see if he understands where I'm coming from, he nods. I think to myself that I've just messed up because I don't want him to think I'm trying to date him or that I only want rich men. "I don't want you to think because of my past that it means I'm trying to get a billionaire. That was just a joke. The next guy I date will be..."

"Will be what?" he asks, staring at me with an interested expression on his face.

"I mean, he'll have enough money that he doesn't need to try and use me for the pittance that I make."

"I pay you a pittance. Do I really?" he asks, smirking.

"Well, you don't exactly pay me a lot."

"Okay. Is that something you would like me to speak to HR about?"

"No," I say quickly. "Are you out of your mind?"

"Why would I be out of my mind, speaking to HR about paying you more?"

"Because we just..." I pause. I can't say made love. We didn't make love. I don't want to say had sex. It sounds so crude. I didn't want to say fuck because that was dirty. "We just banged?" I regret it as soon as the words come out of my mouth.

"Isn't postcoital time the best time to ask for something?"

"I don't want you to think that I slept with you because I want something from you."

"Why did you sleep with me?"

"Why did you sleep with me?" I retort back at him.

"Ah, a question answered with another question." He grins and cocks his head to the side. "I slept with you because I find you to be very attractive, very sexy, and," he licks his lips, "you seemed to be into it. You were into it, right?"

"Yes." I nod. "Obviously."

"Good," he says, and then makes a face. "I forgot to ask you..."

"I'm on birth control," I say quickly. "You're clean, right?"

"Yes," he says, "I get tested every thirty days. You?"

"Yeah, I get tested every time I go to the gynecologist, and I haven't had sex in a while, so I'm good."

"Good," he says, "I kind of liked coming inside of you."

I blush at his frank comment. My entire body is heated. Am I crazy for loving how honest and open he is about everything? "I know you did. But what would you have done if I said I wasn't on birth control?"

"I feel like you would've asked me to pull out or something, right?" He waits for me to answer, then says, "Unless you were trying to trap me with a baby or something. I mean, to be honest, I wasn't even thinking about it. I was caught up in the moment. Fuck, I feel like an eighteen-year-old boy again."

"It's okay," I say. "I make you feel young because I'm so cool and fun—ha-ha."

"You sure are," he says with a nod. "You make me feel fucking hot and horny, too."

"Is that your way of telling me you want to bang again?"

"I don't know if I want to bang, but I sure want to fuck." His palm moves up my thigh and he leans down to kiss me again.

"But that will be the third time, and you have a five-time limit," I remind him, swallowing hard. Why do I feel so comfortable with this man? Why do I feel like I've known him for years?

"I'm not worried about it." His lips are on mine again, and I run my fingers down his back. If he's not worried about it, then neither am I. Because, frankly, I feel like I'm in the best daydream of my life and I never want it to end.

18

Ethan

"Ethan, I am going to go into the shower now." Sarah gives me a sweet little smile as she stands there naked and unashamed. I try not to devour her body with my eyes, but all I want to do is step forward, grab a hold of her and carry her into the shower so that we can make mad passionate love in the shower. I can't seem to get enough of her and I'm pretty certain that she's been mesmerized by my body as well.

"Okay," I say, with a knowing look. My eyes are on her still and I can't seem to look away. "Are you sure you don't want me to join?"

"I'm good. Thank you very much." She giggles and the sound delights me.

"But I can do your back for you." I pause. "I can go

hard and deep." I'm growing as I listen to my own words. I really hope she takes me up on my offer.

"It's okay. I have a long scrubber at home, so I'm able to reach my back." She shakes her head and disappointment fills me. Darn. "Didn't you say you were going to order some Chinese food or something?"

"Yeah. You're hungry, huh?" I want to add "for some of my big cock," to my sentence but I outgrew teenage humor in my early twenties.

"I'm starved. Hello." She nods enthusiastically. "I could eat a horse right now or two or two horses and a cow."

"So I'm taking it that you're just a little bit hungry then."

"Very funny." She smiles.

"So what would you like?" I ask her as I pull out my phone. "There's a Chinese restaurant that I always order takeout from and the food is always delicious, but I don't know if we have the same taste."

"I'm kind of basic." She says wrinkling her nose.

"I find it hard to believe that you're basic about anything, Sarah." I look over at her breasts and lick my lips. "Very hard to believe that."

"Very funny." She shrugs. "I would like sweet and sour pork."

"Okay." I add that to the cart.

"Crab Rangoon."

"Crab Rangoon, eh?" I grin at her.

"What? You don't like Crab Rangoon?"

"I love Crab Rangoon," I say. "Anything else?"

"Ooh. How's about General Tso's chicken?" My lips tremble slightly.

"What?" I say as she pinches me in the shoulder. "You gave me a look."

"What look did I give you?"

"Like I was a basic bitch ordering the most basic food ever."

"I would never give you such a look, darling. Anything else?"

"Yeah, vegetable, Lo Mein, vegetable fried rice, maybe some egg rolls, pork and vegetables."

My eyes widen as she continues. "So you weren't joking about being hungry."

"I do not joke about food. If there's one thing you should know about me, it's that." She giggles. "I can eat."

"I'm glad," I say. "I can eat as well. And I like hanging out with women that don't make me feel like pigs."

"You're going to think I am a pig by the time we're done." She laughs and the sound reminds me slightly of a piglet, but I don't say anything as I'm not sure if she will consider that a compliment. Even though I think the sound is endearing.

"And feel free to add anything else that you want."

"Ooh," she says quickly, "if they have any egg tough custards, tarts, or anything like that, or fried dough, like doughnuts."

"Oh, I've never even heard of such a thing."

"Sometimes some Chinese restaurants have it for

dessert." She says. "I love sweet stuff, but if they don't, it's fine."

"I can order from somewhere else as well if you want. We could get some cupcakes or ..."

"No, then you'd have to pay two delivery fees and I don't want you wasting your money."

"I think I've got an extra couple of bucks I can spare to get you something sweet."

"Okay, well if you don't mind."

"Sarah, I offered. Trust me, I don't mind."

"Then salted caramel cheesecake." She licks her lips.

"Oh my gosh, I love salted caramel cheesecake. Coming up. I'll find a place."

"Okay, go in the shower now." I tap her bare ass and she giggles as she walks into the bathroom. I walk into the corridor and head towards the kitchen. I'm smiling as I grab some plates and put them on the counter in preparation for when our food arrives. I decide to head over to my iPad that's connected to the speakers in the living room and search for Noah Kahan on YouTube so I can listen to one of his songs. Immediately he pops up and I stare at him. "So you're the guy that's got Sarah in a tingle," I mutter out loud as I press play on the first song that pops up in the list. My speakers click into action and I hear the strumming of a guitar before he starts singing, "Love Vermont," he says, And continues crooning." I blink as he continues singing. He does have a nice voice. I can see why she likes him.

I wonder if she wishes she could sing with him. The thought annoys me slightly, but I dismiss the twitch in my heart. I can see why she might want to perform with him. They would have an amazing duet if they were ever to link up. They have a very similar vibe and sound going, and I know that if they were to produce something, it would be even more magical.

I take a seat on the couch and look out at the skyline of the city. The sky is dark now but the city is filled with twinkling lights. There are people in their living rooms and kitchens puttering around their houses. My phone rings and I answer it. It's Jackson.

"Hey, what's up?" I say as if I haven't just spoken to him a few hours ago. There's a happy tone to my voice and I wonder if he notices.

"Yo Ethan, what are you doing for dinner, man?"

"Chinese, I think. Why?"

"Cool. Shall I meet you there? Which restaurant?"

"Oh no, I am getting a delivery." I hope he doesn't ask too many questions.

"Okay, I guess I can come over to your place. In like 30 minutes? Does that work?"

"No," I say quickly, frowning slightly. "I have someone here."

"You have someone there?" He sounds surprised. "What do you mean, like your parents or something? Your grandparents?"

"No, not my parents, not my grandparents. A lady."

"What the ..." He sounds shocked and his voice is loud. "You have a lady in your apartment?"

"Yes. What's the big deal?"

"You never have ladies in your apartment. Is there a full moon tonight?"

"What are you talking about? I'm always with women."

"Number one, you're not always with women, and number two, you never take them back to your place."

"That's not true. I've had women at my place."

"I'm not talking about housekeepers or cleaning women or chefs, I'm talking about women you're fucking." He chortles. "And I assume the woman you're sharing Chinese food with is someone you're fucking."

I press my lips together. Technically he was right, but I don't want to think about that. It doesn't mean anything. Sure, maybe the women I've hooked up with in the past have not been in my home, but they've certainly been to hotel rooms with me, very nice hotel rooms.

I try not to compare the fact that Sarah is here in my private space. About to have a shower in my bathroom. I do not want to think about what that means. "Look, it wasn't actually meant to be a hookup." I say quickly trying to reason it out to myself. "She came over here to do some work and it just kind of happened."

"Who came over there to do some work?" He sounds confused and I don't respond. "Oh shit, Ethan. It's not Edith, is it?" he shouts and I try not to laugh.

"What the fuck, Jackson?" I respond cringing inside that he thinks for even one second that Edith might even be here. "Are you out of your mind? Do you really think I would sleep with Edith?" There is silence on the other end and I'm about to curse him out when he finally responds.

"No, I guess not." There's a hint of amusement in

his tone and I know he's been yanking my chain. "So then who? Wait. No, it can't be who I think it is. Sly dog you."

"What are you talking about, Jackson?"

"Did you fuck that hot girl from copywriting?"

I press my lips together. "I didn't fuck anyone." Technically I did, but it doesn't feel right describing what I did with Sarah as fucking.

"Did you bang nerdy Sarah from copywriting?"

"Her name is not nerdy Sarah and we may or may not have had a romantic entanglement."

"Whoa you totally banged the shit out of her." He laughs as I frown and try not to think about the sound of her wet pussy as I slammed into her deep and hard. "I guess the no fraternization policy at Rosser International is not important, anymore, huh?"

"Really, Jackson?"

"What? You're the one that told me I couldn't bang Angie in accounting. You're the one that told me that I couldn't bang Alice in the marketing department. You're the one that told me I couldn't have a threesome with Jenny and Louisa from the-"

I cut him off. "Really, Jackson?"

"What? I'm just saying, why is it one rule for you and one rule for the rest of us? I mean, I know that you're the CEO, but dude, I thought that we didn't sleep together because that was the plan. We ended up messing around because-"

"Wait a second," he cuts me off. "You ordered Chinese food?"

"Yeah, I just told you that."

"For you and Sarah from copywriting?"

"You could just call her Sarah or Ms. Kahan."

"But you never order takeout for dates, not even in hotels. You say you don't want there to be an expectation of cuddling or-"

"We're not cuddling. I am in the living room waiting for the takeaway to come and she's in the bathroom, showering."

"Showering?"

He pauses for a couple of seconds. "You banged the daylight out of her, didn't you?"

"No, I ... Anyways, what is that supposed to mean?"

"I mean, what woman showers at a guy's place unless her body is stained with cum or-"

"Really?" I say angrily. "That sounds absolutely-"

"What? It sounds like the truth."

"No, it's not the truth." I cut him off. I'm annoyed and I know I shouldn't be. "Look, I don't really want to talk about this with you, Jackson. It's just not appropriate. Sarah's a good girl and-"

"She's a good girl now?" He bursts out laughing. "Are we talking about the same woman that posted on our company intranet that she was looking for a billionaire?" He pauses. "I guess it worked huh? Apparently she got herself one."

"She didn't get herself anything. She knows the rules."

"So you told her that there will be no more than five bang sessions?"

"Yes." I snarl into the phone. "Not that it's any of your business."

"I'm not saying it is my business. I just want to make sure that we're all on the same page here."

"You don't need to be on any page." I hear the sound of a door opening and lower my voice. The last thing I need is Sarah hearing this conversation. "Anyway, I got to go."

"Oh, has your darling Sarah decided to come out and bang you for the fifth time?"

"Bye, Jackson." I hang up, annoyed. I'm not going to pay attention to what he's just said. I take a couple of deep breaths and turn around to see Sarah walking down the corridor wrapped in a towel. Her hair is long and wet and she offers me a small impish smile that makes my heart tug. She really is cute and I don't know that I like the fact that I'm noticing that.

"Hey, I don't suppose you have any conditioner, do you?" She asks me softly and my heart flutters as she looks at me. She's beautiful, really, really beautiful. I realize as I'm sitting there listening to her favorite artists waiting on Chinese food to arrive in my own home, that I love having her here. I love being around her. I love making love to her. I love talking to her. I love just being in her space and a part of me doesn't want her to leave, which is not good. At all.

"Oh yeah. I don't use it that often, it's most probably in the cupboard." I nod gruffly as I jump up. "Come on, I'll get you some."

"Thanks." She says softly. "I didn't mean to interrupt or get water on the floor, but I really need conditioner or my hair just frizzes up and-"

"It's okay." I shrug and can't resist giving her a quick

kiss on the lips. "I'm sure your frizzy hair would still be beautiful. I don't care."

"Thank you for those words, but my frizzy hair makes me look like a scarecrow," she says with a laugh as she surveys my face. I can see she's surprised by my words, maybe even more surprised than I am. I wonder if I should go to the doctor because something is definitely not right in my head.

19

Sarah

Dear Diary,

Have you ever experienced a moment so perfect that it makes you want to cry? Have you ever just felt so connected to one person that it doesn't feel real? Well, of course you haven't. You're an inanimate object. You don't feel anything. It would be weird if you did. Or maybe I'm just weird. That's more likely. But I'm just here to say that I felt something today. And get your mind out of the gutter, I don't just mean Ethan's cock. Hehe, don't judge me.

I mean something special. Something visceral. I felt it in every bone of my body. But it scared me.

It's super scary to know you're getting the feels for someone. It's much like the day when you realize you won't live forever and have no control over anything in life. But anyway, I'm blabbering on. I will tell you more soon. After I laugh and cry.

Sunny and always smiling, Sarah

The smell of hot and greasy Chinese food greets me as I make my way out of Ethan's bathroom and head towards the kitchen. I can hear Noah Kahan's suave and svelte voice carry through the room and I smile. I'm happily surprised that Ethan is playing his music. I hadn't expected that he would actually listen to him.

"Ready to eat?" Ethan says as he hands me a plate, filled with so much food that my heart expands with joy.

"More than ready. I'm so hungry. Thank you." I follow him to the dining table and we sit down across from each other. I watch Ethan dig into his fried rice and then start eating myself. I don't want to stuff my face like a pig, but everything looks and smells so delicious that I just can't stop myself.

"I just cannot stop eating. This food is so delicious," I say as I grab another crab rangoon and stuff it into my mouth. The cream cheese is still warm and gooey and I lick my lips to ensure I don't waste any of its salty goodness.

"Well, you did have quite the workout this afternoon." Ethan has a glint in his eyes and I giggle slightly. I don't know why I'm so happy and so flush, but I'm not going to question it. The afternoon has been fun, but I still can barely believe what has happened or what it means.

"Well, I don't want to say I've had harder workouts." I want to groan as I realize what I've just said. What does that say about me? I was talking about in the gym, but I'm not going to explain that now.

"Really?" He looks at me with a raised eyebrow and narrowed eyes. I can see the surprise in his face and then he chuckles as if I'm joking.

"I don't know if that's a challenge or what." He leans forward and stares at my lips.

"Why would it be a challenge?" I ask him, praying I don't just take my clothes off and throw them on the ground. Do not act like a desperado, Sarah. "A challenge to do what?"

"I don't know." He says slowly licking his lips and standing up. My heart races as he comes to stand next to me and looks down. "Maybe you want a harder workout from me?" He winks. "I'm guessing that's your way of telling me that you'd like to do the work?" He puts a hand in the air like he has a lasso in his hands and I swallow hard.

"What do you mean, I'd like to do the work?"

He bites down on his lower lip and my stomach flips as he grabs my hands and pulls me up. He is absolutely gorgeous, and I know that whatever he says next is going to make me want him more because I'm just stupid and crazy like that. Plus I love a dominant alpha man.

"Well, normally when a woman is on top, she does a

lot more work." He says as he pulls me toward him and the couch.

"Is that your way of telling me you want me on top?" I ask as he falls back onto the couch and pulls me on top of him.

"I'll have you any way that I can get you," he says, with a small wink. I'm about to respond that he's already had me, but even I know I don't want to say that. I thank myself internally for not being a complete blabbermouth as he pulls me up his body so that I'm positioned on top of his hardness.

"So are we done with food and we want to have seconds of dessert?" His hands cup my ass.

"Well, I don't know about seconds. We've already had seconds." I moan slightly as he grabs my hips and moves me back and forth.

"Hmm?" He grunts.

"The way I calculate it, we only have room for one more."

"Oh?" He stares at me for a couple of seconds and I smile sweetly at him. "You said five times and you're out, right?"

"Yes." He frowns "But I say many things, and does this really count as five times, being as it's all been on one day?"

"I think it counts." I nod. "So you can have me on top one time, and then it's done. We're done."

He frowns slightly and shakes his head. "So, what does that mean?"

"You're the one that has the rule that you only do it five times, right?"

"Yes." He shakes his head in exasperation. "I've never had a woman remind me of that."

"I'm not sure why not." I say, feeling like a fool. Why am I going on about this? It's not like I don't want there to be more than five times. I just don't want him to know that I want there to be more than five times. I don't know what sort of game I'm playing, but it doesn't seem to be working out well for me.

"So," He changes the subject. "I think this Noah Kahan guy is as good a singer as you say."

"You're changing the subject?" I groan as I feel him growing harder beneath me.

"I thought that the other conversation was done." He shrugs as he shifts me to the side and stands up. "Would you like another glass of wine?"

"I would. Thank you. That has to be the best cabernet sauvignon I've ever had in my life."

He grins. "It is from Italy. I took a trip there last year and bought quite a number of bottles and had them shipped over to me."

"Ooh, must be nice." I rub my hands in glee. "Money pants." I try to ignore the fact that I miss his body next to mine.

"Well, you knew I had money." He shrugs. "I spend it. Is that a shock?"

"No. If I had that sort of money, I'd be going to Italy and buying bottles of wine as well."

"You've never been to Italy?" He looks surprised as if everyone has the money to fly overseas on a whim. I shake my head. "Do you want to go to Italy?"

"Are you asking me if I want to go to Italy because

you're going to take me?" I respond back giggling. He stares at me for a couple of seconds and then shakes his head.

"No, that's not what I was asking."

"Okay, then." I feel slightly embarrassed and so I stand up and grab the glass from him that he's offering me. "Thank you."

"Do you want to watch a movie or something?" He asks me hesitantly and he looks taken aback by his own statement.

"A movie?" I stare at him in surprise. I didn't think that he would want to do anything else with me right now. I was surprised he hadn't kicked me out already. This was technically meant to be a meeting where I was getting in trouble for posting a personal ad that never should have made it onto the company intranet. Instead it was turning into something else. That I had certainly never expected.

"I just think that it would be nice to relax." He shrugs nonchalantly. "Unless you have somewhere to be, something to do right now." His voice trails off and he looks away.

"Not right now, I don't." I'm not sure what to say. I do want to spend more time with him. I surprisingly like him more than I thought I would. I just don't know if it's stupid to be liking him. He's my boss and I just made love to him several times, and it feels amazing and weird at the same time. Was it really smart to be watching a movie or a TV show with him? Especially considering the fact that this wasn't going anywhere. It wasn't like this was some sort of amazing first date and we were going to make plans for a second and a third and possibly ride off into the sunset and get married.

This man was my boss. He'd already told me that he has no intentions of dating me. He has no intentions of taking me on a date and whisking me off of my feet. He has no intention of doing anything romantic with me.

This isn't going to end in true love.

"Sure." I say, going against my intellect. "Let's watch something."

"What do you want to watch?" He asks as he walks over to the living room. I watch as he picks up a remote control and turns on the TV. "I have every TV station and app available, so anything you wish to see, it should be available to me."

"I have almost every app as well.", I laugh. "I love watching TV." I wrinkle my nose. "Or should I not admit that?"

"No, that's great." He stares at me for a couple of seconds. "Now you can tell me to shut up, but I would love your feedback on something."

"Oh, what?"

"So we're planning on starting an entertainment division at Rosser International. We're primarily interested in getting into the music industry. So we're thinking of starting a record company" My heart races at his words. They're going to open a record label? Would he ever consider signing me? I don't say anything though. I don't want him to think that I want anything from him.

"That sounds cool." I nod. I don't want him to

think that the only reason I am interested or care is because I want him to sign me. There would be nothing worse than him offering me a contract just because I slept with him.

"But we're also thinking about getting into TV production and also getting into possibly starting our own TV channel."

"Oh?" I stare at him. "I had no clue."

"Well, you wouldn't, would you? You're not exactly-" He pauses as if he thinks better about what he's about to say.

"What? I'm not exactly what?"

"You're not exactly privy to executive talk." He shrugs and looks me in the eyes. "Don't get mad at me."

"Oh, I'm not mad." I laugh loudly. "I work in the copywriting department as a junior copywriter. I barely make $50,000 a year. I'm not under any illusion that I am in the upper echelon of people that work at Rosser International."

"You make $50,000 a year?" He looks surprised, like he can't believe it. He most probably spends $50,000 a day.

"Please don't tell me you think that's a lot of money."

"I don't. I think that's not much money to have to live in the city." He frowns.

"Trust me when I say it's hard."

"I know you don't want to talk about your salary or have me go to HR, but-"

"But nothing, Ethan." I shake my head. "You

cannot go to HR and talk about my salary. I do not want you to. I do not want-"

"It's got nothing to do with us sleeping together. You know that, right?"

"Yeah, I know that, but-"

"But what? Do you think other people wouldn't know that?"

"I don't know. I just don't want anyone to think that there was any impropriety. And I don't want you to think that there was any impropriety here. I don't want you to think that—."

"I don't think you came over here to convince me to give you a pay raise." He shakes his head. "Just like I don't think you came over here with the intention of-"

"Ethan, can we just watch a TV show and hang out?"

"Of course. I'd like nothing more." He motions to the couch.

"What was the question you had for me? If it's something I can answer that is not going to be about me getting a raise or anything like that, I'll be happy to do it. But if it's about something else-"

"I was just going to ask you what sort of TV shows you really enjoy? Jackson and I have been debating with paying for several scripted drama shows or reality TV."

"Oh, wow. I love scripted drama shows, but I can't lie I love reality TV as well. In fact, there's this show I've been watching recently called The Traitors, and it's absolutely amazing."

"The Traitors?" He looks at me with a small smile. "Never heard of it."

"We can watch an episode if you want." I stare at him. "You might not like it, but I think it's fun."

"Okay. Let's watch The Traitors." He types it into his TV screen remote and I see the word popping up. "The Traitors USA, The Traitors UK, and The Traitors Australia. Which one do you want to watch?" He asks. "UK, US and Australia. Wow looks like a pretty popular show."

"Yeah, they also have it in Canada and New Zealand, but you can't get that through Peacock. I love the UK one the most, if you want to watch that. Even though US is great too."

"Let's do it." He settles onto the couch. "You want to sit next to me?"

I stare at him and shake my head and head over to the recliner. He looks back at me for a couple of seconds and shrugs, though I can see a look of disappointment on his face.

"Really Sarah?"

"What? You asked if I wanted to sit next to you, and-"

"Get over here, Sarah." He motions to me and points to the seat next to him.

"Excuse me?" My jaw drops slightly.

"I said, get over here. Or do you want me to pick you up and bring you over?"

"You are not going to pick me up, and-"

He stands up and I jump out of the recliner quickly.

"Fine. I will come over and sit next to you, but..."

"But what?" He grins as he grabs my hand and pulls

me into him. "You scared to be too close to me? You're scared the big bad wolf is going to eat you?"

"Why would I be scared about that?" I ask grinning. "The big bad wolf has already eaten me."

"And you loved it, didn't you?"

"I wouldn't say loved it, but-"

"But what?" His hand creeps up my back and tugs on my hair. "You didn't love it?"

"Okay. Maybe I loved it, but you loved it too."

"Fuck yeah." He growls. "I don't know if I should tell you this, but you give the best head I've ever received."

"Wow. What a compliment, Ethan. Maybe that's something I can put on my resume." I roll my eyes. He's so unromantic.

He chuckles. "But you know what, you also could give me the best ride of my life too." He rubs my thigh. "Giddy up, cowgirl."

"Ethan!" I gasp and giggle.

"What? I'm just saying I could help you out. You said you wanted more of a workout."

"Maybe later." I grin, and squeeze his hand. "Maybe before I go."

"Promise?" There's a glint in his eyes as he kisses the side of my face and then looks at my lips. Why is this man so damn sexy?

"Maybe." I say, as I reach down and rub the front of his pants in a direct way. I love how hard he is already and I bite down on my lower lip to stop from dropping to my knees and taking him into my mouth immediately.

"You're such a fucking tease, Sarah." He pants and I can tell that I am driving him crazy. "And I absolutely love it."

"What?" I whisper under my breath as my heart races. I stare at him for a few seconds and then rub my head as my brain processes what he'd just said. For a moment I think he's said he loves me and I am about to say I think I love you too before my brain calls out my wishful thinking and poor hearing.

I really am losing it.

And even worse than that is the fact that I'm pretty confident that I am developing real feelings for this man.

How am I falling in love so quickly?

I really am a hot mess.

20

Ethan

Ever since I was little I knew my mom and dad didn't have a healthy relationship. They were either super lovey dovey or angry. And most times, when they were angry, my father would buy my mother something and she would be happy again. Until the time came that he couldn't buy her what she wanted anymore. And the anger grew and grew. And the tears were plentiful. I can keenly remember the dead feeling inside my stomach whenever I saw my mother crying. I can still feel the sadness in my soul as I sat there helplessly not knowing what to do.

As I grew older, I often wondered why my parents never divorced. It seemed to me that they would both be happier alone. However, I think the fact of the matter was that they were both codependent and couldn't live without each other. I never want to be in a position where I feel like I can't live my life to its fullest without someone else.

I stare at my empty couch for a few moments and then jump up and pace back and forth in my living room. I don't know why my normally homey apartment feels so desolate. Sarah has only been gone for a couple of hours and yet, it feels like I haven't seen her in days. I can't quite seem to focus on anything. I need to get my mind off of how much she makes me laugh. For some reason being around her makes me remember the past. Maybe because she's awoken a part of me that's not just focused on work.

It had been fun having her here. She challenged me to think about more than work. And while a lot of those thoughts were about her body and what I'd like to do to her, a lot of them were about other things as well. She made me think big thoughts. Like what life would be like if I was in a serious relationship or if I had kids. I wonder for too many minutes what it would feel like to be committed to someone.

Would I feel like I was losing myself? Would I feel like I couldn't survive without the other person? Was I that weak? I knew my father couldn't live without my mom; even though he cheated on her all the time. She was his everything. The other women were just there to make him feel better about his sorry life. And mom pretended not to notice, though I knew it still ate her up inside. I didn't want that emotional attachtment to another person. I didn't want any woman making me feel like I couldn't live without her; even when she treated me like shit. I don't want to lose myself.

I grab my phone and call Jackson. I need to get out of my head. More importantly, I need to stop thinking about Sarah.

"What's up, Mr. Loverman?" He answers the phone with a chuckle and I want to hang up, but I don't.

"What are you up to?"

"Not eating Chinese food with my lover."

"Wanna grab a drink?" I ignore his comment. I will not let him rile me up. I will not engage in this conversation.

"Now?" He asks and pauses as if this is a shocking question. As if I never drink. As if he doesn't ask me to grab a drink almost every night of the week. "This is a work night, Ethan or did you forget that?"

"Don't be a dick, Jackson."

"Oof, someone sounds pissed. I take it that nerdy Sarah has gone and now you're wondering where you went wrong."

"Really?"

"I'm guessing the sex wasn't good? Did you not make her orgasm?"

"I made her orgasm plenty," I growl, annoyed by his words. "She's still screaming my name in her head." I tense slightly as I think of the sound of her sweet voice moaning my name. "She'll most probably be dreaming about me and my good loving tonight." I cringe inside. When had I turned into such a douchebag? I'm grateful Sarah can't hear me talking.

"Yet, she was able to make her way away from you and be by herself for the evening."

"I don't think she could handle any more of me today."

"Cos you're *that* good." He chortles, and I squeeze the phone tightly as he starts humming the tune to Baby Got Back.

"I can give you lessons if you want." I pause. "Show you on a diagram how it's done."

"No thanks." He chuckles. "I don't think I need any lessons; they don't call me Jackson, the Sex God of Manhattan, for nothing."

"In your dreams, buddy. No one calls you that, aside from the blowup dolls in your spare bedroom."

"You mean your exes?"

"Funny, not. Do you want to grab a drink or not, Jackson?"

"I can meet you at Used Dishes in 20 minutes." He chuckles, and I hear a beeping in my ear. "I text you the address. It's a new speakeasy. You enter through the kitchen of a Turkish restaurant. Super cool."

"How do you know about all these new bars?"

"Because I have my fingertip on the pulse of the city."

"A model told you?"

"Maybe." He laughs. "Maybe she mentioned something about the place when she offered to have a threesome with me."

"A threesome?"

"I declined." He sounds bored. "How many threesomes can a man have in his life?"

"How many have you had?"

"Enough." He pauses. "So, are we going to talk about what motivated you to call me for a drink tonight, or are we sweeping it under the rug?"

"Sweeping what under the rug?"

"The fact that you're sleeping with an employee?" His voice is lighthearted, but I know he's serious. "Is this an ongoing thing or..."

"It happened once, and it won't happen again. Sarah and I both know that it was a one-off. Neither one of us is looking for anything more." I know I'm being abrupt, but I'm starting to feel pissed off by his questioning. "Please stop bringing this up, Jackson. It's a non-starter of a conversation."

"If you say so. So Sarah knows it was a one-and-done, and y'all are not starting a relationship?"

"A relationship?" I laugh out loud. "After one day of lovemaking? She's not stupid." I'm not 100% sure she realizes this was a one-off, and I'm not sure that I even want that, but I'm not going to let him know that. I mean, it's not like I want anything else from her. That would be a stupid thought. Just because she intrigues me and makes me laugh doesn't mean anything. Even though she's different from most women, she's not going to make me change my philosophy on love. No way and no how.

"All relationships aren't like your parents, Ethan," Jackson says softly, and I cringe at his words. "Some of them are healthy."

"Like your parents?" I ask him and there is silence on the phone. I'm not sure what game Jackson is playing, but I know he's not one to believe in love, either. He knows, as I do, that relationships only make you lose a part of yourself. And often lead to failure or depression. I didn't want to be a statistic. I didn't want to be like my mom, unable to let go of something that made me feel like shit.

"My parents aren't the healthy example I'm talking of no." He says dryly. "But that doesn't mean that all relationships have to be like our parents. We're not the poster children of children born to emotionally healthy human beings. Maybe we don't know how to handle relationships." He sounds thoughtful. "Maybe there's a way to—."

"Jackson, I don't know what you're about to say and frankly, I don't have the mental brainpower to process it. Tonight I just wanna get drunk."

"What happens when you see Sarah tomorrow?" He asks softly. "You'll just be able to pretend nothing happened?"

"She won't be there tomorrow," I say quickly, not wanting to think about Sarah any longer. "I've given her the next couple of days off to work on the jingle for Lord Chambers." I lie and open my text messages to tell her about this new plan. "She's concentrating on work, and so am I," I growl as I press send on the message telling her to take the rest of the week off. "Now, let's go get drunk and see what other honeys we can flirt with tonight so I can show you just how not interested I am in my nerdy employee."

21

Sarah

Dear Diary,
There is no way that I am ever going to live this down. No way whatsoever. I need to leave earth.

STAT!

I don't care if aliens come from the sky and kidnap me and tell me I have to marry a hedgehog. I will do it. In a heartbeat. I won't protest or say no thanks. I will ask if the hedgehog would like some tea with honey or coffee and live out my life on Mars, Pluto, or whatever other planet the aliens came from. I'm sure you are wondering what happened. Don't worry I'm about to tell you.

Ashamed and Red in the face, Sarah

. . .

Have you ever lived your life in fantasyland? Dreaming and hoping that one thing will be true and ignoring reality. That's pretty much how I've spent the last few days. Ethan allowed me to take a couple of days off to concentrate on writing the jingle for the Royal Line of Lights, and I haven't been happier.

I feel so light and excited. I've been in my element, thinking up lyrics and playing different instruments to see what sounds the best. Johnson seems to be enjoying me being at home so much, though I think it's because he's getting an extra walk each day. And an extra treat.

"Get your lights, sparkly lights, make your palace your home." I sing as I dance around the living room, shaking some maracas one of my brothers brought me back from his last trip to Puerto Rico. I don't love the tune or the lyrics, but I am having fun. I am happy to be able to use my creative mind for something that excites me more than boring ad copy for product placement. I try not to question whether I am excited because I am working with Ethan on this project or writing a song.

My body still tingles thinking about Ethan. I wonder if we will ever make love again. Not that I would ever bring it up to him. Not that I would want him to break his rules for me. Not that I even care. Part of me wants to tell him that I could sleep with him 100 times, and it wouldn't make me feel any differently about him. Though I'm not 100% sure if that's true, I think about him a lot. Randomly throughout the day. I think of the way he kissed me. I think of the way his fingers touched me. I think of the way we laughed and joked around and wonder if he also thinks about those moments. I also think about when I thought he'd said I love you. And the way my heart had raced with love for him. I don't want to dwell on that too much, though. Because I don't want to think I'm crazy. How can I be falling in love with Ethan Rosser?

I'm grateful when my phone rings, and I walk over to the coffee table and pick it up. Joy fills me when I hear Ella inviting me out. I need to get out of the house and out of my head. I need to ignore my growing feelings for my boss.

∼

"So, what exactly is going on between the two of you?" Ella asks me, and I can tell from her face that she doesn't know whether to be nervous or excited for me.

I can tell she's super confused by what I've told her about my situation with Ethan, but that's not a surprise because I'm also quite confused. I don't know how to explain the chemistry and magic I feel when I'm with him.

"Nothing's going on," I say, trying not to let my exasperation win out.

"What do you mean nothing's going on?" Ella prods.

"I mean, we hooked up once. Well, more than once,

but it's done. We're not hooking up again. I haven't even heard from him."

"That's so weird," Isabel chimes in and takes a sip of her drink. She's thoughtful for a few moments and then continues. "Why are guys so weird?"

"I wish I knew." I shake my head and play with my hair. Even though I'm in my thirties, I still don't really understand men. I don't want the sadness to fill me because I really enjoyed my time with Ethan, and even though I wish that circumstances were different and that he'd been blowing up my phone and asking me out, I didn't want that to dampen the moments we'd had together. I mean, it wasn't like we had anything special.

"I think he sounds like a real idiot," Ella says. "I mean, I know men just don't get it like we do, but..."

"But nothing," I say, sighing. "He has a five-time rule. Remember?"

"Five dates?" Ella asks with a frown. "Five times of what?"

"I guess it's a combination of five dates or five times hooking up or something." I shake my head. "I don't know. I don't really want to talk about it right now." I freeze as my phone starts ringing. All of us look at the screen. I can't believe it when I see Ethan's name on the screen. Do I have magical powers? I say his name, and then he calls.

"Oh my gosh, it's him," Isabel says, a giddy expression on her face as if she'd been waiting for the call herself.

I laugh slightly at how happy she sounds. I'm the

one that should be feeling giddy, not her. But I suppose that's why she's such a good friend. She's happy for me, and that makes her happy.

"What should I do?" I ask, just staring at my vibrating phone on the top of the table. I want to answer, but I don't want him to know that I'm eager to speak to him.

"Answer it, of course," Ella says, pushing it towards me.

I grab it, take a deep breath and say casually, "This is Sarah. Can I help you?"

"Sarah, it's me."

"Sorry, who's me?" I say as if I don't have Ethan's number saved in my phone.

"It's Ethan, your boss." His tone is clipped, as if he's annoyed.

I try not to roll my eyes. I don't know why he had to add my boss. We both know he's my boss, but I would've hoped he'd think he was more than that now that we'd slept together. Couldn't he have said, "it's me, Ethan, your part-time lover, or something?"

"Oh, hello, Ethan," I say in a stilted tone because I don't want him to know how excited I am.

"What are you doing?" He demands as if he deserves to know the information.

"I am out with my best friends, Ella and Isabel, and we're—."

"Okay, I see," he says, cutting me off.

I frown slightly. I can't stand it when he's a rude, annoying asshole.

"I haven't heard from you in a couple of days," he continues.

"Yeah, well, I've been working and—."

"Is the jingle ready?"

"It's not ready yet, but it will be soon. You gave me two weeks, remember?"

"Well, I thought you might be finished with it earlier than that."

"Well, you thought wrong," I say. I'm starting to feel annoyed now. Why had I been so excited to hear from him?

"I need you to meet me tomorrow," he says lowering his voice.

"Okay, when and where?" I want to groan at how eager I sound.

"4:00 PM at the Champagne Room," his voice is a low growl.

"The Champagne Room?" I ask, my heart racing suddenly. "Are you asking me—."

"I got to go." He clicks and hangs up the phone before I can finish my question.

I stare at the phone for a few seconds in disbelief and then look at my best friends. Their eyes are both wide and I can tell that they want to know what the conversation was about, but they're nervous to ask.

"I think he may have just asked me on a date," I say grinning, widely. I can't help myself, I'm excited. Really, really excited. Maybe this is going somewhere, after all.

"Wait, what?" Ella says. "Like a real date?"

I nod slowly. "He wants to meet me tomorrow at

the Champagne Room." I squeal. "I mean, it sure sounds like a venue for a date."

"Oh my gosh," Isabel says, gawking. "The Champagne Room is only the city's best, most exclusive bar."

"I know," I say, nodding slowly as I remember reading about it in a magazine. "Girls, what am I going to wear? Oh my gosh, I'm freaking out guys. I think Ethan Rosser just asked me out on a real date."

I start jumping up and down, and they both stand up and join me. I grab their hands, and we're all jumping up and down together as if we're 18 years old and the quarterback just asked me to homecoming.

"Guys, what do you think it means?"

"I don't know," Isabel says. "But what I do know is that he's been thinking about you and he wants you and..."

Ella nods. "I think he might be about to change his five-day rule for you."

"Five-time rule," I say, giggling. "I don't know if it's five days or five times in bed or whatever. It doesn't matter. Do you really think so?"

"Girl, you blew his world and now he wants more," Ella says, nodding. "How exciting."

"I know. I'm freaking out. Should I wear my slinky red dress or that short black one I recently got that clings to my body?"

"The short black one," Isabel says, cutting me off. "Definitely. When you walk in that dress, you look like a million dollars. If you bend over slightly, your ass is giving hotness."

"But do I really want to go looking like a hoe?"

"Girl, you want him to stare at that ass," Ella says, giggling. "You want him to look at you and think, holy shit, she is dynamite."

"That's true. I cannot believe that I have a date with Ethan Rosser. Okay, I need to calm down," I say, trying to stop myself from screaming. "And to think, I thought the reason I hadn't heard from him was because he wasn't interested, but it turns out absence does make the heart grow fonder."

"Or the dick harder," Ella says.

I stare at her for a couple of seconds. "What?"

"Or the dick harder." She shrugs, looking a little sad. "I'm not trying to be a bitch, but we don't know if it's his heart or his dick that misses you."

I giggle slightly. "That's true." I shift my legs. I'm starting to feel wet just thinking about his dick. I know that's a crazy response, but the thought of him in bed is enough to turn me on. I grin to myself as I think about him inside of me, growling my name.

"Get your mind out of the gutter, Sarah," I mumble.

I don't want to think about Ethan inside of me, but it was hot, and the grunts and the groans that he made and the way he held my body so tightly was amazing.

"What are you thinking about Sarah?" Ella asks, pinching me in the shoulder.

"What?" I say innocently, blushing.

"Your face just went red and you were making moaning noises."

"No, I wasn't," I say quickly, but Isabel nods.

"You totally were. Were you fantasizing about Ethan just now?"

"No. Maybe. Kind of," I laugh. "Oh my gosh, what is this man doing to me?"

"I don't know," Isabel shakes her head. "But I need to find someone who's going to make me feel that way too."

We all start laughing then and I wonder if Isabel is really serious about trying to find someone. She's been single for even longer than I have, and I love her and I want her to find someone. I make a mental note to see if I can get her to join a dating app or at least go to some bars or speed dating events with me. Even if it's just for some good sex. Ethan has made me realize that even though it's nice being alone, it's even better when you can be with someone.

~

I attempt to pull down the hem of my short black dress as I make my way towards the Champagne Room. I'm excited. I've never been in a bar as exclusive as this one before and I've never been on a date with a billionaire.

I wonder if Ethan's going to bring me roses and chocolates or perfume. I wonder what it is that billionaires bring their dates. I realize I don't know if he's the sort that likes to spoil his women or not, and I don't even know if I am one of his women. It's only a first date and I haven't even heard from him since the phone call yesterday.

I step inside the lobby and look around. A cute man is standing there right in front of the entrance. He's got a man bun, which I normally don't like, but he's so handsome that it doesn't matter.

"Hi," I say as I walk toward him.

"Hi, can I help you?" He looks me up and down and I can see his eyes widening appreciatively.

I had spent hours on my makeup and hair, but I wanted to look my best for my first official date with Ethan.

"Yeah, I am meeting someone here and his—."

"Oh, that's a pity," he says, disappointment in his eyes.

"Sorry, what?"

"I was hoping you were going to say you were meeting a girlfriend or you were just coming to have a solo drink." He chuckles slightly.

"Oh, why is that?"

"Because I get off in a couple of hours and I'd love to take you out."

"Oh, well, I mean, I'm kind of here for a date and..." I blush slightly. Was this cute guy really flirting with me?

"All the gorgeous ones are taken," he says.

"Well, you know." I run my fingers through my hair and laugh slightly. "I'm not quite taken yet, but..."

"Ms. Kahan?" I hear Ethan's voice and I blink. I turn and look around and I see him standing in the corner. He's wearing a business suit still, and there's a blank expression on his face. My heart races slightly as I gaze at him.

"Oh, there's my date," I say, as I lift my hand up and wave slightly.

Ethan steps forward, but he doesn't smile. I see three men following behind him and my heart jolts. Who the fuck are they? I put on a big smile and head towards Ethan.

"Hi, I..."

"What are you wearing?" He whispers to me and I blink slightly as I see his eyes move towards my exposed thighs and back to my face. He shakes his head and then turns to the three men that were standing behind him.

"Gentlemen, this is Sarah Kahan. She works in my copywriting department. I had her come because she has some good ideas for the new campaign. Sarah, this is Bob Discok, Bill Prints, and Joey Santorine."

I swallow hard as my face goes bright red. I'd gotten it wrong. This was not a date. This was a business meeting with clients and here I was looking like a dolled-up prostitute. I knew I didn't look professional. I knew my boobs were about to pop out as well as my ass. I bite down on my lower lip. I can't believe this. I want a hole to open up and swallow me.

"Hi," I say, and I've already forgotten the men's names.

Each one shakes my hand and I just nod as they say something to me. I can't even comprehend what they're saying. My brain is racing. I feel completely out of it. I feel like a fool.

I look over at Ethan and his eyes are narrowed. I know he's pissed. But maybe not as pissed as I am. At both myself and him. Why hadn't he told me this was a business meeting? Why had I assumed it was a date?

"Shall we have a seat?" One of the men says. I can't remember his name, but he looks at me appreciatively. He looks like a slightly younger version of George Clooney. He's very attractive, and even though his hair is gray, I'd decide I'll still flirt with him even though I'm not into older men.

"Yeah, that sounds good," I say as he pulls out my chair and waits for me to sit.

"So Sarah, how long have you been at Rosser International?" The George Clooney lookalike asks me, and my mind goes blank.

"Well," I lick my lips nervously as I attempt to pull the back of my skirt down again. This is not good.

"One second. I just need to speak to Sarah for a moment," Ethan says, as he grabs my arm and pulls me over to the side of the room.

"What are you wearing?" He asks, his blue eyes blazing as they narrow.

"What do you mean what am I wearing?" I glare at him. "Clothes."

"What do you not understand by my question? Why are you wearing," he flickers over my breasts and down my long legs. "This barely nothing piece of material. It's very inappropriate."

I'm not about to tell him I thought he'd asked me on a date. There's no way in hell I would let him know that.

"I'm going out later to a pole dancing class," I say. "And I just wanted to be in the right attire.

"A pole dancing class?" His eyes narrow to a slit. "Is this your way of telling me that you really are a stripper after all?"

"No," I say through gritted teeth.

"This is very unprofessional, Sarah," he says, shaking his head. "You're going to force me to report you to HR."

"Excuse me?" I say staring at him. He's gone way too far now.

"I also saw you flirting with two men when you came in."

"What men?"

"The guy with the long hair."

"Oh, you mean the waiter with the man bun?" I ask.

"Yes," he says.

"I wasn't, I mean, hey, he just wanted to know if he could take me out for a drink later. What do you care?" I say, rolling my eyes.

"I don't care, but it's very unprofessional. When you are on a business meeting lunch, you need to be professional."

"Oh, shut up, Ethan," I say, wondering why he's acting like such a jerk.

"Excuse me?"

"I said, shut up, Ethan. You know what? Just kiss my ass."

"Oh," he says, his eyes glittering. "You'd like that, wouldn't you?"

"Oh, yeah," I say, rolling my eyes. "I'd absolutely love it, not."

My jaw drops as he falls to his knees and I just stare at him.

"What are you doing?"

He looks up at me and winks. "You wanted me to kiss your ass, right?"

He grabs a hold of my thigh and runs his fingers down the side. I swallow hard. I look over towards the gentlemen. None of them are looking at us, but all it will take is one glance and they will see Ethan on his knees next to me.

"What do you want me to do now?" He says. "Sarah, I bet you want me to lift up the bottom of that dress so you can sit on my face?"

My jaw drops, and he chuckles slightly as he stands back up. "But you'd maybe like that a bit too much, wouldn't you?"

"You are so inappropriate, Ethan Rosser." I glare at him. I'm mortified and annoyed and I can see that he's wanting to get a reaction out of me. Well, he's going to have to wait a long time for that.

"Am I?" He says, looking me up and down. "Or are you?"

I just stare at him for a couple of seconds and say nothing because he's right, of course. I'm totally not dressed appropriately for a business lunch. But then again, I had thought it was a date. "To be quite honest, I'm bored of this conversation," I say as I walk away from him. "I have things to do later, so let's just get this meeting done quickly."

22

Ethan

I am pissed that Sarah was flirting with the waiter, and now she's flirting with Bob again at the table. I stare at her blatantly, and I can see she's glaring at me. She hadn't found my facesitting joke funny, but to be quite frank, I didn't find her appearance to be funny either. She looked absolutely gorgeous. Far too sexy to be around these pervs.

As soon as she'd walked in, I'd been blown away. She looked gorgeous, but then, she always does. I love how sexy she is, but I can't help but notice that everyone else is admiring her as well, and I sure don't like that.

I knew I'd made a mistake calling her, telling her to meet me here. I had thought that she might think it was a date, and maybe a part of me wanted to see how she'd react to that. I hadn't expected to see her flirting with every man around, though. Bob was acting way too friendly, and I was growing pissed.

"Sarah, can I speak to you for one second?" I say as I stand up from the table.

"What now, Ethan?" She says. There's an edge to her voice, and I can tell that everyone has noticed.

I look at the other gentlemen as they stare at each other for a couple of seconds, and I frown slightly. "Over here," I say, grabbing her elbow and forcing her up. We move to the side of the room and stop.

"What now, Ethan? Ar you going to get on your knees and try and kiss my ass again?" She's glaring at me again.

"No, that was just a joke. I..."

"Yeah, right. Sure, that was a joke. That's why you got onto your knees and you were..." She blushes slightly. "Anyway, what's the deal? Your business associates are going to wonder what's going on."

"I just want you to know that this is a business meeting and not anything else. I really hope that you didn't have your hopes up that this was a date." I say succinctly. Her face goes red, and her eyes widen. She presses her lips together and then she just starts laughing.

I'm surprised by that. I thought she was going to go off on me. I thought she was going to get angry. That's what I was expecting, almost hoping for. I wanted her to tell me she had hoped it was a date. We hadn't seen each other in a week and I'd missed her, but it seemed that she hadn't missed me at all.

"What's so funny?" I ask her, waiting for her to tell me why she's laughing so much.

"That you thought I would think this was a date." She says, rolling her eyes. "I haven't even thought about you since the last time I saw you." She wrinkles her nose. "So no, I didn't think this was a date. I didn't hope this was a date. And if I had thought you were asking me out, I would've said no because it's inappropriate."

"So fucking you wasn't inappropriate?" I ask her, starting to feel pissed again.

"No, that *was* totally inappropriate. And I'm sure if I reported you to HR, I'd get some sort of settlement." She pauses and gives me a sweet smile, "But I'm not that sort of girl."

"Oh, so you're not a gold digger?"

"No," she says, an edge to her voice, "I'm not a gold digger, no matter what you think."

"I didn't think you were," I say, trying to take control of the situation.

"I just think that maybe the problem here is you're only thinking with your small head." She says, looking at me for a couple of seconds. "And honestly, your small head isn't really that smart or that good, so maybe you should think with your big head after all." She says, tapping the side of my head. I stare at her for a couple of seconds and grab her hand.

"What are you saying?" I ask her, leaning towards her ear and whispering. "Did you change the subject because you want my cock?"

"What do you think I'm saying, Ethan?" She gasps and trembles slightly.

"I think you're saying you didn't enjoy my small head." I pretend to frown.

"Ooh, maybe you are smart after all." She says, grabbing her hand away from me. "Now, let's get back to work. I have other things to do later."

I press my lips together. This is not how I'd expected this to go. For some reason, I'm angry and annoyed, and I just want to grab her, and take her into a room, and bang the living daylights out of her. I want to show her that my small head can work many miracles. Instead, I nod, and we walk back to the table.

"Sorry about that. I was just checking to see if Sarah brought the files. Turns out she didn't." I shake my head. "She's new to the role though, so maybe she'll get better later."

"Excuse me?" Her jaw drops, and then she just takes a deep breath. "My apologies, gentlemen. I didn't even realize that I was going to be coming to this business meeting until very recently. But I will do whatever I can to help out."

"Oh, I'd like that," Bob says eagerly, and I stare at him for a couple of seconds. "How long have you been with Rosser International?" He asks, looking her up and down, and I can see the glint in his eyes. I can see what he really wants. He doesn't care at all how long she's been with the company. He just wants to know if he can get into her pants.

"Oh, a number of years." She says, "But this is my first time in a senior management role." She looks over at me. "Would you say I'm in senior management now, Ethan?"

"No," I say dryly, shaking my head. "But let us have a seat." I said, "Maybe if you can impress our clients today, you'll be in line for a promotion."

"Oh, is that all I have to do to get a promotion?" She says sweetly, glancing at me as we all take a seat. "Just impress the clients today?"

"That's normally how it works," I say, nodding at her.

"Oh, okay. I wasn't sure if I would have to kiss someone's ass, hypothetically speaking." She laughs, and Bob stares at her with a bemused expression. I can tell his thoughts, and I want to punch him.

"That's normally how it goes in these Fortune 500 companies." He says, nodding. "I've seen it time and time again. It's the person that kisses the most ass that seems to rise to the top."

"I guess I won't be rising anywhere." She says, laughing self-consciously and touching her hair. "I'm not really one to kiss ass."

"Oh, really?" I ask her, "That's not what I've heard."

"Oh?" She says innocently, "You heard that I kiss ass? I mean, I've never kissed yours, right?"

I pause for a couple of seconds and withhold the thoughts in my mind. I want to say to her, "Yeah, you've never kissed my ass, but you had my cock in your mouth very recently." But even I know that would be very unprofessional.

She stares back at me, and I can tell she's waiting for me to cross the line. She's waiting for me to be the unprofessional one. Instead, I turn to Joey on the right and ask him a question. We start talking about different faucets, and I'm trying to concentrate on the conversation, but the sound of Sarah giggling is needling me.

I turn to the right and look at her. Bob has got his lips close to her ear, and he's whispering something, and she's laughing like he's fucking Chris Rock.

"Oh, no, I couldn't do that." She says, touching him on the shoulder, and I wonder what she's responding to. What can't she do? What has he asked her? I know I can't actually ask because everyone would want to know why I was eavesdropping, but I'm starting to feel annoyed. I have to hide my emotions, though.

This has been a mistake. Everything about the last couple of weeks has been a mistake. I never should have invited her over. I never should have shown her my painting. I never should have gone to that bar that night and seen her dancing on the tabletop. I never should have slept with her, never should have ordered Chinese food and slept with her again. I never should have let her get into my head. I never should have let Jackson get into my head.

I never should have played this game of inviting her to this meeting, knowing full well that she would think it was a date and knowing full well that it wasn't. Maybe I'd been playing checkers and she had been playing chess all along. Maybe she knew she was needling me. Maybe this was her way to get into my head.

I wasn't going to let it happen. I wasn't going to let her get to me. Just because the sound of her laugh made my heart jump for joy. Just because the sight of her face made me appreciate beauty. I wanted to paint her. I wanted to paint her in the nude and hang it up in my bedroom so I could stare at it every night.

I hold back a smile as I think about what that process would look like, her sitting nude on my couch. I groan to myself at the thought, I need to get my mind out of the gutter.

"Sorry, what was that, Ethan?" Joey asks, and I blink at him.

"What?" I say, having no idea what the conversation we'd been having was.

"I said I can get you some black and some stainless steel faucets for a really good deal, but you said something about painting?"

I realize I must have mumbled something out loud, and I feel even angrier. The fact that I'm not in control of the words coming out of my mouth is not a good sign. I need to end this meeting as soon as possible.

"Yeah. Well, we'll have to work out the details later." I say. "Sarah here is working on some jingles for our new lighting line by some royal family members, and I thought perhaps she could do something for the faucets."

"Oh, yeah?" Joey sounds interested.

"So Sarah, do you think you can come up with as a jingle to sell faucets?" I ask her.

"I don't know," she says, shaking her head, "I didn't even know I was going to be coming up with a jingle making faucets."

She looks at me and I stare at her. Neither one of us is smiling. Bob touches her hand.

"I have an idea for a jingle." He says.

"Yeah?" She looks over at him. "What's that?"

"I don't know. Maybe something about, I can make you wet, wet, wet." He licks his lips deliberately, and I shudder at how he's trying to be sexy and flirty, and he's just coming off like a creep. She stares at him for a couple of seconds, and I can see her lips twitching as she pulls away slightly.

I smile to myself at the fact. So she's not impressed by this douche bag, that's good.

"I guess. Do we want faucets to make stuff wet, wet, wet though?" She says.

"Maybe not." He says, licking his lips again. "Maybe I was just thinking about something else being wet." He runs his finger through his hair and stares at her. "Maybe I was just thinking about you."

"Me?" She says blinking, and I can see her face going red. She pulls back slightly and I wonder if she's going to tell him off.

"Yeah." He says, "I mean, I guess we don't need a faucet to make you wet."

"Excuse me?" She is loud now, and I wonder if I'm going to have to come to her defense.

"I mean, we have shower heads as well." Bob realizes he's crossed the line and that we are all listening. "I mean, shower heads are good too, right?" He blinks, and Sarah nods slowly.

She looks at me and shakes her head, and I know what she's thinking. She's thinking that she's sitting with a bunch of perverted creeps. And I know that she's right. I can't believe that Bob commented to her, but he feels like he can because she's wearing such a revealing dress to a business meeting.

I feel guilty then. I should have told her exactly where she was going. I should have told her that this wasn't a date, even though I kind of knew that she'd assumed that it was. I'd fucked up. I'd gone and played games, and now it was making me feel like shit. But I knew then that I just needed to let Sarah go. I knew then that I couldn't be professional and mess around with her. I was just going to work with her in a business capacity, and leave it at that. That was for the best.

23

Sarah

Dear Diary,

Why do I love dancing on tables so much? Don't answer me. Well, it's not like you can answer me because you're just a piece of paper with pen written on it, and if you did answer me, I think I'd freak out, but I wish I knew why. I really wish I knew why I love to dance on tables so much. Maybe it's because I love the movie Coyote Ugly, but I'm not Piper Perabo. I certainly don't have her moves and I don't have her body. Though, if I'm being quite honest with myself, I kind of like dancing on tables. Maybe it's because it makes me feel sexy and free and maybe it's because every time I dance on a table, something hot happens. Though, that something seems to be happening with Ethan Rosser and I'm not really interested in going down that road with him because he is a jackass. And when I say he's a jackass, I mean he's the biggest donkey going. If he started snorting and sounding like a donkey, I wouldn't be surprised.

However, that doesn't really excuse the fact that I did it with him again and by did it, I mean it. Yes, we fucked. I hate that word though. It sounds so crude, but maybe that's just who I am now. A table dancing, crude hoe. Love, always, sassy Sarah.

I immediately called Isabel as I left the business meeting. I am furious. With myself. With Ethan and with the creep Bob, that made it far too obvious that he wanted to take me to his hotel room after the meeting. I am on my way home, but I am upset and need to speak to someone.

"Hey, Chica, how's it going?" She says as she immediately answers the phone.

"Oh my God. I'm so pissed off."

"Oh gosh, what did that asshole do now?" She cuts me off before I can even finish my sentence.

"What? How did you know?"

"Because it's always Ethan," she giggles. "At least it's always been him the last couple of weeks whenever you're upset."

"He's such a jackass. Girl, he did not ask me on a date. He was not interested in spoiling me. He..." I take a deep breath. "Let's just say that he is the most arrogant, pompous..."

"He's a prick, huh?" She cuts me off again and giggles.

"Yeah, he's a prick and I do not even want to think about him. What are you doing right now?"

"I was just about to watch Love is Blind. The new season is out. Oh my gosh. There is this guy called Jimmy and he..."

"Girl, I don't even want to talk about that right now. You want to go and grab a drink?"

"Another drink?"

"What do you mean another drink?"

"I'm just surprised that you've wanted to go out so many times during work nights for drinks. You don't normally."

"Yeah. Well, I don't normally have to deal with a grumpy jackass of a boss, but I am certainly dealing with that right now."

"Maybe it was better when he didn't know who you were then?"

"I don't know," I say, thinking out loud. "I mean on the one hand, I didn't have to put up with this bullshit. On the other hand, who wants to be invisible?"

"So what exactly happened?"

"I went to The Champagne Room looking all hot, thinking it's a date, and he was there with a bunch of men because it was actually a business meeting, and he got really rude and annoying. Then one of the guys was basically telling me how he wanted to go down on me in front of everyone. Like what a pig. Why are men such pigs?"

"Whoa. Who was telling you that he wanted to go down on you? Ethan or..."

"No, not Ethan. This guy called Bob something.

Maybe Bob Jackson. Not to be confused with Jackson, Ethan's best friend who works at Rosser International." I sigh. "Anyway, I could tell that even Ethan was pissed off, but girl, right at the end he was like, to me, 'I hope you didn't think this was a date because it's not a date.' I was like, 'I didn't think it was a date. I haven't even thought about you.' He was like, 'Well, that's good because I'm not interested in getting into a relationship.' I was like, 'I wouldn't want a relationship with you anyway.'" I take a deep breath. "Anyways. I need a drink so I can forget about him."

"Girl, that sounds like a lot. You want to go to the Owl and the Pussycat again?"

"Fine," I say. "Meet you there in 20?"

"Sounds good. I'll be there, and don't worry Sarah, it will be okay."

"Uh-huh. I know that's what Bob Marley says, but was it okay for him?"

"Touche, though I think he says it will be alright." She giggles and hangs up.

I make my way into my apartment and study my face in the mirror and then I study my body. I do look hot. Totally inappropriate for a business meeting. Totally, totally inappropriate. I want to die. I can't believe Ethan told me that he was sorry that I'd been confused and that I thought it was a date. A part of me was still confused. Why hadn't he said it was a business meeting? And why had he gotten onto his knees when I told him to kiss my ass? Who does that?

"Oh, this man is going to drive me crazy," I say to myself as I shake my head.

I splash my face and take a deep breath before I head into the kitchen and grab some water. I drink two glassfuls and then head back to the bathroom to redo my makeup. I decide to keep on the same outfit because I look good and I'm not going to change, even if I do look really sexy.

Maybe some guys will see me and want to flirt. Right now, I'm ready to flirt with any hotties because I kind of need to forget about Ethan. Obviously, what we had done meant nothing to him. Obviously, it had just been one hot moment, and he had told me he didn't want anything else. As far as I was concerned, I didn't want anything else either. I might be looking for a man, but I'm not desperate and I'm not going to force myself on anyone. I'm not going to make someone want to date me, and if Ethan Rosser is not interested in me, I'm not interested in him.

Just because he makes me laugh, and he's funny, and he's rich and he has the biggest cock I've ever seen in real life, that doesn't matter to me. I'm looking for a man with principles. I'm looking for a man that has compassion and is sweet, and makes me feel like a million dollars. That is not Ethan. Ethan makes me feel like, I don't know. I don't even want to think about it.

I grab my red lipstick and reapply it and head out the door. Tonight I am going to forget I have ever seen Ethan Rosser naked.

"Oh my gosh, you look so hot," Isabel says as I approach her outside the bar. She's standing there looking just as sexy in her short red dress.

"Girl, you are the one that's looking hot. How did you put that on so quickly?"

"I have a supply of hot dresses ready for when you want to go out." She giggles. "You think I look good?" She twirls around and I nod.

"Girl, you look like a fricking Victoria's Secret supermodel."

"Yeah, right," she says laughing. "I wish. More like you do."

"Thank you, but no I don't."

"You're hot, hot, hot," she giggles.

"Come on. First round's on me."

"Ooh, tequila shots?"

"I don't know that we should do tequila shots," I say looking over my shoulder as we enter the bar. "But you know what? I don't even care. Tequila shots, vodka shots, rum shots. Whatever you want, we will do."

"Woo hoo," she says. "This is what I'm talking about."

We dance towards the bar and start singing the Usher song that's playing.

"I feel like tonight's going to be a good night," she sings.

"So do I," I laugh and dance around.

I order the shots, we down two and then we head over to the dance floor. I'm singing loudly, and Isabel is dancing around me. I feel relaxed and even though Ethan is still in the back of my mind, I'm not going to dwell on him.

"I'm going to dance on a table again," I say as I head over to a round table in the center of the room.

Isabel smiles at me. "Are you sure you want to do that?"

"I'm sure. What's that saying? Dance like nobody's watching?"

"There's a whole bar of people watching you," she says, gesturing around the crowded bar.

"Well, that's great because I deserve to be the center of attention. I deserve for people to look at me and want me."

"Girl, every single man in here wants you right now."

"Good," I say as I get up and dance on the table. I don't care what anyone thinks. This is my moment to just be free.

I close my eyes and swing my head back and forth. I'm one with the music. I'm sexy. I'm beautiful, and I won't let Ethan Rosser make me feel I'm not. I'm dancing around, spinning and giggling, and then I feel like someone is watching me. I open my eyes slowly, and my jaw drops as I see Ethan standing there. Looking just as shocked to see me.

"What the fuck?" I say under my breath. Is he stalking me? How is he here again?

He steps towards me. There's a glint in his eyes, and I suddenly start to panic. I step back and twist my ankle slightly.

"Ow," I cry out, as my hands flail and I try to take a step forward to adjust my position. That was the wrong move, and I can see I'm about to fall onto the ground and I have no way to stop myself.

As if in fast-forward, I see Ethan rushing towards me, his arms outstretched as I fall. He catches me in his arms and holds me close to him as he lowers me down to the ground. My heart feels like it will pop out of my chest and my entire body is trembling.

"What are you doing here?" I mutter at him, and try to push him away as he's still holding me.

"That's no way to say thank you," he says, his eyes burning into mine. I feel like I can't breathe.

I swallow hard. "Maybe because I am not going to say that." I glare at him.

"You need to stop being so clumsy, Sarah."

"You need to stop being such an asshole, Ethan."

"You need to stop dancing on tables if you don't have the skills," he says, his lips smirking.

"You need to stop stalking me when I go to bars and dance on tables."

"You wish, honey."

"I certainly don't," I say. I'm breathing heavily now, and I can feel that he's breathing heavily as well. My heart races as I breathe in his deep, musky scent.

"You need to stop being so damn sexy," he says as he puts his arms around my waist and pulls me into him.

His body is hard and warm, and even though I want to pull away from him, I can't.

"You need to stop wanting to touch me," I say,

pressing my palms against his shoulders and squeezing tightly.

"You need to stop being so fucking sexy."

"You need to stop being so fucking hard," I say as I reach down and rub his cock slightly through his pants.

"You need to fucking stop turning me on." He blows into my ear. "Because trust me, darling, you haven't even seen hard yet."

I swallow. I know I'm playing with fire but can't stop myself. I grab a hold of his face and whisper in his ear. "You need to stop making my panties so wet," I say, throwing caution to the wind.

He growls as he grabs my hand and pulls me towards the side of the dance floor.

"What are you doing?" I say, blinking at him, wondering where Isabel is right now.

"Something I've wanted to do since the first moment I saw you dancing on that table," he says.

He grabs me and pulls me down a hallway. He pushes open a door and pushes me inside before closing it. I look around and see a bunch of boxes and bottles. We're in some storage room.

"We can't be in here, Ethan."

"Says who?" He says, pulling me towards him.

"We're in a bar and anyone could..."

"Shut up Sarah," he says, as he grabs my face and pulls me towards him. His lips are on mine before I can protest and I kiss him back. He's hot and hard and I'm horny as hell and I don't care what's going on. Or where we are.

"We shouldn't be doing this," I say, as I run my hands down the side of his arms.

"But you know you want to," he says, as he lifts up my skirt and pulls down my panties.

I feel his fingers between my legs, rough and eager, and I moan as he slips two fingers inside of me.

"You weren't lying," he grunts as he feels my wetness.

He finger fucks me and my entire body trembles. This is going way fast and I don't care.

"Fucking hot. You're so fucking hot," he growls as he pulls his fingers out and sucks on my juices.

He reaches down and unzips his pants and I watch as he pulls his cock out. He looks around and pulls me over to the side.

"What are you doing?" I say, murmuring as he bends me over a stack of boxes.

"You'll see," he says, grunting.

My ass is up in the air and I feel his hand slapping against one of my ass cheeks.

"Ow. What was that for?"

"That was for being a clumsy, clumsy girl," he says, growling as he pulls his cock up against my slit and rubs it back and forth. "Fuck. You want me so badly, don't you?"

"No," I say, as I push my ass against him and he groans. I feel his cock sliding into me and I moan loudly.

"Fuck. You're so hot, Sarah," he says, as he slides into me deep and hard. "Your fucking pussy's been waiting for this, hasn't it?"

He slides out, and I moan as I realize that I want him more than anything in the world at the moment. I wouldn't take it even if I were offered a million dollars to stop.

"Fucking horny as hell, aren't you?" He says as he pulls me back up; I feel his hands reaching up, and he yanks the top of the dress down slightly so that my boobs are free.

"Oh, fuck yeah," he says, as he plays with my nipples. "Hard nipples are such a fucking turn on to me."

"Shut up, Ethan. Just fuck me," I say, and he laughs.

"Okay, your wish is my command."

He bends me back over and slides his cock into me deep and hard, and continues thrusting faster and faster. I hear myself screaming, but I can't stop it. He feels so good inside of me. I cannot believe that we are here doing this. I cannot believe that even though I'm so mad at him, I've let him take me again.

"Fuck yeah," he says, as he grabs a hold of my hips and slams my ass back into him. "Fuck," he says. "I'm going to cum."

"Make me cum first," I say, glancing back at him and he groans.

I feel his hands between my legs and he's rubbing my clit.

"Oh, fuck yes," I say. "Don't stop."

He continues rubbing my clit as he enters me slowly and then he starts thrusting again. I feel myself cumming hard and fast and then I feel him stilling. My orgasm spreads across his dick as he pulls out and spurts over my ass.

"Fuck yeah," he says, his body shaking behind me as he reaches up to play with my breasts again. "That was fucking hot."

He spins me around and looks down at me, presses his lips against mine and kisses me hard. I reach up, play with his hair, pull my dress back down, and then push him away.

"Thank you," I say sweetly and he just blinks at me.

"Sorry, what?"

"Thank you for making me cum. That was a nice surprise, but now I'm going back out and dancing for my admirers."

"Dance for what fucking admirers?" He looks shocked.

"You know, all the men watching me as I was swinging my hips on that table."

"Sarah, don't you dare..."

I step away from him towards the door, look back and give him a small little smile. "Ethan, like you said before, you and I, we're not anything. I'm not looking for an emotional entanglement either. I'm not looking for a relationship. Our fucks, while they've been quite good, haven't been the best I've ever had. So you know what? Move on with your life." I take a deep breath as I return to the dancefloor. My entire body is trembling at my lies, but I am pleased at the shocked expression I've left on Ethan's face.

24

Ethan

"I cannot believe that woman," I say as I stare up at the ceiling from my bed. The previous night had been one of the hottest nights I'd ever had in my life, and yet Sarah had walked away from me as if it meant nothing. She'd gone back out to the bar, and over to her friend, and they'd started dancing and jumping up and down. She hadn't even looked around to see if I was watching, or still there.

I wasn't sure why I'd gone to The Owl and the Pussycat the previous evening. Something had told me to go in for a drink, and when I'd seen her there dancing, laughing like she was having the time of her life, I hadn't been able to believe it.

She didn't seem bothered whatsoever about the fact that the afternoon meeting hadn't been a date, or the fact that I'd said I wasn't interested in a romantic entanglement. Maybe she wasn't interested in me like that. Maybe she didn't want to be in a relationship. Which I knew was not true because she'd put a personal ad.

"She's fricking literally looking for a billionaire," I say as I pull up my phone to look at her ad again. She literally had been looking for me. I mean, maybe not me, but someone that was just like me. Maybe she really wasn't satisfied by me, which I knew was a joke. The way she'd come on my dick the previous evening had told me just how attracted she was to me.

"Maybe it's just a physical thing," I say as I pull the sheets off and jump out of bed. I'm annoyed again, and I'm fed up with feeling annoyed. I'm fed up of Sarah controlling my emotions. I'm fed up with thinking about her morning, noon, and night. This woman has gotten under my skin and I don't even understand why. I'd slept with plenty of women before in my life, hotter women even. But yet, none of them had irked me the way that she does.

There's just something about her, a lightness in her eyes, the way she smiles. Everything about her calls to me. Everything about her makes me want to fall at her feet and kiss them, and kiss up her legs, and have her sit on my face. Fuck, I'm growing hard. I know I need to have a shower. I know I need to get this woman out of my mind. I sigh. It's going to be a long day.

I notice that Jackson's called me several times, and I call him back as I head into the shower.

"Yo, what's up?" I say as soon as he answers.

"What you mean, yo, what's up? You're the one that called me." He sounds groggy.

"I'm returning your calls. There were three of them."

"Oh, yeah." He grunts. "Lord Chambers wants to know if you've come up with the jingle. He wants to hear it because he's got some marketing meeting with his PR company." He groans, "I don't know exactly what's going on, but could you call him?"

"I mean, I'm not the one working on the jingle; that's Sarah," I say, groaning.

"Well, can you ask her when the jingle's going to be ready?"

"I didn't particularly want to speak to her right now," I say as I turn on my shower faucet. I think back to the previous evening. I wish she'd spent the night. I wish I could fuck her in the shower right now and then go about my business.

"Dude, I thought you said whatever you guys had was not going to affect the workplace."

"We didn't have anything, and it's not affecting the workplace."

"Well, you did have something. And there's no point getting an attitude with me, Ethan. I'm just saying Lord Chambers wants to know if you have the jingle. You handed that over to Sarah Kahan, right?"

"Yes," I grunt. "I just said that."

"Well, you need to find out if she's finished the jingle. And if she has, she needs to record it and perform it or whatever so Lord Chambers can hear it. Because right now he's not very happy."

"What do you mean he's not very happy? Do you know how much money we paid him to be able to-"

"Ethan," he cuts me off, "Dude, get it together."

"I've gotten it together. I'll call her and find out." I say. I hang up on him and take a deep breath. I do not want to contact Sarah. I do not want to talk to her. I'm not in the mood to play games with her this morning. But if I'm honest a small part of me is excited to see her.

I call her number before I can think. She answers on the second ring.

"Hello?" She says, sounding groggy.

"Sarah, is that you? Are you still in bed?" I practically bark into the phone.

"Oh, my head. Why are you shouting?"

"This is your boss, Ethan Rosser."

"Yes, sir." She says. "What do you want?"

"As I just said, this is your boss. Talk to me with respect." I don't know why I'm teasing her.

"Ooh, sorry, boss." She says, groaning. "How may I help you?"

"I need you to-"

"If you're about to ask me to meet you in another storage room to get fucked, no thank you."

"You weren't saying no thank you last night."

"That's because I wasn't in my right mind."

"Seems like you're not in your right mind a lot."

"What do you want, Ethan?"

"I want to talk to you about your job. The reason why I pay you?"

"Yes, and?"

"Have you finished the jingle?"

"For Lord Chambers, or?"

"Yeah, for Lord Chambers. He wants to hear it. And before we play it for him, I need to hear it to make sure it's up to standard."

"What, you think I'm just going to produce something that sucks?"

"I don't know, Sarah. I don't know your work ethic, I don't know if you're-"

"What do you mean you don't know? You've heard me perform stuff, you heard me sing. You said that-"

"Not right now, Sarah. See me in my office at 10:00 AM."

"Whatever," she says, "Goodbye."

I hang up and I smirk as I get into the shower. I'd needled her. I could hear it in her voice. And while it shouldn't make me happy, I was glad that I still had some effect on her. I was glad that she wasn't always cool as a cucumber with me. I wonder if she's thought about me since last night. I wonder if she woke up this morning wishing I was beside her. Unlikely, seeing as it sounded like I'd woken her up. The thought angers me and I don't know what to do.

I don't know what I'm thinking. But right now, all I need to focus on is the jingle. And the pendant light range. Once that was resolved, I would focus on the home stores. And maybe I'd take a trip to Japan, meet with some vendors, and get away from everything for a little bit.

I need to get my head on straight. I need to focus on what is important, and that is business. That is making money. That ensured that Rosser International stood long after I was gone.

∼

There's a knock on my office door, and I look up from my desk.

"Come in," I say, my heart racing.

"It's me, Mr. Rosser." Sarah steps in. There's a slightly apprehensive look on her face, and I wave her in.

"Good morning," I say, looking at my watch. "Five minutes late."

"Sorry, sir." She says, "I was just-"

"No excuses, Sarah. Come and have a seat. And please, play me the jingle."

"Okay, I guess no niceties this morning."

"What would you consider a nicety?" I say as I look over at her face. She's wearing her thick black glasses again, and her hair is up in a bun. She still looks beautiful, though.

"You just want me to sing the jangle?" She says.

"The jangle, the jingle, whatever you want to call it. I just hope it sounds good." I say, leaning back in my chair. She takes a deep breath and grabs her phone. "Now's not the time for texting, Sarah."

"I'm not about to text. I recorded a melody to go with the song." She says. "It's not like I could bring my keyboard in with me."

"Touche," I say, nodding. "Play it."

"Well, that's what I was about to do."

"Good," I say. She just stares at me for a couple of seconds and mumbles something under her breath. "What did you say?" I lean forward, crossing my arms.

"Nothing." She says batting her eyelashes at me and glaring.

"No, tell me what you said."

"I said that I can't believe that I slept with you. That you're a douche bag, and a jackass, and I don't appreciate the way that you-"

"The way that I what?" I say, raising a single eyebrow at her.

"Nothing." She says as her fingers touch the screen of her phone. "I found the music if you're ready."

"I've been ready," I say. "I've been waiting."

"I was only five minutes late. Please don't try and act like I was five hours late."

"You would keep me waiting five hours if you knew it wouldn't get you fired."

"No, I wouldn't." She says, though she smiles slightly and I know that's a lie.

My heart twitches for a second, but I ignore it. "I'm waiting."

"Fine." She says, and presses a button on her phone and closes her eyes. I study her for a couple of seconds as the melody plays. It's upbeat and fun, and I can already tell that it's going to be amazing. I don't know why she doesn't want to look at me as she sings, but there's something about observing her in her element that makes my heart soar just a little bit.

"You want to be a royal?" She sings. "You want to be a royal? Light up the lights, light up your life. Light up your every fantasy. Because if you want to be a royal, get Royal Lights. If you want to be a royal, get Royal Lights. If you want to, you want to, you want to be a royal, get Lord Chamber's Lights."

She pauses. Her eyes fly open and she looks at me. She looks apprehensive, and there's silence in the room as I just stare at her.

"Is that it?" I say.

"Yeah. You don't like it." She scrunches her nose. "I'm sorry. I thought it-"

"It's good," I say, smiling at her, "I think it's really good. I think Lord Chambers will love it."

"You think so?" Her eyes widen, and she looks happy. Happier than I've ever seen her before, and I wish she was smiling that way because of something she felt for me.

I ignore the thought immediately.

"It's good. You may or may not have some skill of a songwriter." I say, laughing. "You're a good copywriter."

"I guess that's why I work in copywriting." She says, laughing.

"You could be a singer as well. You have a beautiful voice."

"You're just saying that." She stares at me for a couple of seconds.

"I'm not just saying it. You've got a nice tone."

"Thank you." She is silent for a couple of seconds. "So what do we do next?"

"We call Lord Chambers," I say, "And ask him what he thinks, and if there's anything he wants to change."

"Oh, okay. He gets a say in that?"

"Not really," I say, shaking my head. "But we make him think he has a say."

"Oh," she wrinkles her nose. "I guess that works."

"Trust me," I say. "Even if he says he wants to change some stuff, he won't."

"What do you mean?"

"I mean, this is how the conversation will go. I'll say, "Hey, this is the jingle. What do you think?" He'll say, "Oh, it's amazing. There are just a couple of things I'd like to change. Then I'll say, "Oh, what you want to change? And he'll say, "Can I get back to you in a couple of days?"

She giggles.

"And I'll say, "Sure, take your time." And then I won't hear from him for a couple of days. And I'll be like, "Hey, do you have those revisions you wanted me to make?"

And he'll say, "Actually, I think it's pretty good."

"And I'll say, "Great."

"You don't know that's how it's going to go." She says, staring at me.

"I don't know that it's going to go exactly like that, but 95% of the time it goes like this. He's not a songwriter. He's not a musician. Any ideas that he has or thinks he has won't make sense once he thinks them through. This jingle sounds pretty damn good." I laugh. "Or are we calling it a jangle now?"

"We can call it whatever you want." She says, shaking her head. "I'm just glad that you like it."

"Did you think I wouldn't?"

"I don't know." She says. "I mean, things between us are..."

"Things are what?" I prod her to continue.

"I don't know. I'm just saying that I wasn't sure if you'd like it or not."

"I think it's great. I think you're an amazing songwriter. I mean, you've got a great voice. I just wouldn't dance so much, seeing as you're so clumsy."

"I'm not clumsy." She glares at me. "Trust me."

"I'm saying, it seems like you're kind of clumsy to me."

"I'm not."

"I'm just saying that it's a good thing that you're not a stripper trying to get up and down that pole. Because..." I pause and laugh at the look on her face.

"Excuse you. If I wanted to be a stripper, I could be." She says, glaring at me. "In fact, I could be the best stripper in all of the United States if I wanted to be."

"I don't think so," I say, laughing.

"I could be. I could work a pole. I've got rhythm, I've got moves." She says. "Just because you don't think I do, Ethan Rosser, doesn't mean I don't."

"Put your money where your mouth is," I say.

"What do you mean?"

"I mean, if you think you're so good, prove it."

"Prove it how?"

"Show me."

"Show you what?"

"I think, if you think that you're that great of a dancer and you can work a pole, I'll give you $20,000. If you show me a dance on a pole that is worthy of the best strip club in town, that is."

She stares at me for a few seconds. "$20,000?"

"Yep. No questions asked."

"And I don't have to do anything."

"Do anything like what?" I stare at her innocently. I mean, am I hoping that strip dance will lead to us fucking? Of course. But I'm not going to tell her that.

"I don't have to give you a lap dance or do anything kinky?"

"Nope. You just have to dance. And if I think it's worthy of 20 grand..."

"How do I know that you're going to be fair?"

"I'll be honest." I put my hands up. "I promise."

"Fine," She says. "I will show you that I'm the best dancer you've ever seen."

"Really?" I burst out laughing. "The best?"

"Yes," She glares at me. "I am fly."

"Okie dokie, Sarah. This I got to see."

"Well, fine. Come over tonight, 8:00 PM. And bring the 20 grand."

"Okay. It seems like you really want that money."

"Well," she says, "You offered it. And you don't seem to have faith in my dancing skills." She jumps up out of the chair and spins around, "But I'll have you know, I've been taking classes for the last six months and my teacher says that I am a natural."

She lifts her leg up and tries to touch her toes with her fingers. She doesn't quite make it, and I can see the small grimace on her face. This is going to be an interesting evening.

"And don't be expecting any funny stuff either, Ethan."

"Would I be?"

"Yeah, you would." She says. "Remember last night you fucked me in a storage room and-"

"And you loved it, don't even lie."

"It was fine." She says. "Nothing to write home about."

"Uh-huh," I wink at her. "That's why you were thinking about me all morning, right?" She stands there blushing, and we stare at each other. My heart races, and I realize that being around her makes me feel more alive than I ever have.

25

Sarah

Dear Diary,

I am going to die. Please don't miss me too much. You may visit me at the cemetery anytime. I cannot believe my luck. I guess I really wasn't joking when I said I was a hot mess.

Always yours, sunny and silly Sarah.

"Oh my gosh, Isabel," I whisper to my friend on the phone as I run around my apartment tidying up. "What did I do?"

"I do not know what you were thinking, Sarah," she says, and I can tell that there's a tone of amusement in her voice. "I thought you said you weren't that good yet."

"I mean, I'm not the best in the class, but I'm okay. At least that's what the teacher told me."

"Are you sure the teacher didn't tell you that because she wants to make more money from you?"

I think back to my pole dancing lessons and how the teacher had told me I was one of the best in the class. I bite down on my lower lip because I know what Isabel is saying is correct. I'm not the worst in the class, but that's because the worst woman in the class can't even get up the pole at all.

"Okay. You might be a little bit right, but that's not going to help me right now because he's coming over and I think he'll be here within an hour."

"I mean, who knows? Maybe he will like your moves," Isabel says doubtfully. "Though, I'm very confused as to why you invited your boss over, seeing as..."

"Not now," I glare into the phone and sigh. "Do not ask me why I invited Ethan over."

"I mean, I know why you invited Ethan over," Isabel giggles. "Because you love him, because you want to do him," she sings and I wrinkle my nose.

"I do not love him. Are you crazy?"

"I was just joking, but I think you're being very defensive right now." She pauses. "You're not developing feelings for this douche bag, are you?"

"Would I develop feelings for a douche bag?"

"Yes," she says adamantly. "Yes, you would."

"I know. Okay, so there's something that I have to admit."

"Oh my gosh. Please do not tell me you're in love with this man." She groans. "If you think you're in love with him, you need to send him a message and tell him to go home and not bother coming over."

"I'm not in love with him. I mean, I think he's funny and I think he's cute and you know I have for a long time."

"Yeah, but that was fine when he was ignoring you," she says. "Because then it was just a fantasy in your head. Now he's been inside of you. That means something."

I groan loudly. "Why do I cringe every time you say that?"

"I don't know," she says, laughing. "I mean, how old are you if you cringe when I say he was inside of you?"

"I think I could be 60 or 70 and I would still be cringing thinking about that."

"You weren't cringing when he was doing you though."

"Oh my gosh, Isabel," I scream at her and she bursts out laughing.

"I'm glad I can make you laugh. I'm just trying to lighten the mood for you."

"Should I just tell him I was joking?"

"No. You need that 20 grand, right?"

"Of course I need 20 grand. Don't you need 20 grand?"

"Yes, and if you want to send him over to my house, I'll give him a lap dance for 20 grand."

"Isabel." I frown. "You're joking, right?"

"Uh-oh, are you getting a little bit jealous?"

"No. Why would I be jealous?"

"Because you don't want me giving your man a lap dance."

"He's not my man," I say. I pause as I hear my phone pinging. "Hold on. I just got a message." I open my texts and freeze. "It's Ethan and he says he's 15 minutes away."

"Shit."

"Oh my gosh. I'm about to hyperventilate, Isabel," I groan. "He's going to be here in 15 minutes."

"Well, is everything ready?"

"I mean, my place is as clean as it's going to be. The pole is up. I just need to shave my legs one more time."

"What do you mean you need to shave your legs one more time?"

"Well, I shaved yesterday, but you know hair grows in quickly and I don't want to be upside down and hairs poking out where they shouldn't be."

"Oh my gosh, Sarah," she laughs. "You really are a hot mess, aren't you?"

"Thank you. That makes me feel amazing."

"You've got this. Trust me, he's most probably not even going to be paying attention to your dancing because he's going to be looking at you and you're going to be looking so hot. He's just going to want you."

"Well, he knows that he's going to be hands off because..."

"Because what," she asks.

"Because he's not coming over to bang me."

"Okay, good luck with that."

"What? I'm serious."

"I know you're serious, but the other day you were telling me you never wanted to see him again and he was a jackass, and now he's coming over to your place so you can do some sort of pole dance for him? Like, girl, what is going on?"

"20 grand is what's going on, and he said he's going to bring cash."

"Ooh, 20 grand in cash sounds like a pretty cool thing." She pauses. "If you get it, will you show me?"

"Will I show you what? The pole dance?"

"No." She makes a vomiting sound. "I don't want to see you pole dancing, but I do want to see 20 grand in cash."

"Fine," I say. "When I get it, I will show you. Anyway, I got to go. I'll speak to you later."

"Okay. Good luck, I love you.."

I hang up the phone and quickly rush to the bathroom so I can do a dry shave. I take a deep breath and then put on the outfit I'd had planned. It was a leotard from my tap dancing days and it was slightly too tight. I grab a tutu and wrap it around my waist. If I'm going to be hanging upside down, I do not want my vagina lips hanging out for any reason.

The doorbell rings and I freeze. It's only been 10 minutes. I take a deep breath and head towards the door. Ethan is standing there with a cocky smirk on his face. I stare into his blue eyes.

"You're early," I say.

"Well, much better than being late." He pushes past me and walks into the apartment. "So are you ready to earn that money?" He holds up his briefcase and I just stare at him as I close the door.

"Really, Ethan?"

"What?" He says, looking at me with a confused expression.

"Earn that money? Why don't you just say you want to make it rain on me?"

"I mean, if you want me to, I can throw dollars on you as you're moving up and down that pole."

I lick my lips nervously. I don't know about moving up and down the pole. I can barely get up and do a spin, but I'm not about to tell him that.

"Anyway," I say. "I just want you to understand one thing."

"Yes? What is that?"

"Nothing is going down tonight. This isn't a precursor to sex. This isn't a precursor to a lap dance. This isn't a precursor to any sort of dirty thing that might be in your mind right now."

"I know," he says, looking around my apartment. "We already determined that it was just to see the moves of the best pole dancer in New York City." He smiles at me widely. "I am really excited to see how the best performs."

I narrow my eyes as I stare at him. Why do I have a feeling that he knows that I'm not the best? Maybe because he's seen me dancing on a table and nearly fall, but I'm not going to even acknowledge that.

"You may have a seat on the couch over there," I say.

"Thank you," he says as he sits down. "So are we just going to get right to it or..."

"I mean, that's why you're here, right?"

He smirks. "No drink or anything?"

"What do you mean or anything?"

"I don't know. I know you love Chinese food. I figure maybe you might've ordered some."

"Oh, are you hungry?" I say quickly. "I can get some crackers and cheese for you if you want."

He stares at me for a couple of seconds and shakes his head. "No, but thank you for the offer."

"Would you like something to drink? I have a bottle of wine. I think I have a Merlot and I have a couple of ciders."

"Any beer?"

"No." I shake my head. "I don't really buy beer. I'm not really a beer girl. I mean, I'll drink it sometimes, but..." I pause as I realize I'm mumbling. "Anyway. You don't care about that. Cider or wine for alcohol or orange juice or water."

"I will have a cider, please," he says, leaning back and looking around. "Your place is really nice."

"It's small. Nothing like yours."

"But it's very well decorated."

"Thanks," I say, smiling at him. "I like to think that I could have been an interior decorator in another life."

"Is that something you have interest in?" He says as I head over to the fridge to grab him a cider.

"Oh, no. I mean I like it, but I could never be a professional." I shake my head as I head back with the cider. "Why?"

"Oh, I was just wondering if that was something you were interested in pursuing. You know we have a lot of different avenues and opportunities at the company."

"I know," I say. "But I'm more interested in the writing part, you know, and music."

"I know," he says. "Your jingle was amazing."

"It was okay," I say. "Have we heard anything from Lord Chambers yet?"

He smirks. "Actually, yes. It was like I said, he loved it but wanted to make some changes."

"Oh, what change?" I ask.

"He said he'll let me know. I told you."

"I guess you are the king of knowing all things, huh?"

"Yeah. I think so." He smirks.

I roll my eyes, then head to my phone and turn on my small Bose speaker. "I'm going to dim the lights," I say. "And play some music and then get going if that's okay."

"Perfect," he says. "I'm excited to see you dance."

I take a deep breath and smile and go to my phone and scroll through my music. I'm not even sure what I should perform to. I think about doing Beyonce's new country music song, but the beat won't exactly go with what I have in mind. I then go to Ed Sheeran, but I know that's not going to work. I finally settle on a Lil Wayne song from back in the day. I press play and music fills my apartment.

"Okay," he nods his head. "I feel like I'm at the club."

"Uh-huh," I say, as I head towards the pole.

I close my eyes for a couple of seconds and then

count down in my head, 5, 4, 3, 2, 1. I grab a hold of the pole and twirl around. I can see that Ethan is staring at me intently. I feel powerful. I feel sexy. I love this feeling. I love dancing. I love being admired, especially by someone like Ethan.

I think about what Isabel had said on the phone about my feelings for him, about if I'm falling in love and it's weird because I know it's way too soon to be falling in love. Just because we slept together didn't mean anything, but I definitely have strong feelings for him and I definitely feel a connection.

I can hear Ethan tapping his foot against the floor and I try not to look over at him. I know I'll feel intimidated. Instead, I lift a leg and wrap it around the pole and start making my way up. I'm singing along to the song to try and keep in beat. I'm having difficulty sliding up. I try to remember what my teacher said. I try to be sexy. I try to put on the best show that I can.

As I spin around, I look over at Ethan and I see his hands on his pants and for a few seconds I think he's unzipping himself. He's not about to play with himself, is he? I twist my neck to look at him better and I'm not sure what happens, but the next thing I know, I'm sliding down and falling and my head has hit the ground.

"Ow," I cry out.

I can hear Ethan chuckling as he jumps up. "Oh my gosh. Are you okay?" He says, as he hurries over to me. There's a look of concern on his face.

"Were you about to jack off?" I accuse him as my head starts pounding.

He looks down at me in confusion. "What?"

"I saw your hands on your pants and..."

"I was just smoothing my pants down," he says. "Are you crazy? Do you think I'm some sort of creep? I'm not going to jack off as you try to dance on a pole. Really, Sarah, you think that of me?"

"I don't know. I just..." I press my lips together. I have not felt this embarrassed in a long time. And that's saying a lot.

"Sarah, are you..." He kneels down then and looks at me. "Oh fuck," he says as he touches the side of my face gingerly. His expression changes to one of worry.

"What? What is it?"

"You're bleeding," he says. "You've hit your head harder than you thought."

"Oh, no," I groan. "I can't believe this."

"You're going to have to go to the hospital."

"No," I say quickly. "I'll be fine." I moan as he reaches below me and picks me up. "What are you doing?"

"I'm taking you to the hospital," he says. "I don't care what you have to say. You've just fallen and hit your head and now you're bleeding." He sighs. "I guess I was correct when I said you were clumsy."

"I'm not clumsy," I moan. "I..."

"Sarah, stop arguing with me." He sighs. "I knew this was not a good idea."

"What do you mean you knew this wasn't a good idea?" My head pounds. "Ow, I think I've got a headache."

"I hope that's all it is," he says, staring down at me.

"I will say, you look very sexy, and the beginning of the dance started well, but overall I'm going to give you a four out of 10." He chuckles. "Definitely not the best pole dancer in New York City."

"Thanks a lot, Ethan. Thanks for nothing."

"I'm just saying," he says, as he heads towards the door. "But you know what?"

"What?" I glare at him.

"Let's just get you taken care of," he says quickly. "I want to make sure everything's okay." There's worry in his tone. "Let me take care of you. Okay, Sarah?"

"Fine," I mumble. I'm surprised he's being so caring and I hate how much I love it.

26

Ethan

"I'm fine, Ethan." Sarah squeals in my arms, as I take her out to the street.

"Stop squirming," I say, looking down into her pale, panicked face.

My heart is racing as I stare at the blood on the side of her temple. I really hope that she doesn't have a concussion. I really hope that she hasn't seriously injured herself. My driver pulls up about a minute later, and Sarah looks at me in confusion.

"Wait, what? How?"

"I alerted him." I smile at her.

She doesn't know that I have a button that I press that immediately alerts him to come to the front.

"How did you do that? Was it magic?"

"Would you believe me if I said that it was?" I ask, and she rolls her eyes. I laugh slightly.

My driver jumps out and heads over to us. "Is everything okay, Mr. Rosser?" There's a concerned look on his face.

"She hit her head," I nod. "We're going to take her to the emergency room."

"Yes, sir." He says, opening the back door.

I place her down onto the back seat, close the door behind me, and then walk over to the other side and slide in.

She's sitting up now and glaring at me. "This is really too much, I'm fine."

"You're not fine. You fell and you hit your head and it's bleeding."

"It's just a little wound." She touches the side of her head, and looks down at her fingers at the deep red blood. "Ew." She makes a face. "It's really bleeding, huh?"

"That's what I said," I say, shifting over to her.

She glares at me and closes her eyes. I grab her hand and squeeze.

"Don't close your eyes."

"What? You're so bossy."

"Sarah, listen to me. I don't want you to close your eyes, because if you did get a concussion, I don't want anything bad happening."

"Bad like what?" She says, an attitude in her voice.

"I don't know, like you going into a coma or something."

"It's not that serious, dude."

"Well, I hope not, but better safe than sorry."

"You do not have to take me to the hospital, you really-"

"I do," I say. "I'm not just going to let you go to sleep and possibly not wake up tomorrow."

"Would you care?" She asks, and I stare at her for a couple of seconds.

"What do you think?"

"I mean, I guess you'd be disappointed because you never got to see me pole dancing."

"I don't give a fuck about you pole dancing," I say as the car starts moving.

"Okay, well, tell me this."

"Yes?" I ask her.

"Were you hoping for a lap dance?"

My lips twitch slightly as I stare at her face. "What do you think?"

"I think you were hoping for a lap dance. I think that you were hoping that you were going to get laid tonight."

"Weren't you hoping for the same thing?" I ask her, chuckling slightly.

"No, I already told you that that wasn't going to happen."

"I know that's what you said, but you were on a pole." I stare at her. "In a very skimpy outfit." I lick my lips. "And let's just say I think something may have gone down after you made your twenty grand."

"So you totally came to have sex with me tonight. Is that the only reason you came?"

"I didn't actually come though, did I?" I wink at her, and she groans.

"You're disgusting."

"I don't think I'm disgusting, and I don't think you think I'm disgusting. I mean..." I pause.

"What?" She says.

"Nothing. You're still recovering, I don't want to get you all angry and upset."

"I'm not angry and I'm not upset. I think you should just say it as it is."

"What do you want me to say, Sarah? Do you want me to say that I find you very attractive? Do you want me to say that I think you've got a mouth on you? Do you want me to say that I don't think you're the best dancer in the world, and that you should not quit your day job to take up stripping."

"So what, you don't think I'm a good stripper?" She glares at me.

"I mean, I do not know how to answer that without you getting mad."

Her lips tremble slightly. "Fine, you don't have to answer that."

"I mean, I'd love to see you strip, and I don't care if you're good or not," I say. "I like you naked either way."

"You just want me to be naked, period."

"Am I a bad person if I say yes, I do like to have you naked? It's been more than five times now, so maybe we can do away with that rule."

"Maybe I don't want to do away with that rule." She says. "Maybe I am fine with it. Maybe I don't want to sleep with you more than five times."

"I don't think that's quite true."

"Why, because you're so irresistible."

"I don't know, am I irresistible?" I run a finger down her arm, and she giggles slightly.

"You're totally resistible, Ethan. Trust me."

"Ah, shucks," I say, laughing.

The car stops and I look out and see that we've arrived at the emergency room.

"Good. Wait here. Stay where you are."

"I can get out by myself."

"No." I'm stern now. "Stay where you are. I'm going to get a wheelchair, and I will push you in."

"I do not need to be pushed in, Ethan, I-"

"Please, Sarah." I say softly. "Let me take care of you, at least until we make sure you're okay."

"I'll be fine." She says. "Thank you for caring, but-"

"But nothing," I say as I jump out of the car and rush to the interior of the building. "I need a wheelchair, stat, my..." I pause, not knowing what to call her. "I just need a wheelchair."

One of the nurses points to the corner of the room, and I grab a wheelchair and hurry back out. Sarah is still sitting in the backseat, thankfully. I open the door and reach in to pick her up.

"Please, you do not need to do this. It's so embarrassing." She says, though I can tell she's slightly nervous. Her eyes seem like they're tired, and she gives me a look. "Do you think I'm okay?"

"I hope so," I say. "I really hope so."

I lift her up and put her into the wheelchair, and then I rush her in.

"She needs to be seen immediately," I say, ignoring the sounds of crying and howls of pain from the other people.

"What seems to be the issue?" The nurse behind the counter says.

"She fell hard, cracked her head. I'm nervous that she has a concussion."

The nurse stares down at Sarah and her skimpy outfit and makes a face.

"What was going on?"

"Does it matter what was going on?" I glare at her. "I'm Ethan Rosser, CEO of Rosser International."

"Okay, and?" She says, rolling her eyes.

"And I'm a trustee of the hospital. Last year, I donated fifteen million."

She bites down on her lower lip. "We can get you into a room. I'll call one of the doctors to come and see you."

"Sounds good. Which room?"

She lets out a deep sigh. "Follow me."

I push Sarah in the wheelchair behind her, and then we enter a room.

"I'll be right back." The nurse says.

Sarah looks at me and shakes her head. "You didn't have to pull strings to get me taken care of right away. I know this is an emergency room. I know they most probably have more important cases that they have to deal with, and-"

"This is one of the perks of being rich," I say. "You get taken care of faster."

"But that's not fair." She says. "It's-"

"I know it's not fair, it fucking sucks and I feel bad about it, but we don't know how badly you hit your head, Sarah. I'm not going to sit there waiting with everyone else when I know I can get you to the front of the line." I take a deep breath. "I'm worried, okay? I just need to make sure you're okay."

She stares at me for a couple of seconds and nods. My phone starts ringing and I look at it. It's my mom. I try not to roll my eyes as I put it back in my pocket.

"You can answer that." She says.

"No, I need to watch over for you. I need to-"

"Please, take the call." She shakes her head. "I'm sure a doctor will be in here soon."

"Okay, I'll be right back."

I step out of the room and call my mom back.

"Hey, mom, what's going on?" I ask her. I know my voice is gruff, but I can't help it. If she's asking me for more money or to go on some sort of trip, I will lose it.

"Hey, Ethan, I'm so sorry to disturb you." She stops, and I pause, because my mom has never been sorry about anything.

"What's going on, mom? Is everything okay? Are you okay?"

For a few minutes, I worry that she's going to tell me that she has cancer or something. I lean against the wall. This is the last thing that I need. I can feel my heart trembling slightly as I wait for her to answer.

"Your dad hasn't been home in three days." Her voice is nervous. "I'm worried about him. I've been calling and calling, and now it's just going to voicemail."

"What do you mean he hasn't been home in three days? Do you know where he was going? Do you-"

"I don't know. I'm so sorry to disturb you, Ethan. I know that you're busy, I know that you've got other things to worry about, but I'm nervous. He's never not called before."

"Have you tried to figure out where he could be located? Have you tracked his GPS?"

"What are you talking about?"

Like on his phone, have you done Find My Phone? I know you have iPhones, I got them for you."

"I don't even know what that is, Ethan."

I can tell that she's emotionally spent.

"Okay, let me see what's going on." I say. "I'll call you back."

"Okay. Is everything okay with you?"

"I'm fine."

"Where are you? There's a lot of noise in the background."

"I'm at the emergency room."

"Oh my gosh, Ethan, what's going on? Why didn't you call me?" She starts getting loud.

"Mom, I'm okay. A friend of mine is here."

"Not Jackson?" She says.

"No, a female friend."

There's a long silence on the phone.

"A female friend?" She says. "Like a girlfriend?"

"No, no, she's not my girlfriend, she... I'll call you back, mom, okay?"

I hang up before she can say anything else, and I just stare at the phone. Who is Sarah to me? She's not my girlfriend, I'm not looking for a girlfriend, but she's no longer just my employee, she's no longer just the nerdy woman that works for me. I feel more for her than that, and it's not just because we slept together. I have feelings for her, I'm worried about her, I'm concerned about her, and I get jealous when she flirts with other men. I don't know what it means, and I don't have time to think about it. I quickly call my granddad and wait for it to go to voicemail. I'm pretty certain he's in bed already. Surprisingly, he answers the phone.

"Ethan, what's going on?"

"Have you heard from dad?" I ask, knowing that he'll be straightforward with me.

"Your mom called?"

"Yeah, mom called. She's nervous. She hasn't heard from him."

"Your dad's not doing well." He says with a sigh.

"What's going on?"

"You're going to be a brother."

"What?"

"You're going to be a brother."

"But mom can't get pregnant, she..." And then it dawns on me what he's saying. "He cheated again?"

My granddad sighs. "I don't know what we did wrong. I don't know how I could have made this any different, but yeah, he's not in a good place. He doesn't know how to tell your mom.

"Fuckin' A. Sorry." I say quickly. I hate swearing in front of my grandparents.

"I understand, Ethan. Can you come over? Can you

speak to him?"

"No, not right now."

"Oh." He sounds surprised. "Late night at work?"

"No, something more important than that. I'll be there tomorrow though."

I hang up and just stare at the phone for a couple of seconds. I am quite literally in disbelief. I'm too old to have a new sibling born. My dad is too old to be a dad again. He wasn't even a good dad to me.

"Fuck it." I say, as I head back towards the room.

I'm grateful to see a doctor there with Sarah. He looks up at me and nods.

"Mr. Rosser?"

"Yes?" I say. "How is she?"

"So far, it looks good. It looks like not too much damage."

"She's bleeding though."

"A slight cut by the ear." He says. "We'll run some more tests and check everything, and I want to make sure that you don't have a bad headache tomorrow, but I think you should be okay."

He looks at me. "Will you be able to ensure that she's not alone tonight?"

"Of course." .

"No." Sarah says. "I'm fine, I can be by myself."

"No, I will be with you." I stare at her.

"No, Ethan, you-"

"I will be with you. You can't be alone."

"I can go to Isabel's. I can go to-"

"Sarah." I cut her off, and she sighs.

"Fine."

"I want to make sure you're okay."

"Fine." She says, and looks down, exhausted, and suddenly I realized just how young she looks, and how beautiful, and how vulnerable, and my heart constricts, because I feel something that I don't think I've ever felt before in my life, and I don't even want to question what it is.

About an hour later, we're leaving the hospital, and my driver takes us back to her place.

"You sure you don't want to go to mine?"

"I'm sure." She says. "I know my place is small, but-"

"It's fine, I like it." We get into her apartment and she yawns.

"I'm sorry, I'm just really tired right now."

"It's okay. You can go to sleep, and I'll just do some work, and when you wake up in the morning, we'll grab breakfast, and I'll make sure that you're okay."

"It's very sweet of you to be here." She says softly. Thank you. You really didn't have to stay."

"I know, but I wanted to, Sarah. I really wanted to."

She heads to her bedroom and lies down, and I pace back and forth along the corridor for a couple of minutes, gripping my phone, thinking about calling my dad and speaking to him, asking him how he could cheat on mom and not use protection, but I'm spent. I don't really know what to say.

I head towards Sarah's bedroom to see if she wants something to drink or eat, but she's already fast asleep. I go over and take a seat on the mattress and look down at her. She looks so innocent, so sweet. I watch her stomach rise and fall. I'm grateful that she's okay. I'm grateful to be here with her. I'm grateful to feel something other than lust for business. She's awakened something in me that I didn't even realize had been asleep.

As I sit there and stare at her sleeping, I remember a time when I was seven years old, when my parents had been fighting and my dad had stormed out in the middle of the night. I'd been in bed reading a book, and when he'd left, I'd been thankful that the shouting would stop. I remember waking up at about five o'clock in the morning, and creeping along the corridor to my mom's room, and just standing outside the door listening to her crying for what felt like hours. I remember feeling so alone and cold as I watched her, and then eventually, she fell asleep. I opened the doors and I crept inside, and I remember I watched her sleeping, because I wanted to make sure she was still alive, I wanted to make sure that nothing would ever happen to her.

And as she lay there, I remember her whispering my name in her sleep. "I love you, my darling Ethan. I will never leave, because I love you."

And I remember then how I felt. How I felt guilty and sad, but how I loved her, how I realized she loved me more than life itself, how I realized that I didn't blame her for being weak anymore. I remember creeping into her bed and waking up hours later to her kissing me and hugging me close.

"I love you." She'd said. "I'll always have you, my darling." And I felt warm and protected, and like I never wanted to let her go.

"Ethan." Sarah mumbles in her sleep, and I freeze. "Oh, Ethan." She says, and she's smiling now. I wonder what she's thinking about. "You're not so bad, Ethan." She says, and my heart surges.

I stand up and I walk towards the door, I'm going to go and sleep on the couch, but then I stop. I turn back around and walk towards the bed, and I take my shoes off and lie down next to her. I need to be near her, just to make sure she's okay, that if she needs something, I'll hear her. I lie back down and stare up at the ceiling and wonder what all these emotions mean. I wonder if my mom knows that my dad has gotten someone else pregnant. I wonder if it will break her yet again. I wonder if Sarah knows that we have something that makes me uncomfortable, but also alive for the very first time. I turn to the side and put my arm around her softly, and then before I know it, I'm falling asleep.

A few hours later, I wake up, and Sarah's still sleeping, but she's fully embraced by me. She moans slightly as my hand moves from her stomach, and I realize that she's enjoying the warmth of my body against hers. I realize that she means something real to me, she's worming her way into my heart, and that scares me. I'm not sure what to think or what to do. I don't want to think about it, it's an uncomfortable feeling, and yet, as I close my eyes to fall asleep again, I know that it's the best feeling I've had in a really long time. It's a peaceful, sweet, loving feeling, and I never want to let it go, I never want it to leave me.

27

Sarah

Dear Diary,
I'm writing this from heaven. That is all. My heart is broken. Sad Sarah.

My head is pounding slightly as I wake up. I try to stretch, but I feel that I'm encumbered by something. My eyes open slowly and I realize that Ethan is here in the bed with me. I turn my head over to the side and I gasp as I see that he's awake and staring at me.

"Hey, how are you feeling this morning?" he asks, a look of concern in his face.

I remember the previous evening and how I danced for him and acted the fool, and fallen and bumped my head. How he'd rushed me to the hospital and stayed with me. How he'd brought me back, and here he was still with me.

My heart thuds as I stare at him. "I've seen better days," I say, my head pounding slightly. "I think that I should eat something." I lick my lips. My mouth is dry.

"Would you like some water?" he asks, and I nod slowly. He reaches behind him and grabs the water bottle and hands it to me.

"Thank you," I say, as I open it and take a sip.

My dry throat welcomes the water and I just stare as he stares at me. It's a weird feeling waking up with him in my bed. I don't really know what it means. I don't really know why he's been so concerned, but I like it. It makes me feel closer to him. It makes me feel loved, which is something I haven't felt in a really long time.

"You scared me last night," he says.

"Really? I'm okay, though. The doctor said I'll be fine. I just nicked my ear on something." I roll my eyes. "Just my luck."

"You really should think about..." He pauses and his lips twitch.

"I should really think about what?" I say. "If you're going to diss my dancing..."

"Would I do such a thing?" he says. "I think you're an amazing dancer."

"Liar," I giggle. "I know I'm not that great."

"No, you're better than great," he says. He reaches over and touches my forehead, and then brushes my hair back. "You have really beautiful eyes. Did you know that, Sarah?"

"Really?" I blink at him. "Thank you."

"You're welcome," he says. "You have a really beautiful face as well and a beautiful nose." He kisses the tip of my nose. "And beautiful lips." He kisses my lips. "And a beautiful chin." He kisses my chin. "And a..."

"If you say a beautiful breast or pussy, I'm going to slap you," I say, laughing.

"What does that mean?" He says, chuckling. "You don't want me to suck on your boobs or lick your pussy?"

I stare at him with wide eyes.

"Or is it too early for that? Do you not feel good enough for that?"

"Ethan," I say. "I literally just woke up."

"And?" He says, biting down on his lower lip. "Are you just feeling too sick to be treated well?"

"What do you mean by treated well?" I ask him chuckling.

"I mean, loved on."

My heart races at his choice of words. Is he hinting to me that he likes me like that?

"Why? What are you offering?"

"I'm offering to make you feel good," he says. He shifts slightly and my legs move to the side. I feel his hard cock next to my knee and I rub back and forth gently. "Fuck. You are a tease, aren't you?"

"I don't try to be a tease," I giggle, as he pulls me into his arms and kisses me passionately. I moan slightly as I press my body into his and run my fingers through his hair.

"You always make me feel alive, Sarah," he says, as he runs his fingers down my back. "You love to challenge me, don't you?"

"I don't know about that. This time last month you

didn't even know I existed, and if you'd ever noticed me, it was just as the nerdy woman that worked in the copywriting department. You didn't even know my name."

"Perhaps that's true, but I don't know the names of many people that work for me. But trust me, from that night I saw you dancing on that table, I knew."

"You knew what?" I asked, wondering if he's going to tell me that he knew he was in love with me. That he'd fallen for me at first sight, that he never wanted to let me go. I know I'm being ridiculous hoping for that, but I watch a lot of romance movies. I read romance books, and I even knew a couple of people that had fallen in love at first sight. Why can't it happen for me?

"I knew that you were a sexy, sexy woman," he says.

I feel slightly deflated by his words, but oddly still turned on. "You did now?" I say, touching the side of his face. "Well, I'll have you know that I always knew that you were handsome."

"Oh yeah?"

"Yep," I say. "Even when you didn't recognize me."

"So did you write that ad because you wanted me?"

"I'd already had you," I say. "Well, not technically, but..."

"But what?" He moves back and stares in my face. "Have you had dirty dreams about me?"

"I plead the fifth."

"We're not in court. Tell me, have you had dirty dreams about me?"

"I may or may not have had a dream of us making wild, passionate love on a beach in the Caribbean before you have even said a word to me. Yes." I blush slightly. "Now judge me all you want."

"I'm not judging you. I think I kind of like that," he says. "It makes me even hotter."

"Really?"

"Yeah. So you've really been digging me, haven't you?"

"Oh my gosh. You're going to have such a big head now. I'm not trying to give you a bigger ego than you already have."

"Too late," he chuckles, as he slides his hand up the back of my shirt. "I want to make love to you, Sarah," he says, as he kisses the side of my neck. "And I don't know if you're up for it right now. I don't know if you need to shower, or if you want to sleep, or if you want to have breakfast or you just want to rest, but..."

"I want you too, Ethan," I say.

He growls as he pulls off my outfit, and I reach over and pull off his shirt. I touch his naked chest as he undoes my bra and kisses down my collarbone. I feel his lips on my nipple and I moan slightly as I dig my nails into his back.

"You're so fucking hot. You know that, Sarah?"

"Is that all I am to you?" I tease him as he kisses down my stomach. His tongue licks my belly button and I shiver slightly.

"No," he says. "You're more to me than a quick fuck. You know that, right?"

"How am I supposed to know that?" I say, teasing him some more as he grabs my shorts and my panties and pulls them down.

"Well," he says, and bites down on his lower lip.

"Well what?" I ask.

"I don't know that I'm ready to say just yet." He glances at me and I know in my heart of hearts that he loves me and that he just doesn't know how to say it.

"Fuck me," I say softly, reaching up and grabbing the hair at the nape of his neck. "Fuck me now."

"So demanding," he grunts.

I watch as he pulls off his pants, his fingers moving up and down on his cock, making him harder and harder. He opens my legs and runs two fingers down my slit and my body starts trembling.

"You're so fucking hot," he says, as he positions his and slowly thrusts inside of me. He looks down into my eyes and kisses my lips. "I love being inside of you," he says, growling and I reach up and squeeze his ass cheeks and wrap my legs around his waist.

"I love you being inside of me as well, Ethan," I groan as he moves faster and faster and I can feel my breasts bouncing up and down.

"Fuck," he says. "Why does this feel so good? It's never felt like this before for me," he says, as he increases his pace.

"It's never felt like this for me either," I say, looking up at him.

His eyes are glowing as he stares down at me. There's a smile on his face and I can feel my heart racing. I reach up and touch his chest and I can feel his heart racing too.

"Oh, yes," he grunts. "Oh fuck," he says as he clasps my hands to his. "Oh, Sarah. Yes."

"Me too," I say loudly, my lips parted as I stare at him. I just can't hold it in anymore.

"You too?" He says, leaning down and kissing my lips and then my cheek.

"I love you, Ethan. I love you, too. I'm falling for you. Maybe I've already fallen for you, but..."

"Fuck," he says, as he stills slightly and then slams into me hard two more times.

He pulls out and I feel him cumming all over my stomach.

"Fuck," he says again.

"It's okay," I giggle, thinking he's saying the words because I haven't cum yet. "You can get hard again and fuck me again until I cum. I don't always have to cum before you."

He rolls onto his back and I see that he's closed his eyes. I frown slightly as I glance over at him.

"Ethan?"

He opens his eyes slowly and glances at me. There's a bleak look in them. "I don't love you, Sarah. I already told you I'm not looking for an emotional entanglement right now." He jumps up and grabs his top and boxers as my heart breaks. "Look, I'm sorry. I got to go. Will you be okay?"

"I'm fine," I say, as coldness fills me.

I'm not going to cry. Not in front of him. I'm not going to let him see how hurt I am.

"Look, I'm sorry. We can talk later if you want, but..."

"No, it's fine. Go," I say. "I was just saying that because we were making love and my head is still pounding and I wasn't in my right mind. I don't really love you. I was just..." I bite down on my lower lip and turn away from him. "You should go."

"Sarah, I..."

"It doesn't matter. You know I'm a hot mess. You know I'm emotional. It's fine. Go."

He walks to the door, stops and looks back at me. I turn over and look at him. "Please text me or call me if you need anything," he says. "Okay?"

I nod and don't respond. He sighs and walks out the door. I close my eyes as I wait for him to leave. Once I hear my apartment door closing, I burst into tears. I can't believe I told him I love him. I really am an idiot. I can't believe that he reacted that way. I can't believe that I got it so wrong.

My heart feels like it's never going to be the same, and I just don't even trust the feelings in my brain or my head. How could he have looked at me with such love when obviously he felt nothing close to it?

28

Ethan

Three weeks later.

"So I've been going over the numbers and I think that we're in a really great spot," Jackson says, but I'm barely able to concentrate on the words coming out of his mouth. "Hey, Ethan, are you listening to me?" He asks, and I put my pen down.

"Sorry, I was distracted. I was just thinking about what Lord Chambers said about..."

"No you weren't," Jackson says, leaning back in his chair and shaking his head.

"Sorry. What?"

"No, you weren't thinking about anything Lord Chambers has to say."

"What are you talking about?"

"You're thinking about Sarah from copywriting."

"No, I'm not."

"Sure you're not. You're not thinking about if she's going to come back to the company?"

"I don't know what you're talking about, Jackson."

"So you're not concerned whatsoever about the fact that Sarah has not been into work for three weeks?"

"She said she had a sick family member."

"She told you this directly?"

"No, she told HR she needed to take some time off because she needed to visit with some family. She asked how many days off she had and I told HR to let her know that she could take off for as long as she wanted and it would be paid."

"Must be nice," Jackson says, smirking.

"What? We are a family oriented company and..."

"And so what happened between the two of you?"

He stares at me for a couple of seconds and I just shake my head. I feel sick to my stomach. I don't even know how to tell him what happened. I don't even know how to process it myself. When she told me she loved me, something in me had ignited and then deflated, because I just didn't know if I was capable of handling emotions like that. I just didn't know if I was capable of committing to someone. I didn't know if I was capable of love.

"Hey, you okay, Ethan?" Jackson looks worried. "I know I tease you, but what really happened with Sarah?"

"She told me she loved me." I look at him and make a face.

"Whoa. She really is a hot mess, isn't she?" He says,

shaking his head. "I cannot believe she said that to you. She barely knows you."

"Exactly," I say. "What is going on?"

"How do you feel about her?" He asks.

"What do you mean how do I feel about her?"

"I mean, even I've noticed that you are different."

"How am I different?"

"I don't know. You're edgy. You are bitching and moaning. You're not paying attention. You haven't asked me once in the last couple of weeks what our profit margin is on our last investment or what..."

"Look, I just don't have time for this right now."

"It's okay if you're falling for her. You don't have to hide it from me."

"I'm not falling for her. I just... Fine. I don't know what I feel for her. I like being around her. She's fun. She's different. She's quirky. Yeah, but I just cannot commit to anything. I cannot..." I sigh. "You know what's going on with my parents. It's just a lot. My dad and my mom had the most fucked up relationship and I saw what it did to her and now he's having another baby and it's just not good. Relationships and love suck? They just..." I pause. "I'm not even making sense, am I?"

"I get it," Jackson says. "You're scared to commit. You're scared to give your heart and you're scared to accept love because you see how twisted it can be. I understand that."

"I know. I just feel bad that she's not talking to me and I want to see her, and I want to talk to her, and I want to apologize. What if she just never talks to me again?"

"How would that make you feel?" He asks.

"Like fucking shit. I want to see her. Do you know how hard it's been?"

"What, to not call her?"

"No, I've been calling her. She won't answer."

"Did you leave a voicemail?"

"No, I didn't leave a voicemail because it never went to voicemail."

"Oh," he says, his eyes wide.

"What do you mean oh?"

"She blocked you, dude."

"What? What do you mean she blocked me?"

"If you're calling her and it's not going to voicemail, it means she blocked you."

"Fuck. She blocked me. She hates me."

"Or maybe she just loves you so much that it hurts and she couldn't deal with the fact that you might call her and talk some bullshit to her."

"Fuck., I screwed this up, didn't I?"

"Depends," he says.

"On what?" I ask.

"If you do love her."

"I barely know her. I..."

"Ethan."

"Yeah?"

"Let's be honest here."

"I'm always honest."

"Do you think that you love her?"

"What do you mean do I think that I love her?"

"Do you think that..." He pauses as we hear a knock on the door.

"Yeah," I call out.

Edith opens it. "Hi, Ethan?" She looks hesitant.

"Yeah. What is it?"

"Your mom's here."

"My mom?" I jump up. Jackson looks surprised.

"Yeah. Can I let her in?"

"Sure," I say, rushing to the door.

My mom walks in and I feel nervous. Is she about to have another nervous breakdown?

"Mom, is everything okay? Is dad okay? Is..."

"I'm fine," she says, walking in, a bright smile on her face. "You look handsome."

"Thanks." I'm surprised by her words.

"Jackson, darling." She walks over to him and gives him a hug as he stands up. "So good to see you."

"Always a pleasure to see you, Mrs. Rosser," he says, kissing both of her cheeks. "You look absolutely radiant."

"Why thank you," she giggles. "Can I have a seat?"

"Of course, mom. Do you want anything?"

"No, I'm good." She sits and looks around the office. "Wow. It looks very nice in here and that view," she says, looking out the window.

I chuckle slightly at her comment. It reminds me of what Sarah had said when she'd first come into the office.

"What is it, dear?" She asked me.

"Oh, your comment. It just reminded me of someone I know."

"Oh?" She looks curious but doesn't say anything.

Jackson takes a seat again. "Someone I know as well?"

"Perhaps," I say, glaring at him. I'm not going to continue the Sarah conversation with him now.

"Would you like me to leave?" Jackson goes to stand up again. "Is this a private conversation or..."

"No, you can stay." She beams. "You are Ethan's best friend, and I'm sure he doesn't mind you being here."

"Not at all. I have no secrets from Jackson," I say.

"You don't?" He asks, and I just roll my eyes.

"What's going on, mom?"

"I just wanted you to know that I'm going to India."

"What?" I frown slightly. "What happened? Do you need money? What is going on?"

"I don't need anything dear. I'm going on a yoga and meditation retreat."

"You're doing what?" My jaw drops. "I'm confused."

"I'm divorcing your father."

"You're divorcing dad?"

"He's cheated on me for most of our marriage, he's gaslit me. He's been unfaithful. He's hurt me and I've put up with it. I don't know why. Maybe because I loved him. Maybe because I felt like I needed to give you a two-parent household, which I regret."

"What do you mean, mom?"

"I mean, I think I did you a disservice by staying with dad."

"What?"

"I've never seen you in love. I've never seen you in a relationship. I've never seen you even close to being married, and I think that's because of what you've witnessed with me and your dad. All the nights and days I spent crying and the shopping and the arguments, it had an effect on you."

I pressed my lips together and don't say anything.

"And I'm sorry. I'm really sorry for that. I didn't know how to just be by myself. I didn't know how to be a single mother looking after my son. I didn't know how to not have a man by my side, and yet, you know what I realized?"

"No." I shake my head.

"I realized that even though I had your father, I was still alone. Even though I was a wife, I was still a single mom. Even though everyone thought I had it all, I had nothing."

"You had me," I say softly, remembering all those nights we sat on the couch and watched TV together. And the nights she read me books, and the nights she sang to me and the nights she was too tired and sad to even eat with me.

"I could have been a better mom to you," she says, leaning forward and grabbing my hands. "You have been my everything. I love you so much, Ethan. You have been my savior, your father's savior, your grandparent's savior."

"My savior as well," Jackson says, and I look at him. "Your friendship means a lot to me," he says.

My heart expands and I nod because Jackson has also been my savior, the best friend a guy could ever ask for, but I don't know how to let him know that just then.

"I'm going to India because I've really gotten into yoga and I want to find myself. I want to find my purpose in life before it's too late. I know the two of you see me as an old woman, but I still got some life left in me, yet." She giggles slightly and I frown.

Was my mom giggling like a little school girl? "But you're divorcing dad?"

"It's been a long time coming," she says. "I haven't been happy. He's not been happy, and I don't want this to be my life. I don't want to be on my deathbed and wish I'd done a million things that I haven't. It's time for me to be strong. It's time for me to be independent. It's time for me to open my heart to the world, and I just hope that you can do the same thing."

"You want me to go to India and do yoga with you?"

"No," she laughs. "I want you to let love into your life. I..." She pauses. "Your grandparents told me that when you found out that dad had gotten someone pregnant, you told them you couldn't go. You were at the hospital with someone."

"Yeah, and?"

"Someone important," she says, looking at me with narrowed eyes.

"Maybe. Why?"

"Someone you love, possibly?"

I stare at her for a couple of seconds and then I look at Jackson. He is leaning forward as well.

I nod slowly. "As crazy as this is going to sound, maybe you're right. Maybe I do love her, but maybe I lost her because I was a fool, and I broke her heart and ran away when she told me she loved me and fuck it." I slam my fist on the desk. "I think I screwed up."

"So you do love her." Jackson's grinning now.

"Shut up, Jackson. You knew I loved her."

"Of course, I knew you loved her. I knew you loved her from the very first moment," he says. "It was apparent."

"What do you mean it was apparent?"

"I'm your best friend, dude. I knew the moment you saw her in that bar, you fell hook, line and sinker."

"Really?" I chuckle and he nods.

"I've never seen you look at a girl like that before and I've never seen one respond to you quite like that either."

"What? So you think you knew?"

"Oh, I 100% knew." He laughs. "And by the way?"

"Yeah?"

"She never posted that personal ad."

"What do you mean she never posted it?" I frown. "What are you talking about?"

"All the posts for the company intranet, they go through me." He laughs. "Nothing goes public on our company site without my approval. Are you crazy? We'd have people complaining all the time."

"So wait, what?" I gawk at him. "So you actually

saw what she'd submitted or sent by mistake before it went live?"

"Yeah," he laughs. "Perhaps."

"Why did you make that thing go live? What the hell were you thinking?"

"I needed a way for you to become more invested in the situation. I know you, Ethan. You would have taken years to make a move. I just pushed it along."

"Oh my gosh, this is absolutely crazy. I don't believe it."

"I think she sounds like a special girl," my mom says. "Someone I'd like to meet."

"She's got me on block, so I don't know how likely that's going to be."

"I think if she's the girl for you, it'll work out," my mom says and stands up. "Anyway, I need to go shopping. I've got a lot to get done before I head out."

"When are you going?" I say, feeling slightly sad. This is the first time my mom and I have really opened up to each other since I was a little kid and I'm kind of sad to see that she's going.

"Not until you work it out with your young lady," she says. "I want to meet her. I want to make sure I'm leaving you in good hands."

"Wait, what? I thought you were going sometime soon."

"I have a feeling it will be soon," she smiles. "But if it's not, I can wait. I've been patient this long."

"Mom, you cannot wait on me, on my love life. I..."

"I want to be there for you, Ethan. You've been here

for me my entire life and I love you for it. You're the best thing that's ever happened to me, son."

"Thanks mom. I love you."

"Now I'm going to go shopping."

"Is that your way of telling me to expect some large credit card bills at the end of the month?" I laugh.

"No," she shakes her head. "Those are only for emergencies now."

"What?" I say in surprise.

"I've got a little bit of money that I've been saving through the years, my emergency fund, and I'm going to use that. I need to stop relying on you for everything."

"Mom, it's okay. I am..."

"No, son. I want to see if I can get by myself. I'm fed up of having to depend on people. I want to see if I can traverse the world alone."

"Mom."

"I mean, if I need something and I don't have the money, of course I'll come to you, son, but let me just try this, okay?"

"Okay," I say. "But you know money's no issue. You know I've always got you."

"I know and that's why I love you. You're my safety blanket and I should have been yours."

"You were."

"I hope you know I'm always here for you."

"I know, mom." I get up and walk over to her and give her a big hug. She holds my face and looks at me.

"My handsome, handsome boy. What are you still doing here?"

"What? What are you talking about?"

"Go and get your girl."

"What? Now?"

I look back at Jackson and he's nodding. "In every good romance movie, the guy goes running down the street and finds the girl and declares his love for her, and maybe plays the guitar and sings a song," he says. "I think you should do all of the above."

"You think?"

"Well, maybe not play the guitar and sing a song, but go and find her. Go and apologize. Tell her how you feel."

"I don't even know where she is," I say, biting down on my lower lip.

"I don't know. I'm sure you can figure it out," he says. "I think you know her well enough to know the things she enjoys."

"Well, she enjoys songwriting and singing and..." I laugh. "Dancing on a pole. She takes these pole dancing classes."

"You know where she takes them?" He asks.

I think for a few moments and then think about being at her apartment and looking at the pole when she was dancing. My brain suddenly clicks as I think of a sticker that was on the edge of the pole that had the name of a dance studio.

"I think I may know where she dances, but there's no way that..."

"You never know," he says. "If it's meant to be."

"Am I really going to put my faith in if it's meant to be?" I ask him and he shrugs.

"Do you believe in magic, Ethan?"

I stare at him and then I stare at my mom and shake my head. "No. I don't know that I believe in magic, but I do believe in love, finally. And I do believe in Sarah and I believe in myself, and I believe we're meant to be together. So I'll see you guys later. I love you both, but I got to go and find my girl."

29

Sarah

Dear Diary,

Maybe dreams do come true. Even though you know me better than anyone else knows me in the world, I don't think you realize just how much I've been waiting to find my true love. Or maybe I'm deceiving myself. Maybe you knew better than I did just how much I wanted it. If I'm honest, I never thought I'd find someone that was absolutely perfect for me. I never really thought that I would be the sort of woman that would find the dream guy. I'm not blonde and petite. I don't look like a supermodel. I'm not the funniest or the smartest person in the room. But somehow, just somehow, I was enough and I will always be grateful for that. I will always be grateful that I found a man who appreciates every inch of me. Forever and ever, you're one and only,

Smiling Sarah.

"And okay, everyone. I think we're going to end

class today." Maribel stands at the front of the room and turns on the lights. "How's everyone feeling?"

"My glutes are killing me," Northina says. "And don't ask why or how, but they are." We all start laughing.

"Sarah, you're looking really good today," Maribel smiles at me.

"Please do not say that you think I'm one of the best in the class." I stare at her. "I know I'm not."

"I know you don't believe it, but you're one of the students that has picked this up the fastest. You need to stop being so hard on yourself, Sarah," Maribel continues. "I know you want to be the best, and I know that you feel like you should be good enough to perform in a club or in a show, but it takes those women years and years. You've not been doing it that long. Trust me, you're good."

"Thanks," I say and shrug. I don't want to get all sappy and I don't want to start crying. I've been crying enough as it is.

"So everyone, you have a great evening and I'll see you all next week."

"Sounds good," I say, heading towards the locker room. I walk ahead of the others because I don't really want to chat. I can't even believe that I made it to class today. It's been three weeks since I've been. Really, it'd been three weeks since I'd done anything. I think I must've lost at least 10 pounds because I hadn't been able to eat because my heart had been broken. Isabel and Ella were worried about me and I knew they had a reason to be, but not only was I heartbroken but I was embarrassed and humiliated and I just felt stupid.

How could I have told him I loved him? What sort of dumbass does that after barely knowing someone? Sure, we'd slept together and sure we had an amazing connection, but maybe that's what lust was. Maybe it was nothing more than that. Maybe I was so caught up in the daydream and fantasy of wanting it to be more that I completely over exaggerated everything in my head.

I was looking for jobs because I did not want to go back to Roster International. I did not want to see Ethan ever again. I didn't know how I'd be able to face him. I grab my duffle bag out of the locker, splash my face with some water and head to the main entrance. I debate going for Mexican food or going straight home. I know I should most probably go for the food because it's been a long time since I felt hungry and I know I need some nourishment. I step out of the door and almost immediately collide with Ethan.

"Hey, clumsy," he says, with a lopsided grin and I just glare at him.

"My name's Sarah," I snap. "And what are you doing here?"

"I am here to see you," he says, wrinkling his nose. "I was hoping you'd be happy."

"Why would I be happy that you're stalking me again?"

"Truly not stalking you," he says, "but I think it's fate that you're here."

"You think it's fate that I'm at my weekly dance class?"

"And that I found you here," he says.

"How did you find me here if you're not stalking me?"

"There was a sticker for the club on your pole."

"What do you want, Ethan?"

"You haven't been to work in three weeks."

"I spoke to the HR department. They told me it's not going to be an issue."

"It's not an issue," he says, "but I've missed you."

"Okay."

I take a deep breath. "What do you want? Or do you need another jingle or a jangle or what the fuck ever you want from me?"

"I don't need anything from you, Sarah. I just need you to not be mad at me."

"Well, I am mad at you. I'm pissed off and that's not going to change."

"I hurt you," he says. "I understand that."

"Really? You understand that? Okay, good for you. Yay. Ethan understands that he hurt my feelings. That makes me feel so great."

"There's no need to be sarcastic."

"Okay. How would you prefer me to be? Would you like me to sing and dance and perform some sort of-

"I fucked up. I know I fucked up," he says, "and you have every right to hate me and think I'm a tool and be heartbroken and sad and curse me out, and whatever you want to do. But I want to say something."

"I am listening," I say. My heart is racing now and I'm not sure why. What did he mean when he said he fucked up? I don't want to read anything into it. I can't read anything into it. I don't want to get my hopes up.

"Guess what I have here?" he says, holding up a newspaper.

"I don't know. A balloon?"

"Really, Sarah?"

"A teddy bear?"

He chuckles. "Very good sense of humor, but no."

"Okay. What then?"

"It's tomorrow's paper."

"Okay, so you have tomorrow's paper in your hand. Whoop-dee-doo, good for you. Who are you, Superman?"

"Ouch. I know I deserve this cold treatment from you, but it burns."

"Maybe you should get that checked."

"What checked?"

"You know. The burn? I hope it's not gonorrhea or something."

"It's not," he laughs. He opens the newspaper and shows it to me. I read the headline. **New York's Most Eligible Bachelor Taken**. I frown for a couple of seconds.

"What is this?"

"I'm hoping that you're not going to make me a liar."

"You're going to be a lawyer?" I ask him, deliberately mishearing him.

"I said I hope you're not going to make me into a liar. L-I-A-R."

"Why would I be making you a liar?"

"Because I'm hoping you're the one that's going to be in possession of my heart." He grabs my hands and stares at me. My heart is thudding even faster now. "I'm the billionaire bachelor that is now taken."

"What?" I squeak out. "What are you talking about?"

"I messed up, Sarah. I know I messed up. I know I hurt you. I know I was a fucking idiot telling you that I didn't love you and that I couldn't be in a relationship and..." He sighs. "I was scared. I know that's not a good excuse. I know that that doesn't make the pain go away, but I've never felt like this before and I never expected to feel like this. And I guess I kind of was more of a jackass than I thought I was. I just want you to know that I know I messed up. I know that you deserve better than what I've given you. And I hope I can prove to you that I love you and want to be with you and want to show you just how much you mean to me and how much I need you in my life and how much I love you and how much I never want to let you go and... Am I rambling too much?"

"I don't even know what you're saying, Ethan."

"I'm saying that I love you, Sarah. I'm saying that I've never felt like this before in my life. I'm saying that you have captivated me. You've captured my heart. You've grabbed it from my soul and you've released something in me that I didn't even know existed and it scared me. When I tell you it scared me, I'm not even exaggerating. I mean that it scared me so much that I didn't know what to think. I didn't know what to do. And my parents, they had the worst marriage and my mother, every night she would cry and sob because she loved my father so and he was a jackass and I didn't want to be in that position and I didn't want to put anyone in that position, least of all you.

"And I know none of this is making sense. I know you don't understand. But I want you to know that I will do anything in my power to win you back. I will do anything in my power to make you love me again, to make you give me a second chance, to make you-"

"Ethan," I say, grabbing a hold of his hand.

"What?" he says. "What is it? Is it too late?" I stare at him for a couple of seconds and I don't say anything.

"You got something wrong," I say softly. "What?" I say. "Do you hate me so much that you're not willing to give me another chance? Do you hate me so much that-"

"No, Ethan. I love you. My love didn't go away in three weeks because you told me you didn't love me. That's not how love works. Yes, you broke my heart. Yes, I've been crying. Yes, I've been sorrowful. But I still love you. I love every piece of you. We don't know each other that well, even though it feels like we've known each other for a lifetime, but I love you and of course I forgive you. Of course I understand. I didn't even know that you had a background like that. I didn't know that your parents went through that. I come from a really solid family. I have amazing parents. I have an amazing set of brothers who tease me mercilessly and make me hate them sometime. But I know that they love me and I know that they would do anything for me and I know they always have my back. And I just want you to know that you can always count on me. My love is not going to change. My love is something that will always, always be here."

He stares at me for a couple of seconds. "I don't deserve you. I don't deserve someone as special and as sweet and as loving and as kind as you."

"Maybe not." I laugh. "But..."

"But what?" he says.

"But you have me. Every part of me." I stare at him. "You really love me?"

"I really love you," he nods. "I can't believe it. I fell in love with a mid-thirties, slightly hot mess female that works in my office."

"I guess she got herself that billionaire after all," I giggle.

"I guess she did." He laughs. "Is that your plan all along?"

"Really, Ethan?"

"I'm just joking," he says quickly. "I know that your plan wasn't to try and catch me. I know you didn't post it on the company intranet with that."

"I'm just joking." I giggle. "I know you know that I was not deliberately trying to catch you. And now you also know that..."

"That what?" he says.

"That I've kind of had a crush on you for a long time."

"I know. You couldn't help yourself, though. I'm devastatingly handsome."

"Yeah, you're kind of handsome."

"And you're very beautiful."

"You didn't even notice me before."

"Because I didn't notice anything before," he says. "But once I did notice you, I fell in love with you right away.

"No, you didn't."

"I did," he nods. "Swear to God."

"You fell in love with me right away?"

"I fell in love with each and every part of you," he says. "I fell in love with everything about you. You're beautiful. You're witty. You're funny. You're goofy. You may or may not be the best dancer in the world. But you know what?"

"What?" I say, glaring at him and trying not to laugh.

"You're the best dancer in my world."

"Oh, my gosh. That's so cheesy," I laugh.

"But you love it."

"Only because I love you."

"I'm glad," he says. "I'm really glad."

"So what does that mean?" I say.

"I think it means that we are officially in a relationship now," he says. "So I guess I should ask officially."

"Ask what?" I tremble slightly. If he asks me to marry him, I'm going to faint. I mean, I know he says he fell in love at first sight, but marriage? That seems like it's a step way too fast. Way too soon. Even though a part of me would love to say yes, I just don't want to be a desperado.

"Sarah?"

"Yes, Ethan?"

"Will you..."

"Yes, Ethan?" I stare at him and think about what I'm going to tell Isabel. She will freak out if I get engaged. She will literally freak out. I'm already about to freak out.

"Will you be my girlfriend? My official girlfriend?"

"Your girlfriend?" I squeak and start giggling.

"Yeah." He looks nervous. "Unless you don't want to be. Unless you think-"

"No, I'd love to be," I say, nodding quickly. "I would love to be your girlfriend."

"Okay, great." He smiles at me. "If you're sure."

"Oh, I'm more than sure," I say. "It's all I could have asked for."

"Okay." he nods. "Well, I'm glad to hear that. Is everything okay?" He stares at my face.

"Yeah. Why do you ask?"

"Because you're bright red right now."

"Oh, it must just be the wind," I say, trying not to blush.

"What's going on?" he asks softly.

"Nothing. I don't want you to think I'm an idiot."

"Sarah. Be honest with me. What's going on?"

"I thought you were going to ask me to marry you."

"What?" He starts laughing.

"It's not funny." I hit him in the shoulder.

"You thought I was going to ask you to marry me?

We've never been on an official date. We have not even been hanging out super long together."

"Do not point out all the reasons why it's stupid of me to have thought that," I asked him. "Let's just say I thought that."

"And what would you have said if I had asked you to marry me?"

"I'm not going to answer that question for fear that it may incriminate me."

"You love me. You want to marry me," he says with a small smile.

"Ethan."

"It's okay," he says, laughing. "I kind of like that."

"You kind of like what?"

"I kind of like that you're so into me that you would marry me without having been on an official first date. Because you know what?"

"What?" I say, glaring at him.

"One day I am going to ask you, Sarah, and I'm going to have the biggest diamond ring you could ever ask for. And I'm going to get on my knees and I'm going to stare into your big, beautiful eyes and I'm going to tell you just how much I love you. And you know what else I'm going to tell you?"

"No, what?"

"I'm going to tell you that I knew that you were going to be my wife. And you're going to ask me, 'When did you know?' and I'm going to remind you of this moment because, my darling, you are my everything. You are the best woman that could ever have been made for me. And you know what? You're perfect for me."

"You think so?" I say.

"I know so." He smiles at me. "I love you, Sarah. Thank you for not playing games. Thank you for giving me another chance. Thank you for understanding that I screwed up that day and I made a big mistake. And..."

"Hey, we all make mistakes," I say, shaking my head. "I get it and I understand and I kind of love you enough to forget about it so you don't have to apologize anymore." I pull him into my arms and give him a kiss. And I know that I've never been happier than I am right now.

Thank you for reading Mid Thirties Slightly Hot Mess Female Seeking Billionaire. If you would like to read some BONUS SCENES from the book, please click here.

If you are interested in reading Ella's story, you can get it here.

To ensure you don't miss any of my new releases, please join my newsletter here!